It was almost pitch dark. I called out to him.

"Zuke, where the hell are you?"

I went into the bushes and felt my way through them.

"Come on out!" I urged.

But there was no answer. I stood still and listened. Not a sound. I expected Zuke to be blundering about in the undergrowth but there was complete silence. I moved on more quickly. When I came into a clearing, I soon realized why he had not replied. My foot kicked against a solid object that all but tripped me up.

It was Zuke Everett. Flat on his back.

Something seemed to be sticking out of his chest.

I knew at once that he was dead.

Also by Keith Miles
Published by Fawcett Books:

BULLET HOLE

DOUBLE EAGLE

A Novel by

Keith Miles

FAWCETT CREST • NEW YORK

A Fawcett Crest Book
Published by Ballantine Books

ISBN 0-449-21703-5

This edition published by arrangement with Harper & Row Publishers, Inc.

Manufactured in the United States of America

First Ballantine Books Edition: June 1989

To Colin Murray
who knows a good golfer when he sees one

Wheresoever the carcase is, there will the eagles be gathered together.

—*Gospel According to St. Matthew 24:28*

Chapter One

I've never liked bank managers and I'm bound to admit that they've never really taken to me. Our relationship is doomed from the start. I'm just not their type. What they want are people who deposit more money than they withdraw, self-respecting citizens who are dependable, well-behaved and responsible. I fail on all three counts.

When you try to make a living as a professional golfer, you have to take the rough with the heavy rough. In my case, it's made me about as dependable as a three-legged racehorse and forced me into all kinds of erratic behaviour. As for being responsible, it's an attitude that I simply can't afford most of the time.

The net result is that the average earthquake has more stability than my bank balance. I inhabit a precarious world. The only thing I earn on a regular basis is Bad Risk status. It's the main reason that bank managers don't find me very appealing.

Donnelly is a typical example of the breed. Smug, watchful, offensively polite. He waved me into his office with a podgy hand.

"Come in, Mr. Saxon."

"Thanks."

"Happy New Year!"

"That's up to you."

"Yes." His false affability vanished at once. "Have a

seat,'' he said, resting back in his own chair. ''This won't take long.''

I got the message. Evidently I was being fitted in between two much more important customers. Solvent ones.

While Donnelly looked through my crime dossier, I sat down and glanced around the featureless room. It had an overwhelming sense of order to it. Desk, chairs, filing cabinets, small table, computer, fitted carpet. Bare walls apart from a hideous calendar with a coloured photograph of the Tower of London as its illustration of the month. I tried to remember if it had ever been used as a debtors' prison.

''You didn't need to see me about this,'' decided my host with suppressed irritation. ''Mr. Rhodes could have taken care of it.''

''But he couldn't,'' I said. ''Mr. Rhodes is only an assistant manager and I wanted the top dog. I'm tired of being palmed off with one of your underlings.''

''I can't be expected to handle every account personally,'' he retorted, his flabby cheeks quivering. ''You were passed on to Mr. Rhodes because he deals with this particular area.''

''And what area is that, Mr. Donnelly?''

''Minor disasters.'' His eye fell on my file once more and he let out a sigh. ''This does not make happy reading.''

''Christmas has been a very difficult time for me. I had a lot of additional expenses. You know how it is.'' He nodded grimly. Bank managers know everything. ''Things should even out a bit now,'' I added, injecting a buoyant optimism into my voice. ''They always have in the past.''

''That is patently not true, Mr. Saxon,'' he argued, flicking through the pages. ''Over the last few years, your current account has been consistently high on our problem list. You seem to have no idea how to organise your finances.''

''My income is a trifle irregular, that's all.''

''Doesn't it *worry* you?''

I shrugged. ''It terrifies me. I'm tortured with anxiety. I make at least three suicide attempts a week.''

''This is not a laughing matter,'' he chided, then he

leaned over the desk towards me. "Have you never thought of using an accountant?"

"I've had several but they never seem to last the pace."

Another sigh. "That doesn't surprise me."

"Mr. Donnelly," I said, stating my case in plain terms, "all I ask for is a little understanding and compassion. Bear with me for a short while and I'm certain that everything will sort itself out to our mutual satisfaction. Brighter days lie ahead." A thought nudged me. "Oh, and I'd be grateful if you could have a word with young Rhodes about his itchy trigger finger."

"Trigger finger?"

"Yes. As soon as my account is overdrawn by the tiniest sum, he shoots from the hip and fires off a warning letter. And he doesn't use blanks either! Where do you train your staff—the OK Corral?"

"Our computer monitors any over-spending," he explained, wearily. "Letters are printed out automatically. Mr. Rhodes merely has to sign them. Besides . . ." His third sigh explored a whole new octave of regret. "Besides, Mr. Saxon, we're not talking about an account being overdrawn. We're discussing an overdraft facility which has been—to put it mildly—cruelly abused."

"Christmas comes but once a year," I reminded him.

He sat back heavily and appraised me with that mixture of antagonism and bewilderment that I have put on so many faces in the banking fraternity. Donnelly resented me because I came between him and his complacence.

"Do you have any other assets?" he asked, bluntly.

"Fourteen golf clubs and a winning smile."

"What about property, investments, stocks and shares, premium bonds, accounts with building societies and so on?"

"Nothing," I admitted. "Apart from a controlling interest in ICI and the two million quid I've got stashed away in Switzerland." I flashed my winning smile but it lost out immediately. "Last year was a bad one, Mr. Donnelly: this one will be much better."

"How do you know that?"

"I have this sixth sense."

An acerbic note intruded. "It's never seemed to work before."

"Now, that's unfair!" I protested.

"This is not the first time you've assured us that your financial situation was going to improve, Mr. Saxon, but we're still waiting for the great day to dawn."

Anger reduced me to pomposity. "It may interest you to know that I've had some highly successful seasons as a tournament golfer."

"Not since you became a customer here."

"Those two facts may not be unrelated, Mr. Donnelly!"

"So you think we've brought you bad luck, do you?" he blustered.

"Let's just say that you'd never pass for a rabbit's foot."

Covert dislike had now matured into open hostility and we glared at each other across the desk. When I had reached this point with previous bank managers, they usually invited me to leave the premises for good and to take my account with me. Donnelly resisted the temptation and sought instead to wound my pride.

"What puzzles me is why you didn't save more when you were actually making it," he observed with condescension. "I believe you were quite famous twenty-odd years ago."

"Very famous," I replied with measured calm. "And it wasn't that far back."

"So what happened?"

"Marriage. A child. Divorce. Three giant steps towards total bankruptcy." I shook my head dismissively. "But that's my problem."

"And ours, Mr. Saxon. For the time being." He pursed his lips and stole another glance at my file. Then he came to a decision. "I will give you one last chance."

"Thank you," I murmured.

"We'll increase the overdraft facility by £500—but only temporarily. The bank is not prepared to go on subsidising your financial mismanagement. You *must* get your act together."

"How long have I got?"

"Six weeks."

"It'll be enough," I promised.

"It had better be. If we don't see a marked improvement by the end of that period . . ."

"You'll start bouncing my cheques like beach balls."

"We'll do much more than that," he threatened. A curt nod signalled that the interview was over. "Goodbye, Mr. Saxon."

"Goodbye." I was on my feet at once.

"Oh, one thing . . ."

"Yes?" I paused at the door.

"Have you ever considered giving up golf altogether? Before it gives *you* up, I mean?" He smirked at me. "Have you?"

"Many times."

"Then what makes you keep on playing?"

"People like you, Mr. Donnelly."

"Me?"

"I enjoy proving you wrong."

Before he could answer, I went out of the office at speed.

When I left the bank and stepped out into the street, cold air hit me like a slap in the face. I suddenly realised what I had done. With the easy confidence of a man who has unlimited funds at his disposal, I had blithely undertaken the Herculean labour of sorting out my money worries in a mere six weeks. It was like volunteering to pay off the national debt by the following Saturday. I quailed.

The first few flakes of snow began to fall rather aimlessly out of a swollen sky but I hardly noticed them. Inside my head, a blizzard was raging. I walked along the pavement in a daze.

There was, of course, a solution.

That's what I kept telling myself, anyway. All I had to do was to play four brilliant rounds of golf and earn a large, life-saving cheque. It sounded so easy. Unfortunately, I wouldn't even get the chance until the Safari Tour started in the middle of February. Over a month away.

And leaving aside the vexed question of how I'd raise the cash to get to Lagos to compete in the Nigerian Open, there was the problem of my persistent lack of form. It had dogged me for the best part of a year.

Could I still turn it on when it really mattered?

I consoled myself with the thought that I had actually played four superb rounds the previous summer. Each one was a gem that sparkled in the memory. Powerful drives, brave approach shots, deadly putts. Vintage Alan Saxon. Had those four rounds been in the same tournament, I would undoubtedly have won it by a record margin.

As it was, each day of magic had occurred in a separate event. A single immaculate round had not been enough to redeem the three indifferent ones with which it was partnered. In each tournament, I finished out of the money and out of sorts with myself.

Why should it be any different in Nigeria?

This mood of fatalism took me around a corner and into the side street where I had parked Carnoustie. Snowflakes were settling gently on her windscreen. She looked cold, bored, neglected. I unlocked the door and got in behind the driving wheel. After switching off the alarm system, I turned on the ignition and moved slowly away. When I reached the junction with the main road, Carnoustie stalled.

I gunned the engine again, waited for a gap and then swung left. Carnoustie responded without enthusiasm. A motor caravan is not the ideal means of transport in suburban London on a busy afternoon. Instead of picking my way through heavy traffic in a bulky vehicle, I could have come in by train. It would have been much quicker and far more restful. But it would also have exposed me.

In becoming Open Champion up at Carnoustie all those years ago, I did more than just find a name for the Bedford Adventura that is now my home. At a stroke—283 strokes, to be precise—I changed from private man into public property. My unusual height and prematurely grey hair made me instantly recognisable and thus a ready target for the total stranger with the knowing grin. Fame is trial by ordeal.

As a result, I've learned to hide my grey hair beneath a hat and to travel in the secrecy of my mobile refuge. Only a stern summons from the bank could have got me into London at all. I tend to keep a very low profile. So does my income.

At the first set of traffic lights, Carnoustie stalled again. I gave her some choke, coaxed the engine back into life and edged forward with caution. Carnoustie was long overdue for a major service and she took every opportunity to remind me of the fact. I would have to nurse her carefully. It was going to be a long journey to St. Albans but I had plenty to think about on the way.

I had reached crisis point.

It was not only my bank balance that was ruinously overdrawn. My emotional capital was severely depleted as well. Christmas was to blame. The festive season began—as it always does—with a vicious wrangle about how and when I could see Lynette. My teenage daughter is eager to be with me and I'm desperate to spend time with her but there's a brick wall between us.

Rosemary. My ex-wife.

You never get divorced from a woman like Rosemary. All you do is to redefine the marriage. Though we haven't lived together for a number of years, she remains as crucial a part of my world as ever. A subversive presence. The court awarded her custody of our only child and the right to supervise my access to Lynette. She takes full advantage of that right.

Christmas always brings out the worst in her and she had a special reason for being obstructive this time. Katie. I should have known that Rosemary would never understand someone like her. It was a mistake even to try to explain.

Katie Billings had brought sunshine back into my life for the past three months. Her charms are not immediately apparent. Tall, willowy and red-headed, she has the kind of subdued loveliness that creeps up on you and catches you unawares. It certainly took me by surprise. We met at a party in Hatfield given by some mutual friends. At the beginning of the evening, I hardly noticed Katie. She looked rather dull and submissive. By the end of the party, I thought she was the most beautiful woman in the room and I was lucky enough to drive her back to her house in St. Albans.

She invited me in for coffee. I'm still there.

What I like about Katie is her devastating honesty. She has no time for those petty evasions and half-truths and wilful self-delusions that the rest of us seem to need. Over medium roast percolated coffee, she explained that she was a personnel officer in a local factory and that she was only interested in serious long-term relationships with men. Having recently parted from her live-in lover, she was now searching for his replacement. Later that night, she interviewed me for the post. By morning I had got it.

The honeymoon continued for week after glorious week. I came to believe that I could stay with her forever. Katie Billings had all the qualities I admire in a woman, including an ability to see me in the kindest possible light. Also—a decisive factor—she wore silk pyjamas. I was hooked.

Then came my tactical error. I whisked her off to a quiet hotel in the Cotswolds for a romantic away-from-it-all Christmas. With a reckless disregard for the tremors it would send through my bank account, I booked the suite with the four-poster and had a bottle of their best champagne awaiting us in an ice bucket. A frenzy of last-minute spending bought me armfuls of presents to shower upon her.

It should have been the most perfect Christmas.

Instead, it was a disaster. While we could be relaxed and happy in a semi-detached house in St. Albans, a quiet hotel in the Cotswolds made us tense and furtive. We had lost the very domesticity that had drawn us together.

Besides, Katie had wanted Christmas at home. Sainsbury's turkey with all the trimmings. Christmas pudding served with flaming brandy. Wine, crackers, laughter, celebration. Gentle love-making in front of the James Bond film on the telly. Washing up together.

We stayed one night at the hotel then cut our losses. I

never did get to enjoy the wondrous combination of silk pyjamas and four-poster. The honeymoon was over. My days were numbered.

As I drove back to St. Albans now, I wondered how much longer it would last. Donnelly gave me six weeks: would Katie allow me as much time as that? I doubted it.

The snow had thickened now, road conditions worsened and the British motorist was given every chance to prove just how stupid and inconsiderate he can be. As Carnoustie chugged along in low gear, we passed various examples of the national death wish. Some cars had collided head-on, others had merely exchanged dents and a lorry had spun off the road. At a major intersection, a bakery van had somehow managed to overturn itself. Delays were inevitable. Frustration levels were high. It was early evening before we finally reached the familiar cul-de-sac and groaned to a halt.

Katie owned a small, neat, modern house in red brick. I let myself in, put on the lights and basked in the warmth of the central heating. The telephone rang on the hall table. I lifted the receiver with a gloved hand.

"Hello?"

"Alan?" The voice was unmistakable. "Is that you?"

"How the hell did you get this number?" I demanded.

"That doesn't matter," said Rosemary in her usual brisk way. "I rang to let you know that Lynette has decided to go back to school a few days early."

"But I haven't seen her properly."

"That's not my fault."

"Of course it is. You do your damnedest to keep us apart!"

"Please don't shout," she replied with irritating coolness.

"I'm entitled to have access to my own daughter."

"It just hasn't proved feasible this holiday."

"Rosemary, we have a spare bedroom here," I argued. "Lynette could have stayed as long as she wished."

"I'm not letting her share a house with you and one of your lady friends. Think of the effect it might have on her."

Her tone of sophisticated venom made red mist appear before my eyes. I didn't dare to speak while I was in the grip of such rage. Rosemary had lost none of her power to wound me to the quick.

"Alan?" There was a pause. "Are you still there?"

"Yes," I grunted.

"You do understand my position, don't you?"

"Let me speak to Lynette."

"She's not here at the moment."

"Don't lie, Rosemary. Put her on right now."

"She goes back on Friday. If you're that keen to see her, you'll have to come up to Little Aston."

"No," I asserted. "That would mean having to see you as well."

"In that case, you'll have to arrange a visit to Benenden one weekend." The venom returned. "And please don't take anyone with you, Alan. You mustn't embarrass Lynette in front of her friends."

"Who gave you this bloody number!" I hissed.

"Miss Billings."

She hung up on me and the line went dead.

I was shaken. Katie had *spoken* to her? I felt utterly betrayed. It was minutes before I could even replace the receiver. The thought that Katie might have taken sides against me was like molten metal coursing through my brain. She knew all about Rosemary and yet she had talked to her behind my back. It was a sickening blow.

Stumbling into the living room, I reached for the last of the Christmas brandy and poured it into a glass before slumping into an armchair. Still wearing hat, anorak and gloves, I sipped disconsolately and brooded. I did not have long to wait. Katie's Metro scrunched up on to the drive outside and its engine was killed. The car door slammed and was locked, the front door was opened and closed, then a cheerful call came from the hall.

"Alan, I'm back!" I could hear her taking her coat off to hang it up. "How did you get on at the bank?"

"Not as bad as I expected."

"A reprieve?"

"A stay of execution."

"Look, why don't you let *me* loan you some money?"

"Against my principles."

"But I want to help."

Katie sailed into the room wearing a smart blue suit and a kind smile. Instead of getting her usual kiss and glass of sparkling wine, she was confronted with a morose figure sprawled in an armchair. She read the situation at once and volunteered the truth.

"Rosemary phoned me at the office this afternoon."

"How did she know where you worked?"

"You told her."

"I did no such thing!"

"You did, Alan. Indirectly. She knew my name and you mentioned that I ran a personnel department in a small factory. She rang almost every business in Hertfordshire before she finally tracked me down. Rosemary is a very determined woman."

"What did she want?" I pressed.

"To explain about Lynette."

"And you *let* her?"

"What else was I supposed to do?" she asked, reasonably. "Hang up on her? That would hardly have been the way to convince her that I was a fit person to meet your daughter." Katie looked me in the eye. "Besides, I had a lot of sympathy with her point of view."

"Sympathy!" I croaked.

"Maybe it wasn't such a good idea to invite Lynette here."

"Katie, you *agreed*."

"That was before Christmas."

"And before Rosemary poured her poison into your ear."

"It wasn't like that."

"Then what was it like?"

"Well—"

"Did the two of you simply have a cosy little chat about me?"

"No."

"Then what? Tell me."

"Alan," she said, taking a deep breath, "I'm sorry but I'm just not ready to play Happy Families."

"So you gang up on me," I accused, rising to my feet.

"Don't be silly."

"I expected better of you, Katie."

"Circumstances have changed."

"Yes. Until today there was only one woman trying to stab me in the back. Now there are two of you!"

She winced at the sting of my words but she did not lash back at me. Katie did not believe in violent rows. She liked everything to be on an even keel. A sad smile flitted across her lips.

"The neighbours are complaining about Carnoustie."

It was over as easily as that. Three months of sustained fun and togetherness had suddenly come to an end. Further argument was pointless. I went straight upstairs to pack my case and collect my golf clubs. When I came down to the hall, Katie was waiting for me with a faint hint of regret in her eyes.

"Let's keep in touch," she whispered.

"Yes," I sneered. "We can exchange messages through Rosemary!"

As soon as the words slipped out, I wished that I'd never said them. But it was too late. Her face crumpled and she opened the front door for me. I went out into the snow and let myself into Carnoustie.

Without looking back, I drove noisily away.

Road conditions were more treacherous than ever now and we soon had our first skid. It was not an evening to be out and about. I made for a nearby park and worked my way around its perimeter until I found a fairly secluded spot. Carnoustie rolled to a stop glad to have a safe mooring for the night.

Donnelly. Rosemary. Katie. I've known better days.

The righteous indignation which helped me to stalk out of the house now gave way to remorse. I hadn't really let Katie defend herself and I saw that I'd been far too aggressive. Now that I'd left her, I realised just how much she meant to me. At a more immediate level, I began to miss my creature comforts. I'd forgotten that Carnoustie was in no state for owner occupation. The heater was broken, the water tanks were empty and there wasn't a scrap of food in the kitchen.

In every sense, the cupboard was bare.

I pulled out my thickest blanket and wrapped it around me as I sat in front of the television. Absent-mindedly switching the set on, I ignored the programme completely. My mind was preoccupied with its favourite pastime of devising a suitably dramatic end for Rosemary. Death by high-speed golf ball had a definite appeal. There would be poetic justice in that.

She had blighted my private life again. Katie Billings was the latest name on her long hit list. There would be others.

A couple of hours drifted past. When I came out of my reverie, I was watching an episode of "Cagney & Lacey." It had reached the obligatory Harv scene in which the viewer gets an insight into the domestic problems of a policewoman's life. Christine Cagney then appeared on the screen and I let myself fantasise about the pleasures of being arrested by her and kept in her flat for questioning. Just when she had got me to the point where I was willing to confess to anything, there was a loud knock on my side door.

"Alan!" Impossibly, it was Katie. "Let me in!"

"Hold on!"

Hope flickered as I crossed to pull back the bolt. Perhaps she'd come to make an abject apology and beg me to go back to her. As the door swung open, I resolved to be magnanimous about the whole thing. Katie stepped in out of the swirling snow. She wore fur hat, long coat, scarf, gloves and boots.

"How on earth did you know I'd be here?"

"An inspired guess. I didn't think you'd drive far in this weather. The park seemed the best bet. I'm glad I've found you."

"Why?"

"Urgent phone call from Clive."

"Oh." My disappointment was evident. "Is that all?"

"You're to contact him at once."

"I'll do it in the morning."

"Tonight. He insisted. A matter of life and death."

I was cynical. "The last time I got a message to ring Clive Phelps as a matter of life and death, he simply wanted to boast that he'd finally scored with the receptionist at the Charing Cross Hotel. A Maltese girl who seemed to have a by-line with half the journalists in Fleet Street." I picked a snowflake gently from her nose. "I'm sorry you had to come out, Katie, but I am not jumping to his call."

"Even though it means a lot of money?"

"Money?" My attitude changed at once. "For me?"

"A chance for you to play golf somewhere, he said."

I moved involuntarily towards my own telephone and then remembered that it was out of order. Pulling off a glove, I felt in my pocket for small change. I couldn't wait to speak to Clive now.

"Where's the nearest call box?"

"At my house." Her expression gave nothing away. "Follow me. I know a short cut."

Carnoustie was unhappy about the move and stalled twice but we eventually got under way. Following the rear lights of the Austin Metro, we were towed back slowly to the cul-de-sac. Katie handed me the receiver as I stepped into the hall, then she vanished into the kitchen. I dialled the Fleet Street number I knew by heart.

Clive Phelps is a very special friend. He spotted me in my early days as a promising amateur and his faith in me has never wavered. When sober, he's one of the best golf writers in the business, but when he's had a few drinks—his normal state—he's out on his own. His explanation is that alcohol helps his creative juices to flow. Warts and all, I love him.

"What kept you, Saxon?" he snarled at the other end of the line.

"Sorry."

"And why doesn't that bloody phone of yours work?"

"Somebody snapped off the aerial."

"Well, get a new one fitted."

"I can't afford it, old son. It'll have to wait its turn in the queue." My impatience made me gabble. "Now-what's-all-this-about-a-matter-of-life-and-death?"

He chuckled. "Remember that waitress I told you about, at the Savoy? The one with the prize-winning thighs and the bouncy tits? You'll never guess what she served me for dessert today."

"Clive," I warned, "if you've dragged me to the blower to tell me about your latest sordid little conquest . . ."

"I'm just throwing that in for scenic interest." He became serious. "Okay. Here's the deal. Have you got an American visa?"

"Yes. Why?"

"Because you're off to sunny California."

"When?"

"Tomorrow. Day after. Soon as poss."

"Is this some kind of joke?"

"No, it's a firm commitment. I accepted on your behalf."

"Clive, what are you on about?"

"Golf, matey. You know, that game where you try to hit a small ball into a hole with a club." I heard him take a sip of something. "Alan Saxon is flying off to Los Angeles. First class. All expenses paid. There's even some appearance money for you."

"Appearance in what?"

"The inaugural event at the new Golden Haze Golf Club in the San Fernando Valley. An amazing place, by all accounts. They dreamed up this Tournament of Champions so that they could get off with a bang. You must have read about it in my column."

"I did, Clive. Last time I bought fish and chips. As I recall it, they had some pretty big names lined up."

"Yes. But they didn't get promises from those big names before they announced them. It caused a lot of bad blood. Some of the stars have pulled out."

"So I'm being hauled off the subs' bench, am I?"

"No," he soothed. "You were only left off the original

list by a clerical oversight, Alan. They meant to ask you all along.''

''Pull the other one.''

He chuckled again. ''All right. You're an eleventh-hour replacement. So what? It gets you out to LA and it gives you a chance to fight for a first prize of $100,000. How does that sound?''

''Bloody marvellous!'' I admitted.

My imagination ran riot. I had a vision of Donnelly reeling back in astonishment from the counter as I banked the cheque. It would enable me to clear my overdraft, settle my other debts, treat Carnoustie to the thorough overhaul she deserved, fend off my statutory panic attack when I next had to pay Lynette's school fees and buy myself the peace of mind to enjoy my golf properly.

''Now for the good news,'' resumed Clive.

''There's more?''

''It comes in two halves. First, *I'll* be jetting out to cover the tournament before going on to the Phoenix Open. That means you'll have the joy of my company, the benefit of my advice and the chance to refill my glass whenever you see it empty.''

''You're on,'' I agreed. ''What's the other good news?''

''You'll be staying with Zuke Everett.''

''Great!''

''He's the one who got them to invite you to the party, Alan. You owe it all to Zuke so don't forget it.''

''I won't, don't worry.''

It was not the first time I'd had reason to be grateful to Zuke Everett. In a world as nakedly competitive as that of tournament golf, players don't always go out of their way to befriend and help each other. Zuke was the exception. As well as being one of the top Americans on the pro circuit, he was also among the most generous and likeable. To stay with him and his gorgeous wife, Valmai, made the trip to Los Angeles even more irresistible.

''Listen carefully,'' ordered Clive. ''Here are the details.''

As he talked, I noted down the salient points on the telephone pad. The organisers were certainly not afraid to scatter their money around. I was being featherbedded from start to finish. I can take a lot of that kind of thing.

"Have you got all that?" he asked.

"I think so. Oh—and thanks, Clive."

"Zuke is the person to thank. When they couldn't contact you, he suggested they might try me. Learn your lesson. Because your telephone was out of order, this New Year bonus nearly trickled through your fingers. Fix yourself up with an answering service that will take messages for you."

"I've got one," I reminded him. "He's called Clive Phelps."

He growled a few expletives at me and then hung up. I put the receiver down and let the wonder of it sink in. From snowy St. Albans to sunny Los Angeles. From dire poverty to unexpected solvency. From enemies like Donnelly and Rosemary to true friends like Zuke and Valmai. From the inactivity I hated to the game I loved.

From hell to heaven by courtesy of Trans World Airlines.

"Was it worth making the call?"

"What?" I turned to see Katie in the kitchen doorway. "Oh, yes. Well worth it. I'm off to California to seek fame and fortune."

"That's nice," she said, genuinely pleased for me.

"They want me there immediately."

She shrugged. "That's it, then, isn't it?"

We traded a long look and weighed the implications. My trip to the Tournament of Champions would mark a complete break from Katie. I would be going out on a high, whereas all she would be left were my wet footprints on the hall carpet.

"Alan . . ."

"Yes."

"Do you remember what you said when we met?"

"I said lots of things."

"You asked me to promise something."

"Yes," I recalled. "That when it was all over, we wouldn't just slink off in opposite directions. We'd end it in style."

"You had another phrase. In a blaze of glory."

"That sounds like me."

We stood in silence for a long time, our eyes locked and our differences forgotten. Katie then glanced towards the front door.

"You don't have to spend the night out there."

"Won't the neighbours complain about Carnoustie?"

She gave a slow grin. "Who cares?"

Golf is a funny old game.

One minute you're down, the next you're riding on air.

Chapter Two

Heavy rain greeted us as our jumbo jet touched down on the tarmac at Los Angeles International Airport and taxied on hissing wheels towards the TWA terminal. After a long flight stuck next to the garrulous sales director of a Californian soft drinks company, I was more than glad to get off the plane, stretch my legs and escape any further lectures on marketing strategy. I cleared customs, then pushed my trolley towards the exit.

A sizeable crowd was waiting to meet friends and relatives. I looked around in vain for a chauffeur holding up a placard with my name on it. A young woman forced her way towards me, flung her arms around me and gave me the sort of kiss on which I thought Katie Billings held the patent. It was an electrifying moment.

"Welcome to LA!" she said.

"Thanks."

"Zuke told me to give you a ticker tape reception."

"You certainly did that."

"I'm Mardie Cutler," she introduced, resorting to the formality of a handshake. "I was asked to come and pick you up."

She waved to a short, bull-necked man, who grabbed my suitcase and golf bag and led the way towards the car park. A minute later, we were getting into the rear of a large and luxurious Buick. The chauffeur started the engine but it was almost inaudible as we pulled away. He spoke over his shoulder.

"What d'ya want, lady? Freeway or Lincoln?"

"Lincoln."

"Ya got it."

As we turned on to Lincoln Boulevard and headed north, I had a closer look at Mardie Cutler. Slim, lithe and of medium height, she had a small, sharp-featured face that was lit by a pair of aquamarine eyes. Short brown hair was circled by a thick white ribbon. She wore a baggy shirt above tight jeans and somehow reminded me of a ballet dancer. I put her in her early twenties.

"How was the trip?" she asked.

"Tiring."

"Do you always wear a track suit when you fly?"

"Most comfortable way to travel."

"I guess so. One thing, anyway. I had no problem picking you out."

"What do you mean?"

"Zuke just told me to look for him."

I smiled and nodded. Superficially, there was a definite resemblance between Zuke Everett and me. He was also tall, thin and grey-haired and had something of my gait when he moved. From a distance, we could be mistaken for each other and it had sometimes caused a little confusion among television commentators. Close to, his face was much longer than mine, his nose more aquiline and his teeth more prominent. Again, his distinctive, roguish grin was something I could never match. It was the essence of the man.

There was another major difference between us. Zuke Everett was one of the most successful golfers around. I was not.

"Sorry about the rain, Alan."

"I forgive you."

"We had bright sunshine this morning." She glanced out through the window. "Been to LA before?"

"Quite a few times."

"Like it?"

"Well, I always love coming here," I said, "but I'm usually ready to leave after a few days. Bit too overwhelming. I could never live in a pressure cooker like Los Angeles."

"That's what I used to think, yet I'm still here. After five years. It's got a grip on me now. And it sure is one hell of a big improvement on Pocatello."

"Where's that?"

"Where I come from. Pocatello, Idaho."

"So what brought you here?"

"College. I stayed because of my career."

"You work for Zuke?"

She giggled. "No, I couldn't do that. He makes me laugh all the time. We're just friends. Mrs. Everett is a client of mine. That's how I got to meet Zuke. He's a terrific guy."

"Mrs. Everett is a client of yours?"

"Yes. I go to the house at least twice a week."

"For what?"

"Workouts. Aerobics. That's how I earn my bread."

I hadn't been too far off target with ballet dancing. There was a vitality about Mardie that suggested a high level of fitness and a real commitment to the work she did.

"LA keeps me very busy," she continued. "My clients all need to look good and feel good. That's where I come in. I keep them slim and healthy and on top of the world."

"I wouldn't have thought Valmai was into aerobics."

"Valmai?"

"Zuke's wife."

"Mrs. Everett's name is Helen."

"Since when?"

"As long as I've known them. Three, four months."

"What happened to Valmai?"

"I didn't even know that was her name. Zuke never mentions his first wife. They just split up, I guess."

I was at once surprised and disturbed.

Zuke and Valmai Everett had almost convinced me that there could be such a thing as a happy marriage. They seemed ideally suited. While he was the effervescent entertainer who loved the spotlight, she was the loyal and devoted stage manager. Zuke once told me that he'd have got nowhere without Valmai. She brought calm and sanity and a sense of purpose into his life.

Valmai also brought luck. Wherever he played golf—in any part of the world—she went with him. Her presence always inspired him and his reliance on her was touching. I noticed it particularly because it contrasted so starkly with my own marital situation. I found it impossible to play well in front of Rosemary and stopped her coming to any tournaments.

Golf thrust us apart as surely as it drew them together.

Yet now they had broken up as well. It seemed inconceivable. Intelligent, kind, warm-hearted, Valmai had the sort of gentle beauty that slowly increases with age. Only a very remarkable woman could have supplanted her.

"What's his second wife like?" I wondered.

"Helen? Oh, she's quite something." There was a slight reserve in her voice. "A real stunner in every way."

"Is she younger than Zuke?"

"About ten years or so."

"Which part of the States is she from?"

"No part. She's Mexican. Used to be an actress."

"What was her stage name?"

"Helen Ramirez."

It rang a bell but I couldn't remember why.

Some of the excitement had now gone out of my visit. Instead of staying with two friends whom I liked immensely, I was intruding on a second marriage that completely baffled me. I began to feel highly uncomfortable.

It was well over a year since I'd met Zuke Everett. He'd been a member of the victorious Ryder Cup team which had humbled us in the heat of Florida. On that occasion, Zuke had been Zuke. Friendly, full of fun, ruthlessly competitive out on the course. Valmai had been there to cheer him and the US team home. The couple had seemed as unashamedly in love as ever.

I couldn't believe so much had changed since then.

Mardie chatted on amiably about the Everetts. Though it

was the wife who employed her, she was clearly much fonder of the husband and described some of the practical jokes that he'd played on her. In those, at least, I caught a glimpse of the old Zuke.

The rain eased off and the sun made its first appearance of the afternoon. We'd reached Santa Monica now and were gliding along Ocean Avenue with the Pacific below us on our left. Mardie gazed out as Palisades Park loomed up on our right.

"Almost there," she observed.

Another surprise. The Everetts had owned a beautiful mansion further up the coast in Malibu and Zuke had always sworn that he would never part with it. Yet we were slowing to a halt in front of a hacienda-style dwelling that commanded a view of the ocean. It was a big, dramatic building in bleached-white stone, but it didn't compare with the Malibu home.

Our chauffeur sounded his horn and waited until the wrought iron gates were opened electronically from inside the house. The car slid through the archway and around the crescent drive, stopping in front of the porch. We got out. Almost immediately, Zuke came bounding through the door and grabbed me in a bear hug.

"Hi, Al! Great to see you!"

"Good to be here."

"How was the flight?"

"I survived."

"You made it—that's the main thing."

He released me and stood back to appraise me. There was no apparent change in him. Casually elegant in blue slacks and sweatshirt, he still conveyed his usual charm and zest. The famous grin was intact.

"How's the weather in England?"

"Cold enough to freeze the balls off a brass monkey."

He laughed. "We'll have to thaw you out."

Mardie had got the chauffeur to put my luggage in the hall. As they came out of the house, she gave him a tip, then came to join us. She looked from Zuke to me and then back again.

"No," she decided, shaking her head, "you don't really look alike side by side. I'd never mix you guys up."

"That's a relief," noted Zuke, slipping an arm familiarly around her shoulders. "Did you get a proper welcome at the airport, Al?"

"Couldn't fault it."

"That's my girl!" He gave her a kiss, then turned towards the house. "Let's go inside."

We followed him into a large hall with a tiled floor. Mardie checked her watch and made straight for the telephone that stood on an elaborately carved table. Her manner showed that she was completely at home there.

"Mind if I use your phone? I'm going to be late for Mrs. Hahn."

"Cancel her and stay for a drink," he advised, easily.

"You don't cancel a woman like Mrs. Hahn."

"Okay. Have it your way."

Mardie took an address book from her shirt pocket, flicked to the right page, dialled a number. Zuke handed me my golf bag and picked up my suitcase.

"Lemme show you your room."

"Nice place," I admired as I trailed him across the hall. "How long have you been here?"

"Almost six months."

"Very different from the Malibu house."

"That was the idea."

He led me into a bedroom which ran to a matching wardrobe and chest of drawers, an upright chair, two heavy armchairs and a coffee table with a scene from a bullfight painted on it. There was a colourful duvet on the bed. Apart from an ornate mirror, the white walls were bare.

"Bathroom through there," he said, indicating a door, then he nodded to the arched window. "Feel free to use all the facilities."

I looked out at the luxury swimming pool that was surrounded by wrought iron tables and chairs. The sunshades were still wet from the rain, and water dripped steadily. Beyond the pool was a long, wide lawn that stretched on to a cluster of palm trees and some thick bushes. Something was glinting in the sun between the tops of the trees but I couldn't make it out.

"Must dash," called Mardie, popping her head into the room. "Good to've met you, Alan."

"Yes . . ." I began.

But she was already gone. A second later we heard the front door open and slam. Zuke slapped me affectionately on the shoulder.

"Come and see the rest of the house."

"I'd like that."

"You'll have to get used to Mardie flashing in and out," he explained as we strolled back into the hall. "That kid is a human dynamo. Never stops buzzing."

We went into the living room in time to see a Renault 5 shoot past the window and out through the open gates. Mardie Cutler was evidently in a hurry to reach her next client.

"What d'you think?" asked Zuke, as if needing reassurance.

"Fantastic," I said, gazing around.

"Isn't it terrific?"

"Very impressive."

"Wait till you see the dining room."

We continued the tour of the ground floor. Apart from the ultra-modern kitchen, all the rooms were the same. Large, imposing and with an exotic-primitive feel to them. Brightly coloured rugs scattered over tile floors. White walls covered in tapestries or Aztec paintings. Minimal furniture chosen for its bulk and solidity. Stoneware lamps and pieces of sculpture.

None of it spoke of the Zuke Everett that I knew.

"I bet you could use a drink," he offered.

"Just lead me to it."

"Let's go in the den."

The last room into which he showed me was the smallest so far but easily the most comfortable. Shelves supported an amiable clutter of books, magazines, trophies and golfing memorabilia. Photographs and golfing prints stood or hung everywhere. The place was warm, inviting, pleasantly untidy and exclusively masculine. It was identical to the room I remembered at the Malibu house. Zuke had brought his old den to his new home.

There was one significant difference. He no longer had any photos of Valmai on display. She'd been lost in transit.

He waved me to a leather armchair and opened a cupboard.

"What'll it be?"

"Have you got any white wine?"

"Sure."

"Medium dry, please."

"On its way."

He reached into the nearby refrigerator to pull out a bottle and uncorked it as we talked. Now that he was in his private sanctum, he was totally relaxed and sounded genuinely pleased to see me.

"Been a long time."

"Florida," I noted. "Don't remind me who won."

"We take the European challenge more seriously these days."

"You'd better, Zuke. We intend to snatch the Ryder Cup back when you come to Britain later this year. Spread the warning."

"I will."

"I was hoping to see you last summer," I continued. "Not often you miss an Open Championship. What went wrong?"

"Few things to sort out at this end," he said, offhandedly.

Parting from a wife of twelve years' standing. Marrying a new one. Moving to Santa Monica. Changing his whole lifestyle. A few things to sort out. It was the euphemism of the month.

"Here."

"Thanks." I took the proffered glass of wine.

He poured himself a neat vodka and flopped down in a chair beside me, then raised his glass to clink mine.

"Welcome to Dreamland, old buddy!"

"I'll drink to that."

The Californian wine was excellent and chilled to perfection.

"How's the jet lag?" he asked.

"I can still see you out of one eye."

"Say, maybe you ought to grab a few hours' sleep while you can. Something tells me it could be a long night."

"What could?"

"There's a big party at the club. We're expected to join in the celebrations and say all the right things to the press and to the sponsors." He pulled a face. "Especially to the sponsors. Could be a real drag but it'll give you a chance to meet everybody and to take a look at the Golden Haze set-up."

"Count me in."

"We don't need to leave until around nine."

"I'll be ready." I sipped more wine. "Is it true what Clive Phelps told me? There's only thirty of us in the tournament?"

He grinned. "Means that none of us'll have the embarrassment of missing the cut because we'll all play four rounds. Mind you, the field may be small but it's classy. There'll be some good golfers out there. They were chosen either because they'd won something on last year's tour over here or because they'd picked up a major championship along the way. Like you."

"Yes, I still haven't thanked you properly, Zuke."

"For what?"

"Putting my name forward."

"It was nothing," he said with a shrug. "I made a few phone calls, that's all. What else is a pal for?"

"The invitation couldn't have come at a better time."

"We needed you, Al," he argued. "They're selling this goddamn tournament on the strength of its international stars yet they had no British golfer in the line-up. Except Bob Tolley, that is, and I don't count him. That guy practically *lives* here!" He drained his glass, then put it down. "Whole thing seemed crazy to me. So when Horton Kincaid was forced out with that bad back of his, I jumped in and suggested Alan Saxon."

"Can't tell you how grateful I am, Zuke."

"Then don't even try," he said, punching me playfully on the arm. "Besides, I get my cut out of the deal. Off the course, I got you all to myself. Be great having you around again. Just like old times."

"Just like old times."

But it would not be and we both knew it.

Zuke's grin slowly faded as he looked into my eyes, then he lowered his head as if collecting his thoughts. When he raised it again, he seemed to be on the point of confiding in me but the words never came. A car horn beeped outside and he stood involuntarily. Zuke became the genial host once more.

"That'll be Helen. Come out and meet her."

"Right."

"She's been with her hairdresser all afternoon."

As we got to the hall, the front door swung open. Helen Everett did not so much come in as make a grand entrance. When she saw me, she stopped in her tracks and posed in the open doorway. The effect was quite startling and it made me blink.

Tall and shapely with a full bust, she was dressed in a vivid red suit with matching red fashion boots. Her glistening black hair fell in ringlets to her shoulders and large red earrings peeped out from beneath it. Dark round eyes were set in a face of almost classic beauty. Perfect white teeth showed in a dazzling smile.

I began to understand what had happened to Zuke.

"Hi, honey," he called. "This is Al."

"Hello," she said, extending a hand towards me.

"Pleased to meet you," I replied, shaking it and feeling the delicate warmth of her fingers. "Very kind of you to put up with me."

"Zuke's friends are always welcome. As long as they don't expect me to go and watch them play that silly game."

Her English was good but her heavy accent seemed forced.

"Helen doesn't care too much for golf," explained her

husband, beaming fondly at her. "Haven't got her house-trained yet but I'm working on it. She'll come round."

"Don't bank on it," she warned.

"I believe you were an actress," I observed.

Pride came into her voice. "I still am an actress."

"This is the famous Helen Ramirez," teased Zuke. "One stage play, six commercials and bit part in *Rocky IV*."

"I have been on the brink of stardom for years," she retorted with eyes blazing. "They said I could be a second Katy Jurado."

"Honey, I was only joking," he appeased.

"Well, your joke is not very funny."

"You're a fantastic actress. One of the best."

"Excuse me!"

Her exit was even more theatrical than her entry. With a dignified fury, she surged past us and swept up the stone staircase as if she had rehearsed the move a hundred times. A bedroom door soon slammed.

Zuke's grin looked decidedly nervous around the edges. "Sorry about that. Helen tends to fly off the handle."

"Would it be okay if I took that nap now?" I asked.

"Sure thing. See you later."

As I withdrew tactfully, he went upstairs to calm her.

After closing my bedroom curtains and slipping off my trainers, I lay on the duvet with my hands behind my head. That name. Helen Ramirez. It rang a bell again.

A second Katy Jurado.

It came to me in a flash. Just before Christmas, the BBC had screened a series of Gary Cooper films. *High Noon* was the first and we'd watched it one night at St. Albans. The film still worked superbly. What puzzled me, however, was why our hero chose the repressed Grace Kelly character in place of the tempestuous Mexican Katy Jurado. Ice instead of fire. I know which one of them I'd have taken off in a buggy.

Katy Jurado had played the part of Helen Ramirez.

The new Mrs. Everett was still playing it.

I wondered what her real name was.

* * *

The Golden Haze Golf Club occupied a prime position in the San Fernando Valley and had the sort of facilities that put the majority of its competitors to shame. Inside the vast, domed, futuristic clubhouse were four bars, two restaurants, a coffee lounge, a hairdressing salon, a crèche, a gymnasium, a swimming pool, saunas, offices, store-rooms and apartments for senior staff. There was also a golf shop the size of a small trade exhibition and, at the rear of the clubhouse, a magnificent driving range.

By the time we arrived, it was too dark to see anything of the course itself but opinions about it were being voiced on every side. Golden Haze seemed to attract extravagant praise or outright condemnation. There was no middle ground.

"Take it from me, Al. It's a killer."

"As bad as that, Howie?"

"Some of the meanest holes I ever saw. Only a sadist could design a golf course like that one."

"Well, he has to get his kicks somehow."

"Listen to me. Wise up fast. You play in that tournament, check your life insurance first."

Howie Danzig was a short, wiry, untidy man in his sixties with a squashed tomato face and a wry view of the human condition. He'd managed Zuke Everett from the start and taken him right to the top. I'd always liked Howie. His abrasive manner and deep love of the game made him a lively companion. He'd aged since we last met and I was sorry to see that he now used a walking stick.

His scorn, however, was as healthy as ever.

"This tournament stinks!"

"Then why did you let Zuke enter it?"

"I didn't, Al. Warned him against it like I warned a coupla my other players. *They* had the sense to pull out. Not Zuke. Got hold of the idea that he had to win the first ever Kallgren Tournament of Champions and that was that."

"So what's wrong with the event?"

"This place for a start," he snapped, waving his stick

around. ''Space age golf. Look at it, will you? Then there's that deathtrap out there they call a golf course.'' His features hardened. ''Most of all, there's Kallgren himself!''

The party was being held in the conference room and it was in full swing. Howie and I stood in a quiet corner while the two hundred or so other guests drank, ate, talked, laughed, argued, circulated or simply listened to the band who were providing background music with a Latin flavour.

At the centre of it all, holding court with benign aplomb, was the man who conceived and built Golden Haze. Tall, suave and immaculate in a light grey mohair suit, Rutherford Kallgren had the kind of easy authority that only comes with the possession of immense wealth. Queening it beside him was his wife, a handsome woman with a blue rinse and a dress that cost more than my entire wardrobe. The Kallgrens had to be around Howie's age but both looked fifteen years younger.

I'd never been that close to so much money before and I found it rather intimidating. Howie Danzig was in no way abashed.

''There ought to be a law!'' he snarled.

''Against what?''

''Guys like Kallgren. I mean, you let them into the game, where does it end? They want every goddamn piece of the action.'' He gestured with his stick again. ''How much d'you think it all cost?''

I shrugged. ''Millions of dollars, I suppose.''

''Bigger bucks than that, Al. You're standing on some of the most expensive real estate in California. Millions went on simply buying the land. Then there were all the development costs and consultancy fees. Five years' work on site to build the course and stick up *this* place. Now, I know—as sure as there's shit in a goat—that Kallgren isn't going to lay out all that dough just to have a golf course where he can take his smart Hollywood friends. That guy only spends it to make it. He's in golf to bleed it dry.'' He put his glass down on a table. ''This party's not good for my blood pressure. I'm off.''

"Before you go, Howie," I said, anxious to get his opinion of something. "The second Mrs. Everett."

"What about her?" His tone was gruff.

"You tell me."

"Man wants a nice piece of Mexican ass, it don't come any nicer."

"That's not what I'm asking."

"Zuke's private life is his own," he asserted, fixing me with a glaucous eye. "But I liked it better when he used to win."

Howie gave me a nod of farewell and hobbled off.

When I looked across at my hosts, they were still revelling in the occasion. Helen wore a low-cut, tightly fitting dress of white satin that gave her an almost bridal radiance while Zuke had opted for a red, open-necked shirt beneath a white tuxedo. Both were happy and animated as they chatted to a group of friends. For the first time, the couple seemed really together.

I was glad to be able to linger on the fringes of it all. Too much champagne and too little sleep had combined to make me quite groggy and I was in no mood to socialise. I was especially grateful to dodge all the media attention. This was focussed on the American stars like Zuke and Phil Reiner and Dayton Willard, and on the sensational young Egyptian golfer, Gamil Amir, who had astounded the USPGA tour the previous April by winning both the coveted Masters and the Sea Pines Heritage Classic within the space of eleven days.

Though still in his early twenties, Amir was handling all the attention with great coolness. His striking good looks were a magnet for every camera, and almost every woman in the room had mentally photographed him as well. As I glanced across at him now, he was still surrounded by adoring female company.

I suddenly missed Katie Billings. I was jealous.

"Come and join the party, Al."

"No, I'm fine where I am, thanks."

"But you need to meet people," said Zuke, who had strolled across to me. "Lemme introduce you to someone."

"I have actually spoken to lots of people," I pointed out.

"Kallgren?"

"We shook hands when I first arrived."

"Tom Bellinghaus? You gotta meet the course architect."

"I already have, Zuke," I replied, stifling a yawn. "I've also talked to Phil Reiner, Bob Tolley, Norman Underwood, Howie and many others. I even had a few words with a man who could have passed for James Garner."

He chuckled. "That *was* James Garner."

"The film star?"

"Kallgren knows everybody. If your eyes weren't half-closed with jet lag, you'd have noticed Telly Savalas, Andy Williams and Lee Majors here earlier on. And they reckon Stallone may drop in later. That's what Golden Haze is going to be, Al. A home for the Hollywood set." He slapped my shoulder. "Let's face it. They're the only ones who can afford to join." We shared a laugh. "By the way, don't ever play against Garner in a pro-am. That guy is some golfer on his day."

"I'll remember that." I suppressed a second yawn. "Any chance of me taking a taxi back to the house? I'm bushed."

"We'll all go soon," he promised. "There's just one more person you have to meet. Suzanne Fricker. Come on."

"Who is she?" I asked as he guided me through the crowd.

"Works for Kallgren. One of his head honchos. Suzanne is a bit special. That's her in the black dress."

I'd spotted her earlier. If Helen Everett hadn't been in the room, Suzanne Fricker would have been the most attractive female. Slim and svelte in a black evening gown, she had a face that could have come straight off the cover of a glossy magazine. Short hair flecked with grey was brushed back from her forehead in porcupine style. Even across a large room, I had seen how much jewellery she was wearing.

Zuke embraced her and gave her a kiss on each cheek.

"Hi, babe. Want you to say hello to my good friend, Alan Saxon." He turned to me. "Al, this is the boss lady of the whole tournament—the beautiful and talented Suzanne Fricker."

"Good to have you with us, Alan," she said, flashing a smile.

"Thanks," I replied, shaking her hand and finding it rather cold. "It's a real bonus for me to be here."

"We'll be seeing a lot of each other this week."

"Can't be bad," I remarked, manufacturing a grin. "And are you really the boss lady?"

She shook her head. "Not yet. I'm just part of the Kallgren team. I handle the contractual side of things."

"Suzanne is a hot-shot lawyer," explained Zuke, putting an arm casually around her waist. "You watch out, old buddy. She can tie you up so tight in legal jargon, you'll need an escape clause to go to the john."

Her laugh was immediate but quite hollow.

Suzanne Fricker lost a lot of her attraction close up. There was an artificial quality about her that went beyond the heavy make-up and the careful poise. When her face slipped into a smile, her eyes remained detached and watchful. She reminded me of something.

A Barbie doll with a law degree.

"What do you think of the clubhouse?" she asked me.

"If we had places as luxurious as this in England, we'd never go out and play golf." Her gaze never left me. I was being assessed. "How long have you been with Mr. Kallgren?"

"Eighteen months. It sure beats court work."

"Court?"

"Suzanne was at the US Attorney's office," said Zuke. "Her job was to send some poor bastard to the state penitentiary."

"That's right," she agreed. "Especially when some poor bastard embezzled millions of dollars. I was with the Special Prosecutions Unit. Had its moments. I was into large-scale fraud."

"So what's changed?" teased Zuke.

Another empty laugh, then her eyes flicked across the room.

"Hey, buster, you got competition."

"What?"

"Not that I blame Helen. That guy could charge stud fees."

Zuke's manner altered at once. As soon as he saw Gamil Amir talking to Helen, then kissing her hand with excessive courtesy, he let go of Suzanne and raced off. We watched him say something to the Egyptian, who tensed angrily in reply before nodding politely to Helen and moving away. Suzanne kept her eyes on Amir and spoke softly to herself.

"Six foot two and handsome all the way down! Oh boy!"

We left the party soon afterwards.

The drive back was hair-raising. Zuke took his Mercedes well over the speed limit, zigzagging through the late-night traffic with complete disregard for our safety, doing his best to provoke some sort of response from his wife. None came. Helen remained silent and vengeful in the rear of the car.

When we reached the house, she went straight upstairs and he chased after her. A row erupted in the bedroom and I took my cue to slide off to my own room. As I prepared myself for bed, muffled shouts continued and then ended abruptly. I was relieved. Marital bickering always reminds me of Rosemary.

I got into bed, switched off the light and snuggled down. There was a knock on the door and Zuke came in. Rage had left him now and he was in high spirits. He pulled back my duvet.

"Come on, Al, one last drink. Help me unwind."

"Zuke, I'm all in."

"Just one. Be a pal."

He ushered me along to his den, installed me in an armchair and poured two glasses of brandy. Unlocking a drawer in the oak desk, he took out a video cassette and laughed with childish delight as he slipped it into his recorder. After pressing buttons, he flopped into the chair beside me and pointed at the television screen.

"This is what we need, Al. Wait till you see it."

The film was called *Country Pleasures*. It was made with a low budget and high seriousness. The opening shot gave us a Porsche haring along a country road and then gradually slowing. A close-up of the dashboard confirmed that the petrol tank was empty. The car halted and the driver got out. Since he had the sort of physique that would have enabled him to kick sand into Arnold Schwarzenegger's face with impunity, I couldn't understand why he didn't just lift the car on to his shoulder and carry it off to the nearest garage.

Instead, he took a petrol can from the boot and began to walk. Cut to a wooded area. Excited female noises. Muscle man registers curiosity and crosses to peer through the bushes. The girls, of course, are stark naked. One black, one white. More reaction shots of the voyeur, then into the heavy breathing.

Zuke began to laugh and sat forward on the edge of his chair.

I fell asleep during the first orgasm.

I awoke next morning to a double surprise. Someone had put me to bed and a pop group was using my skull as a rehearsal studio. When I sat up and shook my head, I realised that the pounding music was, in fact, coming from the living room and that its din was intensified by a rhythmical thumping and a series of high-pitched yells. All was explained when I crept into the hall and followed the noise.

Mardie Cutler was leading Helen Everett in a strenuous workout. They were bending, stretching, leaping and kicking in time to the venomous beat blasting out of quadriphonic speakers. Both wore leotards that advertised their natural charms and both were caught up in the hysteria of their ritual.

I felt exhausted just watching them but the indefatigable Mardie had enough breath to yell commands to her client. Her voice kept to the music and rose above it.

"So we stretch to the right on a count of ten—one, two, three, four, five, six, seven, eight, nine, ten. Then we stretch to the left and do it again—one, two, three, four, five, six, seven, eight, nine, ten. Now we keep on dancing and stay on our toes, then we lift those knees and . . ."

I sneaked away before they noticed me.

An hour later, I'd shaved, showered, dressed, breakfasted and was being driven northwards on the San Diego freeway in a Grand Wagoneer. Zuke was much more subdued and said very little. It gave me the chance to look around and take stock.

The San Fernando Valley is a quintessential part of the burgeoning megalopolis known as Los Angeles. Covering an area of 177 square miles, the Valley runs from the Ventura County line on the west, to the San Gabriel Mountains on the east and north, to the Santa Monica Mountains on the south. Geography is an inadequate description, however. The Valley has a psychic importance. Its fertility, its beauty, its prosperity and its infinite variety help to shape the minds of Angelenos.

As I watched craggy mountains rise up ahead of us in the morning sunlight, I felt my spirits surge. Even when viewed from a busy freeway, the Valley could stimulate and liberate.

It eventually brought Zuke out of his untypical silence.

"Valle de Santa Catalina de Bononia de los Encinos."

"Sorry. Don't speak Spanish."

"Old name for this place. When a guy called Father Juan Crespi first climbed over the Sepulveda Pass in 1769, he saw what he described as 'a very pleasant and spacious valley.' " Zuke gave a mirthless laugh. "That was before the Kallgrens of this world moved in."

We left the freeway and headed for the Golden Haze Golf Club.

When I first saw the card of the course, it had induced quiet panic in me. It was less about golf than about a reign of terror.

HOLE	PAR	YARDAGE
1. Spyglass Hill	5	600
2. Cascades	3	158

3. Pinehurst	4	345
4. Firestone	4	465
5. Winged Foot	5	515
6. Merion	4	420
7. Desert Inn	3	206
8. Baltusrol	4	365
9. Pebble Beach	4	450
10. Harbor Town	4	453
11. Olympic	4	427
12. Westchester	4	476
13. Augusta	5	485
14. Butler National	4	429
15. Medinah	4	318
16. Cypress Point	3	233
17. Oakmont	4	322
18. Doral (Blue)	4	425
	72	7092

It was a roll call of some of the toughest holes in America. I had come to grief on several of them during my years on the US tour.

The gargantuan opening hole at Spyglass Hill demands superhuman stroke play to achieve par. I once took twelve at Pebble Beach's notorious 9th and saw why it was nicknamed the Old Heartbreaker. Perched above the restless ocean, the 16th at Cypress Point is the most beautiful but deadly hole I've ever encountered, a true test of nerve and technique. When the north wind hits the Monterey Peninsula, all three holes are invincible.

Other names stirred other memories for me.

Winged Foot needs rifle accuracy. Merion is strategically trapped around the green. The prevailing winds in San Francisco are cunning pickpockets who rob you freely of strokes at Olympic. The 12th at Westchester is a giant par-four that's strewn with hazards. I've lost count of the number of balls I've put into the creek at Augusta's unlucky 13th, and the challenging 14th at Butler National has also had me in deep water. As for the Blue Monster at

Doral, there are few more daunting finishing holes than this one in Miami.

My quiet panic had soon given way to relief.

I realised that Golden Haze was not an amalgam of exact replicas, because it would have been impossible to reproduce some of those unique holes. What Tom Bellinghaus had done was to keep strictly to their yardages while copying only a feature or two from them. Golden Haze, he claimed, was a celebration of the best of American golf.

As soon as I began my practice round with Zuke, I realised that Bellinghaus was a disciple of that legendary course architect, Robert Trent Jones. There were the same hallmarks—lush velvet fairways, manicured roughs, huge tees and massive, undulating greens guarded by water and contoured bunkers. It was pretty but punitive. Bellinghaus had toughened it even more with some vicious dog-legs that created blind shots and some uniformly cruel pin placements.

Howie Danzig had been right. It could be a killer.

Realistically, I had no chance of winning the tournament. I'd been brought in at the last moment and had only two days to master a perilous course. It was over a month since I'd played any golf and I was pitted against quality opposition. The best I could hope for was to give a good account of myself and stave off humiliation.

To achieve this, I was lucky enough to have the help of an excellent caddie. Jerry Bruford was a short, sturdy, bullet-headed man in his forties, a gum-chewing philosopher who'd studied the course carefully and found much to respect but nothing to fear. His comments were invaluable, his judgement of distance faultless and his advice about club selection sound. We liked each other straight away.

Zuke had recommended the caddie and I was grateful. With Jerry Bruford in my corner, I felt safe.

"This is the suicide hole," he warned.

We'd reached the 13th. Augusta. The centrepiece.

"By the end of the tournament," predicted Jerry, surveying the great expanse of water in front of us, "that lake will have more balls in it than the entire United States Army."

The kidney-shaped lake ran almost from tee to green. What made it especially hazardous was the fact that the unusually small green was set on a raised plateau. Too long a shot would take you on over into a bunker while an under-hit ball was certain to roll down the sharp incline and into the lake.

"Don't try any heroics," said Jerry. "Keep right and stay clear of the water. That way you get a good look at the flag when you try to hit the green with your third shot."

"Okay," I agreed.

It was a baptism of fire. I hooked my tee shot into the lake, lost a second ball when I under-hit my approach shot to the green, then found a bunker on the far side of the plateau.

I finished with a bogey six. Jerry was sympathetic.

Zuke managed a creditable par at the hole. His massive tee shot went to the right of the lake, then he cut diagonally across it at its narrowest point. All he could see of the green when he hit his third shot was the tip of the flag, but his ball landed obligingly on the edge of the putting surface and he sank it with two putts.

His mood had changed the instant we began the practice round and he was now jaunty, talkative and brimming with confidence. Dressed flamboyantly in yellow shirt, red trousers and white shoes, he made me feel almost invisible in my dark colours and baseball cap. Whenever he was in the public eye, Zuke liked to cut a dash.

I hit dozens of balls during the round and made many serious mistakes but I was not disheartened. There's always a special thrill in tackling a new course for the first time and I knew that I could improve every time I got out on it. I learned a lot from listening to Jerry and from watching Zuke, and I took the trouble to make copious notes in my little pad at each hole.

We adjourned to the locker room.

"What's the verdict, Al?" asked my host.

"It's a tough bugger and no mistake, but it might have

its weaknesses." I grinned at him. "Just wish I knew where they were."

"I'll find them," he announced. "Come Thursday, that course is going to lose its virginity good and proper. And *I'll* be the guy responsible."

"Are you sure of that?" asked a mocking voice.

Gamil Amir had come into the locker room and overheard us. He sauntered over and studied Zuke through dark brown eyes. Small white teeth showed beneath his black pencil moustache.

"How will you take its virginity?" he teased. "From what I hear, you don't have the balls for it any more."

Bristling with anger, Zuke leapt up to face him.

"Why don't you just hop on your camel and get your unwanted Arab ass out of here?"

"I live in America now," replied the other with smiling control. "I know your customs well, I speak your language perfectly and I play golf better than any of you."

"Only one problem, Amir. We don't fucking *like* you!"

"Some of your men don't," he conceded. "But your women like me. They like me a lot. Ask your wife."

Zuke's punch caught him on the side of the jaw and sent him staggering back. I threw my arms around my friend to prevent him from diving after Amir.

"Calm down, Zuke!" I urged. "Take it easy, will you?"

Blood trickled from the corner of Amir's mouth and down on to his fawn sweater. He looked in a mirror and stemmed the flow with a handkerchief, then he swung round to confront Zuke again. Amir's voice was deep and menacing.

"Don't ever come to my country," he warned. "You're the sort of man who would end up floating in the Nile with a knife through his throat!"

He turned on his heel and stalked out quickly.

When Zuke eventually calmed down, we had a late lunch in the clubhouse. He then excused himself because he had to see Howie on business that afternoon. I took Jerry out for another practice round and worked hard for some hours. We spent a long time at the troublesome 13th. I was determined to crack it before the tournament.

Zuke returned to drive me back to the house. After dinner with him and Helen, I sloped off for an early night.

The next day followed the same pattern. A practice round with Zuke in the morning, lunch together, then a solo foray in the afternoon to try to iron out some of the many difficulties I was still having. It was evening before I finally packed in and went to the bar. A familiar figure hailed me in rasping tones.

"Hurry up, Saxon! You owe the barman eight dollars."

It was Clive Phelps. Lounging against the counter, he was as shabbily dressed as ever and his thick curly hair needed a trim. A cheroot was jammed between his lips and it had burned down so low that it was in danger of setting fire to his thick moustache. Ash decorated his shoulder and sleeve.

I pumped his arm to show how delighted I was to see him and ordered drinks for us both.

"Thought you were coming yesterday, Clive."

"So did I," he moaned, stubbing out his cheroot. "Fog at Heathrow. Cancellations. Delays. Total bloody chaos. I was lucky to get here at all."

"So you haven't had a chance to see the course yet?"

"Someone drove me round in a golf cart. Looks a right sod."

"It won't take prisoners."

I explained why and Clive absorbed all the details like a sponge. A good golfer himself when he allowed himself to be, he was full of pertinent questions about the finer points of Golden Haze. Our drinks arrived and I settled my debts. We toasted each other and drank deep. His eyes rolled comically.

"What's the scandal?"

"None so far."

"Come on!" he complained. "What is this? I was the one who got you out here, remember. I expect a bit of quid pro quo, old son. Spill the beans. Who's been fucking whose wife? Where are the backhanders going? Is it true Kallgren's tied in with the Mafia?"

"Everything's completely above board, Clive."

"Bollocks!"

I pondered. "Well, there is one thing," I admitted.

"Tell me all. Whisper it into my shell-like lughole."

After swearing him to secrecy, I told him about the incident between Zuke Everett and Gamil Amir. He was enthralled.

"We could be in for some fireworks, Alan."

"Why?"

"Because Amir is clear favourite to win. Everybody's tipping him. Man can't lose. Now, my question is this." His eyebrows rose quizzically. "If Zuke takes a swing at him over a chance remark in the locker room, what in God's name will he do to Amir when the bugger slaughters him out there on the course?"

It was an alarming thought.

Pomp and ceremony surrounded the start of the Kallgren Tournament of Champions. The media were there in force and the large crowd around the first tee contained more than a sprinkling of Hollywood stars and VIPs. Resplendent in their uniforms, a US Marines band gave us rousing extracts from the Sousa repertoire. Along with the twenty-nine other players, I was lined up in front of the dais. The *Titanic* could not have been launched with more fuss and pretension.

Using a pair of silver shears to cut a giant ribbon, the Mayor of Los Angeles declared Golden Haze officially open, then posed for the cameras. Rutherford Kallgren came forward to make a short speech of welcome to us all and expressed the hope that the inaugural event would put his pride and joy firmly on the golfing map. Kallgren was far too plausible for my liking and had the sort of self-effacing manner that subtly draws attention to itself. I was happy to play in his tournament but I would have hated to work for such a man.

Tom Bellinghaus now took his turn at the microphone.

Big, sleek and completely bald, he spoke with the beaming arrogance of a man convinced that he is supreme in his chosen field.

"Golden Haze is *my* course. I created it. I wanted it to be the most comprehensive test of golfing skills in America and I believe that I have achieved that objective."

He paused to bask in the spontaneous applause. I noticed that none of the players clapped. Tom Bellinghaus noticed too. He aimed his next remarks directly at us.

"You are the cream of the golfing world and you will all be out to tame my course. I defy you to do so. To prove I have faith in my handiwork, gentlemen, I will put my money where my mouth is. The crucial hole at Golden Haze is the 13th. It will break many of you and hold all of you at bay. Let me throw down a challenge to you. I will pay $500 to anyone who gets a birdie at the 13th hole." He quelled the immediate buzz of interest with outstretched hands. "And I offer a prize of $5000 to the player who gets an eagle."

Applause mingled with excited speculation as he sat down. Tom Bellinghaus had thrown down the gauntlet. Evidently, he did not expect to have to part with a cent of his money. It was up to us to wipe that complacent grin off his face.

"He could regret that," muttered Zuke, standing beside me.

"I hope he does," I said. "Somehow I doubt it."

The first round began shortly afterwards.

When the draw had been made I was fortunate to be partnered with Phil Reiner, the quiet man of the US tour. Tall, muscular and impeccably smart, Reiner had a pleasantly anonymous face that was hidden behind large, gold-framed spectacles. He was a consistently good rather than a brilliant golfer and always finished near the top of the USPGA tour rankings. He was the ideal partner. Cool, polite, professional.

It was a measure of the course's unforgiving meanness that I played well and still finished eight strokes over par. Phil Reiner was in impressive form and actually managed a par round. Two strokes ahead of him was Gamil Amir, the instant crowd favourite and the only player to beat par. Zuke Everett's name ended the day in fourth place.

The 13th hole never looked in the slightest danger of yielding a birdie. Bellinghaus beamed on. His wallet was undefiled.

Pairings were altered for the second round so that the leading players went out last. Thanks to Jerry's guidance and a more aggressive attitude, I shot a 74 that boosted my confidence a great deal. I was teamed with the luckless Mr. Chung, a somnolent Korean who hit two shots into water and lost a third ball in some pine trees.

By repeating his performance of the first round, Amir stayed at the top of the leader board with a cushion of three strokes. Reiner was second on 143 with Dayton Willard breathing down his neck. Zuke had a disastrous second round and slipped right back. It was galling enough for him to have Amir in the lead but he was in an even fouler mood when the Egyptian collected $500 for a birdie at the 13th.

He was miserable company that night at the house.

The third round changed everything. A fierce wind stiffened some already impregnable defences and scores began to tumble. I was struggling from the first tee. Zuke, by contrast, was in his element. I was not too thrilled at having him as my playing partner when we set out but I soon revised my opinion because I became an awe-struck witness to a truly remarkable round of golf.

Zuke Everett had always been a player who responded to pressure but this time he surpassed himself. Defeating the wind with a low trajectory, he drove with a blend of power, accuracy and sheer determination. No hole was safe when he was in that form. He had picked up three birdies before we reached the back nine.

His charge continued all the way to the 13th hole.

"This is the big one, Zuke," I observed.

"I'm ready for it."

"Good luck."

Augusta was truly the death hole.

During the first two rounds, it carried out a series of cold-blooded character assassinations that left even great players looking like ordinary ones. Since it was expected to draw even more blood, it had attracted a huge crowd and the stands around the green were packed.

Sitting among the other ghouls was Tom Bellinghaus.

Gasps of disbelief went up from the gallery when Zuke Everett addressed his ball on the tee. Instead of driving to the right of the lake to secure a good position from which to cross it, Zuke was going to try to carry the water with his tee shot. Since he was aiming diagonally across the widest part of the lake, his ball had to stay in the air for the best part of three hundred yards. Even though the wind was now at our backs, it was a frighteningly audacious shot.

Zuke drew his driver back with utmost concentration and then brought it whistling down with a fierce plunge of speed. His ball flew through the air like a bird for several long seconds and then it all but skimmed the water's surface before hitting the safety of the bank. Ever the showman, Zuke turned to acknowledge the uproar with his club held aloft. A birdie—even an eagle—was now possible.

After Zuke's incredible tee shot, my own was an anti-climax. Opting for safety, I stayed to the right of the lake, content to pick my way around and give myself a good view of the green.

We split up and headed for opposite sides of the lake.

"Go on, Zuke," yelled a fan. "You can walk on water!"

"No," he called back. "I can only turn it into wine."

Since I was much further from the flag, I now played first and hit my best iron shot so far to find an excellent position from which to attack the green. Zuke and his caddie were trying to work out the precise yardage to the pin. The monster drive stirred us all but it left him with what was virtually a blind shot to the green.

From across the lake, I watched him take out a lofted club and try a few practice swings before addressing his ball. Back went the club in a fluent arc, then down it came with measured violence. The ball sailed high into the sky and was lost for a moment in the glare of the sun. Pandemonium around the green told us what happened next. After landing on the putting surface, it had rolled straight into the hole.

Zuke Everett had achieved an impossible double eagle.

I laughed as I imagined the look on the Bellinghaus face.

The remainder of the round was a march of triumph for Zuke. News of his miraculous play on the 13th flashed to all parts of the course and our gallery swelled as spectators deserted other contests to watch ours. Except that it was no longer a contest between two golfers. It was a shoot-out between two deadly rivals.

Zuke Everett and the Golden Haze course.

When he walked off the 18th green with his name near the top of the leader board again, he'd done what he promised. Taken its virginity. In recording an unbeatable 64, he'd also jumped back into the limelight. Gamil Amir, dropping strokes further back down the course, was a usurper who had been thrust aside.

Rutherford Kallgren was the first to congratulate Zuke and told him they would put his name on a plaque at the 13th hole. Lean and gorgeous in a pink suit, Suzanne Fricker rushed up to throw her arms around the hero. He accepted her kiss and then said something into her ear that made her smile harden slightly but she recovered her composure at once. The contract lawyer in her came to the fore.

"How much does Tom Bellinghaus owe you, Zuke?"

"Plenty."

"$500 for a birdie and $5000 for an eagle." Her teeth shone in the bright sunlight. "I'd say you have a pretty good case for claiming $50,000 for that double eagle."

"At least that."

"Mr. Kallgren brought you luck, after all," she argued.

"No, Suzanne," he corrected. "I brought myself luck."

Once again her smile froze slightly.

Fans milled around and fought to shake his hand. I ducked out of the throng and found myself next to Clive

Phelps. Even a cynical, battle-hardened, seen-it-all-before veteran like him was carried away by the excitement.

"That was out of this bloody world, Alan!"

"I couldn't be more pleased for Zuke."

"Some idiot in the press tent called him Fluke Everett but I told him he was talking through his arsehole. Zuke deserved everything he got out there today."

"*I* can vouch for that."

"He played mad, marvellous golf."

"Who'd have thought he'd climb back up the leader board after what happened yesterday?" I asked. "Quite frankly, I'd written off his chances completely."

"Somebody had faith in him."

"What?"

"First thing this morning—while everyone else was laying out their folding stuff on Amir—someone put $10,000 on Zuke to win the tournament. Seemed like lunacy at the time."

"Who was it, Clive?"

"Haven't a clue. Just one of those juicy snippets I tend to pick up in my line." He gave a rich chuckle. "Tell you what, though. It certainly wasn't *that* silly sod." He pointed at Tom Bellinghaus. "Look at him. I bet he'd like to murder Zuke Everett."

Bellinghaus was some distance away but we could see his ferocious scowl. As he glared at Zuke, he was not looking at the golfer who relieved his beloved course of its virginity.

He glowered at the man who raped his daughter in public.

Tom Bellinghaus wanted retribution.

Celebrations which began in the bar continued back at the house in Santa Monica with a superb meal by candlelight. Zuke, Helen, Mardie Cutler, Howie Danzig and I were treated to the finest Mexican cuisine as prepared by Dominga, the diminutive housekeeper and cook. Because the old woman spoke only Spanish, our compliments had to be translated by Helen into her native tongue.

It was wonderful to be in the house when it was filled with such happiness. Helen was ostentatiously loving towards her husband and he was glowing. Mardie giggled at almost everything and Howie told us some very funny jokes.

Zuke Everett was back on the winning trail again.

Everything was all right.

"I still don't understand about this double eagle," complained Helen, who had refused to watch any of the tournament. "How does it work and why is it so special?"

"I'll show you, doll," promised Zuke, kissing her on the forehead before darting out of the room.

I tried to explain. "A double eagle is three below the par for a hole. Otherwise known as an albatross. It's special because it's much rarer than a hole-in-one. With a double eagle, you have to play *two* magic shots in succession. I've had a few holes-in-one, Helen, but I've never got a double eagle in a tournament."

Drink had mellowed Howie Danzig, who spoke gently for once.

"When I was a scrawny kid back in the thirties," he said, "Gene Sarazen had an amazing double eagle at the Masters—or the Augusta National Invitational, as they called it in those days. They reckon that Sarazen's second shot was one of the greatest ever played on a golf course." He sat back in his chair. "I think that Zuke matched it out there today."

"Okay, everybody! Up you get!"

Zuke marched back into the dining room and lifted us up from the table. Wearing my baseball cap, he carried a pitching wedge and a couple of golf balls. The women laughed as he shepherded us out to the rear of the house. He gave me a broad wink.

"Hope you don't mind me borrowing these things, Al. Your bag was in the hall. Mine's locked up in the garage."

"Help yourself. Cap looks great on you."

It was cold outside on the patio but that did not deflect him. The swimming pool was lit but the lawn was largely in shadow. At the far end of the garden, we could just make out a small birdbath set in a concrete circle.

"Right," announced Zuke, swaying a little. "We're on the 13th tee. The pool is the lake. And that birdbath down there is the hole. Up on a plateau. See?"

"You're going to hit a ball *into* the birdbath?" Mardie was torn between wonder and amusement. "Nobody could do that, Zuke."

"I can. Two shots. Stand back."

He dropped a ball on to the paving, trapped it with his foot, stepped back to address it, then swung the club. He sliced the ball straight into the deep end of the pool. The female laughter made him quite annoyed.

"I'll do it properly this time!" he insisted. "So watch, will you? *Watch!*"

Zuke put the second ball on a rubber mat and took more care this time. With a swing of the club, he chipped it over the water and into the middle of the lawn. Mardie clapped but Helen had seen enough.

"It's cold out here. Let's go back in."

"One more shot," said Zuke. "Stay right there."

He lurched across the grass and sized up his next shot. He was only twenty yards or so from the birdbath when he swung his wedge again. It connected too hard and the ball went shooting off into the bushes at the far end of the garden. Mardie laughed and Helen jeered but Zuke was adamant that he should be given another chance.

Swaying more than ever, he lumbered off into the bushes.

"He'll never find the ball in the dark," I noted.

Howie agreed. "He's so liquored up tonight that he'll need two hands to find his own ass. Go get him, Al."

"Bring him back inside," added Helen, impatiently. "I'll organize some fresh coffee."

The women went back into the house and Howie waited for me as I went down the lawn to retrieve my host. Beyond the birdbath, it was almost pitch dark. I called out to him.

"Zuke, where the hell are you?"

I went into the bushes and felt my way through them.

"Come on out!" I urged.

But there was no answer. I stood still and listened. Not a sound. I expected Zuke to be blundering about in the undergrowth but there was complete silence. I moved on more quickly. When I came into a clearing, I soon realised why he had not replied. My foot kicked against a solid object that all but tripped me up.

It was Zuke Everett. Flat on his back.

Something seemed to be sticking out of his chest.

I knew at once that he was dead.

Chapter Three

The shock was like a punch in the solar plexus. It took my breath away. I knelt beside the body for several seconds and fought against the urge to be sick. A close and valued friend had been murdered in his own garden. On one of the greatest days in his career, a brilliant golfer had been separated from his game forever.

It was devastating. The sense of waste overpowered me.

I began to retch.

A car started up in the distance and moved off at speed. The sound got me back to my feet at once and brought me out of my daze. Zuke Everett's killer was making a run for it. Anger blocked out all other feeling. Determined to strike back, I charged headlong through the undergrowth in the direction from which the sound had come.

I did not get very far.

As I went hurtling past a cluster of palm trees, I hit something hard and metallic that sent me bouncing backwards. The force of the impact made my head spin and drew blood from my nose. It also produced a loud ringing noise that was heard by Howie Danzig.

"Come on, you guys!" he called. "Quit horsing about!"

"Bring a torch!" I shouted.

"Why? What's the trouble, Al?"

"There's been an accident. A bad one."

"Zuke?"

"Keep the ladies away!" I ordered. "And bring a torch. *Quick*!"

"Yeah, yeah. Okay, Al."

While Howie went off into the house, I used a handkerchief to stem the flow of blood, then tried to identify the barrier into which I had run at full tilt. It was a high chain-link fence that surrounded a tennis court. The thick wire had left its imprint on my forehead and its sting all over my body. I realised that it must have been the fence that I saw glinting in the sun above the trees on my first day in Santa Monica.

My eyes were more accustomed to the gloom now. I picked my way carefully back to the clearing and stood beside Zuke. The handle of a knife was protruding from his chest. He had been stabbed through the heart. As I gazed down at him, I seemed to feel the blade sliding in between my own ribs.

It was a squalid end to his day of glory.

"Al! Where are you?"

Howie Danzig was hobbling across the lawn on his stick. He had a flashlight in his other hand and its beam cut through the bushes.

"Over here!" I said.

"What's going on?" he asked, anxiously. "Is Zuke hurt?"

"Worse than that, I'm afraid."

He came into the clearing and I took the flashlight from him. When I shone it down on Zuke, there were fresh horrors to comprehend. Blood had gushed freely from the wound to darken the front of his shirt with vivid effect. His body had not behaved itself in death. Vomit ran in a stream from his open mouth and his trousers were stained with urine.

Howie Danzig staggered back a few paces.

"*Jesus!*"

"Are you all right?"

"Not Zuke!" he protested, a hand going to his own heart. "He was the most beautiful guy in the world."

"Take it easy," I advised.

"Who would do *that* to him?"

I caught Howie as he stumbled forward. His eyes were bulging, perspiration was oozing from him and his breath was coming in short gasps. Easing him towards a tree, I rested him gently against it. Then I switched off the light so that the corpse could be decently covered by a blanket of darkness.

Howie's voice became a hoarse whisper.

"Jesus H. Christ!"

"Just relax," I soothed.

"Did you see him? The man is dead!"

His whole frame shook uncontrollably for an instant and I held on tight. I could feel the blood trickling down over my lips but there was nothing I could do about it. Both my hands were needed to support Howie. It had been a massive blow to him. He had been much more than a manager to Zuke Everett. He had been mentor, friend and father figure.

A fifteen-year relationship was stretched out obscenely on the grass nearby. His grief was understandable.

Hard practicality at last asserted itself and he shook me off.

"I'm okay now, Al."

"Are you sure?"

"Yeah. I'm fine." He gave a grim chuckle. "Don't worry. You won't end up with *two* stiffs on your hands."

"That's good news."

"I gotta call the cops," he decided.

"Let me help you back to the house," I offered.

"No," he replied, pushing my arm away, "I can manage. You stay here, Al. I won't be long."

"Helen mustn't see this," I warned. "Nor Mardie."

"*Nobody* oughta see it!"

"Don't tell them just yet."

"I've gotta tell them something," he argued.

"Say it's an accident," I counselled. "Whatever happens, keep them inside the house."

"I'll try, Al. But it may not be that easy."

I used the flashlight to guide him back to the edge of the lawn and I dabbed at my nose with my handkerchief.

Howie Danzig went struggling off across the springy turf. Before the police arrived, I wanted to take a proper look around myself and so I swung the beam downwards to begin my search.

I soon found what I was after. My pitching wedge was lying on the ground near some thick bushes. Zuke Everett was about ten yards away with his head pointing towards the tennis court. Between the golf club and the body, the grass was heavily scored.

Something else caught my attention and it jolted me.

Zuke was still wearing my baseball cap. It had simply not registered when I had first seen him in the glare of the flashlight. Knife, blood, vomit and urine had dominated. Now it was the turn of my cap. I was at once afraid to touch it and keen to reclaim it.

Reaching out tentatively, I caught hold of the peak and tried to tease the cap off but it would not come. I put the flashlight on the ground and its horizontal beam gave a new perspective on tragedy. One hand still on the peak, I slipped the other under Zuke's head to lift it. As soon as my fingers made contact with a sticky substance, however, I withdrew them. Blood was pouring from the back of his skull and the cap was saturated with it. I explored the ground near the head but it seemed relatively soft.

After a thorough examination of the position in which he was lying, I made my way towards the chain-link fence. When I let the light play on it, I saw that it belonged to one of several tennis courts that acted as a boundary line at the end of the adjoining gardens. I noted a more significant fact. A jagged hole had been cut in the fence that bordered on Zuke's property. It explained how his killer gained entry.

Though I stooped down to squeeze through the gap, I still managed to catch my collar on the wire. I moved swiftly across the hard court until I reached the steel door. The chain and padlock which had held it shut were now on the ground. Wire-cutters had been used to sheer through the links.

A large, empty car park confronted me. Beyond that

was the dim outline of the clubhouse itself, a long, low building. When I got to the main gates, I found them securely locked, but the perimeter wall that fronted the club posed no real problems to anyone of normal agility. I shinned up the wall with ease and looked over into a quiet, tree-lined road. It was an ideal place in which to hide a getaway car.

Further investigation was cut short by a scream.

Mardie Cutler had seen the body.

I dropped down from the wall and sprinted back to the garden. As I raced up to the clearing, I found the two women involved in a strange reversal of roles. Mardie was weeping copiously and behaving like the distraught wife while Helen, one arm around the girl, was acting as the comforting friend. Helen was directing the beam of her torch on to Zuke's face.

"You should have stayed inside," I advised.

"He was my husband," said Helen calmly. "I have a right."

Mardie went into fresh paroxysms of grief and Helen enfolded her in both arms, patting her gently and trying to calm her down. Howie Danzig came stumping through the undergrowth.

"Sorry, Al. They heard me calling the cops."

"I have a right," repeated Helen.

Her composure was both unreal and unsettling.

"There's nothing we can do out here," I reasoned. "Why don't we all go back into the house?"

"Yeah," agreed Howie. "I could sure use a drink."

Mardie wailed as she stole another glance at the body.

"Come on," added Howie. "This is no place for you."

He took the girl from Helen's arms and led her firmly away. Mardie Cutler's scream had been a powerful one. Lights had come on in neighbouring houses and voices were calling from other gardens.

Helen Everett shone her torch on Zuke once more and stared down at his face. I put my hand on her shoulder but she refused to budge. It was some minutes before she was ready to take her leave. With a rueful shake of her head, she whispered one word at her husband.

"Angel . . ."

It was not how I would have described him.

The police arrived in numbers soon afterwards. They moved with the casual efficiency of people who are used to being summoned to a murder scene in the middle of the night. When a ring of lights had been set up, the forensic team got to work at once. They searched, measured, photographed and bagged for removal. After thorough examination by the pathologist, Zuke Everett was wheeled away on a stretcher.

The steward of the tennis club was hauled out of his bed in Westwood Village and brought over to inspect the damage to his fence and to switch on the car park lights so that the detectives could extend the area of their search. Neighbours were pacified and sent away. The press was kept at arm's length for the time being. Two uniformed police officers guarded the front door of the house.

While all this was going on, the four of us sat in the living room and tried to come to terms with the enormity of what had happened. Dominga flitted in and out with liquid refreshment. Helen and Mardie drank endless cups of black coffee, I opted for chilled orange juice and Howie launched a full-scale assault on a bottle of bourbon.

I'd washed all the blood from my face now but the memory of my encounter with the fence still lingered. The ugly red weals on my forehead had not yet faded and the knuckles on one hand were raw where they had made contact with the wire.

We were not alone for long.

In response to telephone calls from Howie, a doctor, a lawyer and a Catholic priest soon rolled up at the house. All were surprisingly young men and none of them seemed discomfited by the late hour. The doctor attended Mardie and prescribed sedatives for her. She was still in distress and hardly able to speak without sobbing. The lawyer stayed deep in conversation with Howie. A dead golfer raised all kinds of legal problems for the manager and his brow became progressively more furrowed as he talked with his visitor.

The priest was there for Helen's benefit. He stroked her hand and spoke to her quietly in Spanish. She listened intently and nodded at what was being said but she was still remarkably unruffled.

I had to draw solace from my orange juice.

My own grief began to gnaw away at me. Zuke's friendship had been important to me over the years and it was the reason that I had got to Los Angeles in the first place. I felt loss, outrage, pain. Only hours before, the house had been echoing with his laughter. It now seemed cold and empty without him. I had seen the best of Zuke that night. It had been extinguished forever.

I was hurt, humbled, alone.

Eventually, it was time to give our statements to the police. Since I had actually discovered the body, I was the first person to be interviewed by the two detectives leading the investigation.

Lieutenant Victor Salgado and Sergeant Patch Nelms.

Salgado was a lean, swarthy, once handsome individual who was failing to keep middle age at bay with hair dye and flashy clothes. There was a slightly seedy air to him and the gold tooth did not help. Nelms was a big, solid black man in a dark blue suit and spotted tie. Watchful and somnolent, he reminded me uncomfortably of my father. He had the same steady, unflattering gaze.

We were in the dining room. Salgado was at the head of the table in the chair that had earlier been occupied by Zuke, and Nelms sat beside him with his brawny arms folded. Each had a notepad in front of him and there was a small cassette recorder on the table.

Salgado gave me a brief glimpse of his gold tooth.

"Take a seat," he invited with brisk charm.

"Thanks." I lowered myself on to the chair indicated.

"It could be a long night."

"It already has been."

"You got something there." He stifled a belch. "Never get a job on Homicide. Ruins your digestion."

"I'll remember that."

He switched on the recorder and tested me for voice level, adjusting the position of the microphone as he did so. Then he rewound the tape and kept his finger on the start button.

"Ready?" he asked.

"What do you want to know, Lieutenant?"

"*Everything*. Nice and slow. Got it?"

"I think so."

"And keep it simple. We're as tired as you are."

"Right."

"State your name first."

I cleared my throat and he pressed the button. My voice was flat and unconvincing. Both of them made random notes and Salgado threw in another belch by way of a sound effect. I told the story exactly as I'd rehearsed it in my mind, leaving out details that I wanted to keep to myself and amending others slightly.

My performance was conditioned by the fact that they were policemen. I simply *couldn't* tell them everything. There was no point in trying to explain why because I didn't fully understand the reasons myself. They were far too complex and contradictory.

Law enforcement had weighed on me heavily from the start. My boyhood had none of the fun and freedom that my friends managed to enjoy. Wherever I looked, my father was on point duty, holding up a hand to stop me most of the time and motioning me forward only when he felt like it and always at a speed that he dictated.

Policed into a show of submission, I was forced to give statements on a daily basis. My father did not use a cassette recorder but he always made mental notes on a pad. Conversation with him was in the nature of an interrogation. I learned to lie, to conceal, to adapt. I felt myself doing it now all over again.

My story was too neat and over-prepared. The two

detectives looked equally unimpressed. Salgado jabbed a finger down on the stop button, then glared across at me.

"What is this, Mr. Saxon?" he protested.

"I'm trying to tell you what happened."

"Don't give me that shit!"

"Everything I've said is *true*."

"But I want the *whole* truth," he emphasised, "and not just the bits of it that suit you. That story of yours has more fucking holes in it than a chorus line—only not nearly as pretty."

"What do you mean, Lieutenant?"

"Give me the details you missed out."

"Such as?"

"Tell him, Patch."

"The baseball cap," grunted Nelms. "It was yours."

"How do you know?" I challenged.

"You wore it for the last three days in the tournament," he said, his Bronx vowels coming in sharp contrast to the light Californian drawl of his superior. "I watched the highlights on TV. It's yours."

"So why didn't you mention it?" pressed Salgado.

"Must've slipped my mind."

"Along with a few other things, Mr. Saxon."

"Maybe," I conceded.

Salgado glared at me for a few moments, then got up and paced around the room to relax the tension. When he came back to the table, he leaned over so that his face was close to mine. He examined the red marks on my forehead.

"Still hurt?"

"Only when I laugh, Lieutenant."

"Then we'll have to make sure you *don't* laugh," he rejoined. Dark, fiery eyes explored my own. "You don't like cops, do you?"

"No," I admitted.

"We can always tell."

"It's nothing personal."

"Then what have you got against us?"

"My father is a policeman."

"Your old man is a cop?" he translated. "So what? Mine

was a trucker. When I was a kid, he used to kick my ass for the sheer hell of it. I hated the bastard. Doesn't mean I gotta hate *all* truckers."

"This is different," I said.

"Why?"

"That's my business."

"What did he do to you?" he asked with heavy sarcasm. "Put the cuffs on you? Knock you around with his night stick? Throw you in the slammer and feed you on bread and water? What in god's name did the sonofabitch *do* to you?"

"Much as you're doing now, Lieutenant."

"Me?"

"Yes," I replied. "My father used to browbeat me."

"Is that all?"

"He treated me as if I was a criminal."

Salgado's eyes flared but he bit back his retort. He sat down again, glanced through his notes, then pointed at the recorder.

"Okay," he said, drily. "Let's try again. Only this time, give us the *full* version. You don't have to like us, Mr. Saxon, but you do have to help us. We'll be listening."

He pressed the start button and I talked into the microphone again. My account was substantially the same but I conceded a number of details that I had held back before. They were still not satisfied. When it was all over, they exchanged a look.

"Patch has a question for you," announced Salgado.

"That baseball cap," said Nelms. "Yankees. You a fan?"

"Not really, Sergeant."

"Then why do you wear it?"

"That's a long story."

"We got all the time in the world."

"I have this friend in New York," I explained. "He's English but he's lived in the States for over twenty years now."

"Well and truly polluted then," added Salgado with a grin.

"Ian always used to tease me about my golf. Said it was

such a boring game to watch. He reckoned that baseball was much more exciting. First time I came to New York, he took me along to Yankee Stadium. Ian was right. It really *was* exciting. We certainly got our money's worth that day. I don't remember who the visiting team were but it was an absolutely cracking game. There was nothing in it until the final innings. Then the Yankees came good and hit a string of homers. The crowd went delirious and I must admit that even I got a bit carried away. There was pandemonium at the end. Everything was thrown up into the air—hats, scarves, programmes, popcorn, the lot. That Yankee cap dropped right down in my lap. Nobody came to reclaim it. So I kept it. Just my size. If the cap fits, I thought, I'll wear it. From that day onward, I never played a tournament without it. Like most golfers, I'm very superstitious. That cap brought me luck. At first, anyway."

"It didn't bring Zuke Everett much luck," observed Salgado. "By the way, I should have told you. Patch is from New York."

"The Bronx," confirmed his colleague.

"He thinks the Yankees are crap."

"I prefer the Mets," grunted Nelms.

There was a long pause. They sat there appraising me with unfriendly eyes set in stone faces. Both of them looked like my father now. It was quite unnerving. Thousands of miles away, he could still get back at me. I was being judged and found wanting. As usual.

"Will that be all?" I wondered.

"No," answered Salgado.

"What else can I tell you, Lieutenant?"

"Plenty."

"Don't you believe my statement?"

"Up to a point."

"Which point?"

"The discovery of the body," he said, consulting his pad again. "You claim that you almost tripped over it in the dark."

"I described it exactly as it happened."

"But you didn't, Mr. Saxon," he corrected. "You gave us

two versions on tape. Okay, they're very similar but there were differences. Second time round, for instance, you tell us you saw him lying there and knew instinctively that he was dead.''

''I did, Lieutenant.''

''Could be another explanation for that.''

''Could there?''

''Oh, you found Zuke Everett when you went into those bushes,'' he conceded. ''No doubt about that. Question is: was he still alive when you got to him?''

The directness of the accusation rattled me.

''Are you saying that *I* killed him?''

''It's a possibility we have to consider,'' he replied, easily.

''But he was my *friend*!''

''Hey, come on now!'' he returned with a shrug. ''You're not *that* wet behind the ears. Murderers often turn out to be friends, wives, husbands, mistresses, business partners, somebody close. It's the people we ought to love that we can hate enough to kill.'' He gave me a knowing smile. ''Look at you and your old man.''

''I did not murder Zuke Everett!'' I asserted.

''Then what are you hiding from us?'' he demanded.

''Nothing.''

''Knock it off, Saxon.''

''*Nothing*, Lieutenant.''

''Gimme facts, will you? Something I can stick my dick into.''

''I've told you all I know.''

''Boy, you must think we're fucking dumb around here!'' he snarled, slapping the table with his hand. ''You really expect us to believe that cockamamie story of yours?''

''What's wrong with it?''

''What's wrong with it, he asks! What's fucking *wrong* with it!''

''It just don't make sense,'' explained Nelms, seriously. ''That's what's wrong with it. According to you, the deceased was kidding around on the lawn with a golf club. He loses his ball in the bushes and so he goes to find it.

Only there just happens to be this killer waiting in there for him with a stiletto.''

''Put like that, it does sound unlikely,'' I admitted.

''It stinks like last week's chicken shit!'' sneered Salgado. ''*You* took that knife into the bushes with you. Guy didn't know what hit him. You rigged the whole goddam thing. That's how it reads to me.''

''Lieutenant, I swear that I didn't kill him!''

''Then who did?'' he challenged.

''A professional,'' I decided, throwing all my guesswork at them by way of defence. ''Zuke Everett was set up tonight by someone who's connected with the world of golf. The killer knew that he'd be here. Celebrating his triumph. Off guard. The man could have been waiting out there all evening until he got his chance. He probably couldn't believe his luck when Zuke actually strolled towards him.''

''Go on,'' encouraged Salgado.

''He had to be a pro because it was done so quickly. Even in the dark, the killer needed only one thrust to find the heart. I didn't see any other entry wounds.''

''There weren't any,'' corroborated Nelms.

''That's more or less all I can tell you about him,'' I said. ''Except that he's very strong and quite short.''

''How do you make that out?'' pressed Salgado.

''He had to be strong because he knocked Zuke out with one blow and caught him before he crashed into the bushes. Howie Danzig and I heard nothing. The killer dragged the body about ten yards—you can see the heel marks in the grass—so that he could lay it down in that clearing without any noise. My guess is that he slipped the knife home then. While Zuke was unconscious. I know the man is short because of the size of the hole he cut himself in the fence. I couldn't get through it without snagging my collar and I was bent right over.''

The two detectives traded a covert smile and I realised that I had been tricked. They had pressurised me so that I'd volunteer everything I knew or suspected. I felt betrayed by the police. Again.

"That's pretty good," remarked Salgado, writing something on his pad. "You think like a cop. Your old man'd be proud of you."

"Just one thing you missed," added Nelms.

"Is there, Sergeant?"

"That baseball cap."

"You seem obsessed with it," I observed.

"Only because it's so important, Mr. Saxon."

"Important to us," reinforced Salgado, "and important to *you*."

"In what way?"

"Spell it out for him, Patch."

"We think the perpetrator could've been a hit-man."

"I just told you that, Sergeant."

"Guys like that, who handle contracts. Don't usually know much about golf. They got other games."

"So?" I asked.

"So," continued Nelms, solemnly, "he's never seen his victim before. Never heard him speak. All he's got is a name on his stiletto and some mug shots. With me? He gets into the garden. Watches the house. Waits. Four people come out. One of them looks like the guy in the mug shots. Wearing this baseball cap. The hit-man is in the bushes. Sees his victim against the light around the patio. Long garden. With me?"

I nodded. My mouth was now too dry to form words.

"Like this," concluded Nelms. "I see you playing in that tournament on TV, I thought you were Zuke Everett at first. Works both ways. The hit-man's watching from a distance. In that light—in that cap—the deceased was Alan Saxon's double."

"That's how we know you didn't do it," explained Salgado, airily. "Because you were probably the intended victim."

"Why *me*?" I protested.

"Why Zuke Everett?" countered Nelms.

"But what *reason* would anybody have to kill me?"

"This is America," rejoined Salgado, wryly. "They don't always need a reason to rub you out over here. They do it for kicks. Get their rocks off.'' He hunched his shoulders. ''Maybe someone didn't like your face. Or your baseball cap.''

''Wait a minute,'' I argued, grasping at something that would disprove their theory. ''The killer would have heard Zuke's voice. He would have *known* it wasn't me.''

''Only if he spoke English,'' noted Salgado.

''What do you mean, Lieutenant?''

''Use your eyes,'' he advised. ''This is not a real city. It's another United fucking Nations. Throw a stick in LA, you hit some dumb immigrant. My old man was one. So was almost everyone else's. And they still keep coming. We got bimbos here who can't even wipe the shit off their ass in English!'' He pursed his lips and studied me for a few moments. ''Know what I think, Mr. Saxon?''

''What?''

''Our guy could be just off the plane from Sicily.''

''Sicily?''

''That stiletto,'' he said with casual interest. ''Used to be a favourite murder weapon of the Mafia.''

The implications were all too much for me. I sat there for some minutes in a state of fear and bewilderment. All I had done was to come to California to play four rounds of golf and I was now caught up in a murder inquiry.

As a possible victim who got away. This time.

Patch Nelms broke the silence with a partisan comment.

''Bet you wish you never went to Yankee Stadium now.''

Another hour or more passed before the house began to empty. The doctor went first and gave the still shaken Mardie Cutler a lift back to her apartment. Howie vanished with the lawyer, still haggling together over fine details. The Catholic priest slipped away unnoticed.

Having completed their initial enquiries, Salgado and Nelms took their men away but left one uniformed officer on guard outside the house. Helen went straight to bed and so did Dominga. It was time for me to bring a horrendous night to its close as well. I got to my room and locked the door behind me.

Sleep refused to come. I was aching with fatigue as I lay in the darkness but I was kept awake by the same recurring questions. At length, I gave up. Putting the light back on, I got out of bed and went to draw myself a bath in the hope that it might relax me. The hot, soapy water brought relief but no escape.

The questions continued to torment me afresh.

Who murdered Zuke Everett? Had the killer been after me?

I tried hard to believe that I was not in danger. To gain a kind of perverse comfort, I did my best to persuade myself that Zuke had in fact been the intended target. Though he was renowned for his friendliness, he did have enemies as well. When I searched for people who might hate him enough to want him killed, I came up with two names.

Gamil Amir and Tom Bellinghaus.

The golfer had actually threatened Zuke in my hearing and even mentioned death by stabbing. Though the course architect had made no verbal attack, his expression had said everything. He wanted revenge.

The more I thought about it, the more certain I became that the murder was connected with the tournament. It was no coincidence that Zuke had been cut down in his finest hour. His double eagle had been a gesture of defiance at Gamil Amir and a gross insult to Tom Bellinghaus. It had put him back into the reckoning and somebody was determined that he would not win.

My mind went back to the locker room. What was it about Amir that had prompted Zuke to behave so violently? There was a personal enmity there that went much deeper than professional rivalry. How had it arisen and what part did Helen play in it?

No answers offered themselves.

I was working on gut reactions and not on facts.

The water eventually began to soothe my mind as well as my body. Fears subsided. Anguish slowly diminished. Exhaustion soon washed all over me. Without trying to resist, I fell gratefully asleep.

I was awake again within minutes.

There was a knock on the bedroom door and the handle was tried. Lifting myself quickly out of the bath, I grabbed the white robe from its hook and pulled it on. I felt that I was in mortal danger. It never occurred to me that a potential killer was unlikely to announce himself by tapping on my door.

There was a second, louder knock.

"Alan?" It was Helen Everett. "Are you there?"

"One moment," I called, tying up my belt as I crossed to the door. "What do you want?"

"Let me in!"

The plea in her voice made me unlock the door at once and pull it open. Helen Everett was framed there for a moment. She was wearing a silk nightgown and looked as striking as ever. The mourning she had kept at bay had now claimed her. Circles under her eyes showed that she had been crying and her mouth was trembling.

She stepped into the bedroom and shut the door behind her.

"Thank you," she said.

"Trouble sleeping?"

"My husband is dead," she whispered, as if realising it for the first time. "Zuke is gone."

Tears came again and she flung herself into my arms. I patted her gently and eased her down so that we were sitting on the edge of the bed. Mardie Cutler had been inconsolable when she saw the dead body. It was now Helen's turn to weep and moan and blame herself. I pulled some tissues from the box on my bedside table and gave them to her to dab at her eyes.

When she had sobbed her fill, she sat up and made an effort to pull herself together. Helen was no longer the poised actress with confident charm. She was a frightened, vulnerable young woman who had been thrown into a state of total confusion. Even her voice had changed. It had lost both its heavy accent and its Latin brio.

"Zuke was the only one who cared," she murmured.

"Was he?"

"The others were all the same. Pigs. Slobs. But not

Zuke. He was the first man who was really *kind* to me." Her eyes moistened again. "I wish I'd been kinder to him now."

"How did you meet him?" I wondered.

"On a film set. I was working as an extra." She gave a bitter laugh. "This guy I was dating, some hot-shot studio executive, he promised to get me into the big time. Ha! Shall I tell you what his idea of the big time was? Two tiny scenes in a crap movie that never went out on release."

"Why was Zuke involved?"

"There was a golf sequence. He was supposed to advise on how the shots were played but the leading man didn't know one end of a club from the other. So Zuke ended up hitting the shots for him. Best part of the movie." A reflective smile lit her face. "We got talking one day. That was all it needed. Zuke was just so easy to be with. Happy, full of life. I'd never met anyone like him. What's more, he didn't try to take advantage." The smile gave way to a sad frown. "I'm a wetback, Alan. Do you know what that means?"

"An illegal immigrant."

"It means you're cut off from your own country and hunted down in somebody else's. You never stand still, never take it easy. All the time, you have to look over your shoulder."

"How long have you been here?" I asked.

"I was thirteen when we came," she recalled. "We were like lots of other Mexican families. Very poor, very ignorant. We believed that life in America would be wonderful." Her lip curled sardonically. "If only we had known the truth!"

"How did you cross the border?"

"One night, we got through a gap in the fence near Tijuana. About forty or fifty of us. I was with my mother and my little brother. Our father had died. It was a terrible night." Her face went taut as she remembered it all. "They were waiting for us in a ravine. Bandits. Mexicans from our own *patria*! They were animals. They took everything we had. Then one of them, the leader, he said, "Find the pretty ones!'' They grabbed about half a dozen of us. I was the youngest. When my brother tried to stop them, they knocked him to the ground. I begged them not to kill him. The leader said he would make up his mind afterwards. Then he dragged me off into the bushes.'' She stared down at the floor. ''That was my welcome to America.''

I waited patiently until she was ready to go on. As she talked, she began to play with her wedding ring. Her voice was subdued.

''We were wetbacks,'' she said simply. ''We had no rights. If we'd reported it to the police, they'd have told us it was our own fault. It happens all the time. We'd have been sent back across the border and we had nothing to go back to by then.''

''What did you do?''

''We went on. My uncle lived near San Diego. He took us in for a while. We got jobs. When we lost those, we moved on.'' She looked up at me. ''That's how it was, Alan. Job after job. And men.''

''When did you take up acting?'' I said.

''That came much later. After I'd split up with my family.''

''Split up?''

''My mother didn't like some of the things I did.'' She gave a little shrug. ''*I* didn't like them either but I had no choice. There was always someone. My mother called me bad names and we had these terrible rows all the time. In the end, I couldn't take any more of it so I walked out. She never forgave me. When I sent money, she sent it back.'' Helen winced. ''She even refused to come to the wedding.''

''And the acting?'' I reminded.

''One thing led to another. I met this man who said he could turn me into a top model if I lived in LA. I stuck it for six months and saved up enough to take voice lessons. Then there was this other friend. He was nice at first. He made TV commercials.'' Sarcasm took over. ''That's how it all started. My brilliant career as Helen Ramirez!''

"What was your real name?"

She was so taken aback by the question that it produced another bout of tears and she buried her head in my shoulder. I brought my arms around her again for comfort.

"Zuke took me away from all that," she whispered. "Ever since I've been in this country, I've been afraid that someone would come and get me. Until Zuke. He made me his wife. He gave me a *right* to be here. I was safe. I was someone at last."

"You've *always* been someone," I reassured.

"And now he's dead. Because of me."

"Now, that's silly. It was nothing to do with you."

"But it was," she insisted between sobs. "If he hadn't married me, Zuke would be alive now. It's all my fault."

"Of course it isn't," I soothed.

I tightened my grip on her as the weeping intensified.

The embrace seemed to last interminably. Her silk nightgown was smooth beneath my fingers. Her body was warm. I could feel the beat of her heart. My cheek was against the delicate softness of her hair. The subtle fragrance of her perfume invaded me.

Her tears died away and she began to sway gently to and fro as if trying to lull herself to sleep. I found that I was moving with her in a steady, unforced rhythm. She looked up at me through moist, doleful eyes. Her voice was a murmured plea.

"*You* won't come and get me, will you?"

I shook my head and kissed her on the temple.

The effect was startling.

Helen reached up to fling her arms around my neck and her lips fastened on mine. In that first, long, luscious moment, my resistance was swept aside. I made a token attempt to ease her away but it only served to intensify her need. We fell back on the bed together. My fatigue was forgotten now as I matched her frenzy and joined with her in trying to blot out the horror of what had happened.

In the shadow of death, we were attesting life.

We were soon naked and the wetness of my body lent an added excitement. When I slid into her, she gave a cry of pleasure that aroused me even more. I arched and plunged with gathering momentum until she suddenly quivered violently all over, let out a deep, searching moan and dug her fingernails into my flesh. The racking urgency of her orgasm brought me with it and our voices mingled in celebration.

Eyes closed, we lay there entwined and gasped for breath. For a time, at least, we had shed the burden of grief. It soon returned.

"Oh, Zuke," she whispered. "That was wonderful."

Not daring to speak, I squeezed her by way of reply.

"I need you, Zuke. I need you so much."

I went cold. In her desperation, Helen was willing me to be her husband. I was being taken for Zuke Everett yet again.

She leaned over to kiss me and her eyelids lifted. When she realised who I was and what we had just done, she was seized by panic. Fear and revulsion distorted her features.

"You're not Zuke!" she accused.

"Helen—"

"Get off me!"

She shoved me away and leapt up from the bed. Without pausing to collect her nightgown, she opened the door and fled down the corridor. I threw on the bathrobe and went after her to calm her down. She was halfway up the stairs by the time I reached the hall.

"Wait!" I called.

"Go away!" she screamed.

"Helen!"

I heard the door of the bedroom slam behind her. When I got to it, I spoke through the timber but she would not reply. I tried the handle but the door was locked and bolted.

"We'll talk about this in the morning," I promised.

There was silence inside the bedroom but a noise came from directly behind me. I turned round to see that another door had opened. The small, anxious face of Dominga appeared. She'd heard the raised voices and saw me standing there half-naked. No words were needed.

The picture carried its own translation.

She closed her door again and locked it behind her.

Circumstantial evidence against me was damning. I felt quite mortified. Guilt competed with self-disgust. What had I *done*?

Within hours of Zuke's death, I'd made love to his widow.

I pulled the bathrobe around me and went slowly downstairs.

It had been an extraordinary night but there was still one more surprise in store. As I made my way to my room, I came to Zuke's den, the only part of the house in which he seemed to belong. I opened the door and switched on the light. This was how I wanted to remember him. The place was quintessential Zuke Everett. His personality was stamped all over it and I was filled again with a sense of acute loss.

Then I saw that there had been an important change.

Photographs of Valmai were everywhere. Those featuring Helen had vanished altogether. The den was now virtually a carbon copy of the one in the Malibu home.

In his private sanctum, Zuke had reinstated his first wife.

A couple of hours of shallow sleep left me feeling weary and nauseated. I had a cold shower to freshen myself up and took some aspirins to clear my head. Breakfast was waiting for me but there was no sign of Dominga. Along with Helen, she was keeping out of my way.

I was saved the trouble of calling a taxi to take me to the course for the final day's play. Clive Phelps rang to say that he was picking me up in person in his hire car. Having seen the news of the murder on breakfast television, he was eager to corner me and get the inside story. I was grateful for his company as we drove along the freeway. After an abrasive session with the police and hostility from the two women, it was good to be with a friend again.

Clive's attitude was highly reassuring.

"I don't think the killer was after you," he declared.

"Hope you're right."

"Certain of it. Who'd want to bump off Alan Saxon?"

"My bank manager, for a start."

"No," he corrected. "Bank managers don't stab their customers. They prefer to roast you slowly over a hot overdraft. It's more fun."

"That's true," I conceded.

"Zuke Everett simply *had* to be the target."

"Why?"

"Because he was the man in form. Not you, old son. There's no money riding on Alan Saxon in this tournament."

"Not even yours?" I complained.

"Especially not mine."

"Thanks for your loyalty and moral support!"

"All part of the service," he said with a broad grin. "Anyway, there's your number one suspect."

"Who?"

"The bloke who accepted that $10,000 bet on Zuke yesterday. At that point, Zuke didn't seem to have a hope in hell of finishing at the top of the leader board."

"What were the odds?"

"Something like twenty-five to one," he replied. "Now, what would *you* do in that bloke's position? Shell out a quarter of a million dollars when Zuke won? Or buy yourself a stiletto?"

"You may have something there, Clive," I agreed. "Listen, I want you to do me a favour. Find out who placed that bet and where."

"How am I supposed to do that?"

"You're the newshound. Sniff out the information. Oh, and while you're at it, there are two other things I need to know."

"Do your own detective work," he bleated.

"First—what is Helen Everett's real name?"

"You're staying with the woman. Why not ask her?"

"I tried," I admitted, "but she clammed up on me."

I said nothing about the circumstances in which I'd put the question to her. Though I'd given him a reasonably full account of the killing itself, I suppressed all mention of my intimate moments with Helen. I knew that Clive would never understand.

I wasn't even sure that I understood it myself.

"What's the last thing?" he asked sourly.

"Get me Valmai's address and telephone number."

"Are you organising a wives' reunion or something?"

"Just see what you can do, please."

"I make no promises," he stipulated. "Surprising as it may seem, I actually have a job to do here. I didn't come to LA for the sole purpose of acting as your information centre. Chances are I won't be able to come up with *any* of the answers."

"You won't let me down," I assured him.

Further conversation was curtailed when a truck pulled out directly in our path. Clive braked, pressed his horn viciously, flashed his headlights and issued a stream of expletives at the driver.

We left the freeway at the next exit.

Murder was good for business. In being forced out of the tournament, Zuke Everett had maximised public interest in it. The crowds swelled and the police presence was correspondingly larger. In addition to the golfing press, the news media had now descended on Golden Haze in force. As soon as we reached the car park, we were surrounded by reporters and cameramen. I got out to face a barrage of questions.

"Say, Al, what's it like back at the house?"

"How is Mrs. Everett taking it all?"

"Can you remember the last words Zuke said to you?"

"Any idea who could've done it, Al?"

"How d'ya feel about playing a round of golf today?"

Before I could tell them that I had no comment to make, I was rescued by a uniformed security officer who slung my golf bag over his shoulder and bullocked a way for us through the crowd. His pug-nosed determination got me safely inside the clubhouse.

"Thanks a lot," I said.

"Yeah."

He handed me the bag and went to stand guard at the door.

''We thought you might need some help,'' explained a voice.

I turned round to see Suzanne Fricker. She looked quite arresting in a casual suit of pale blue cotton. Her face had the same polished beauty and her eyes still refused to join in the smile.

''Our newsmen can be a pain in the ass,'' she added.

''So I noticed.''

''We'll make sure you're not bothered by them.''

''I'm grateful.''

''You've got enough on your plate as it is.'' The smile gave way to a serious frown. ''I think you're very brave, Alan. In your position, a lot of golfers might not have turned up today.''

''I need the money,'' I joked.

''The pressures on you must be terrific.''

''I can't feel them yet, Suzanne. Haven't woken up properly.''

''Mr. Kallgren would like a private word with you,'' she said.

''Of course. Now?''

''After the tournament.''

''Fine,'' I consented.

''Zuke's death has come as a great shock to him.''

''That goes for all of us.''

Suzanne Fricker nodded in agreement and lowered her head for a few seconds. When she raised it again, tears welled up in her eyes. I was surprised and touched by this sign of human fallibility. She went up in my estimation at once.

I hadn't realised that Barbie dolls could cry.

''Zuke was a special kind of guy,'' she confided, wistfully. ''He and I got close for a time. *Real* close. I'll miss him like hell.'' Her manner became businesslike. ''Okay, then. I'll tell Mr. Kallgren that you'll see him afterwards.''

''My pleasure.''

''Thanks, Alan.''

She turned on her heel and moved swiftly away.

I stood there wondering when the affair had taken place. Her tone seemed to imply that it had been fairly recent. After Valmai and before Helen Ramirez? Or did it overlap with his second marriage?

I was still trying to work it out when Jerry Bruford strolled up and took my bag from me. His gum-chewing nonchalance was just the tonic I needed. He jerked a thumb towards the course.

"You wanna go out there and play some golf?"

"Why not?"

"Then get your ass into gear." He led the way towards the locker rooms. "You don't play, I don't get my dough."

"It's worse than that, Jerry. I don't get *mine*."

"Check."

My caddie saw it as part of his job to keep my mind on my game. He made no reference at all to Zuke. He chatted easily about the technical problems that faced us out on the course and suggested ways to overcome them. As I listened to him, I underwent a transformation. When I left the house that morning, I was in no state to play golf. Ten minutes with Jerry Bruford not only restored my confidence. It revived my competitive instinct and made me want to get out there and battle on.

The mood among the players was sombre. I collected several muttered condolences and sympathetic nods. Zuke's death had cast a dark shadow over the whole tournament and every golfer was deeply affected.

The exception was Gamil Amir. He showed no sorrow.

"They tell me Zuke has cried off," he remarked.

"One way of putting it," I said.

"He was afraid I'd beat him. That's why he's not here."

"I don't find that very funny, Amir."

"You English have no sense of humour."

"That's where you're wrong," I countered. "We're still laughing ourselves silly over the Suez crisis."

His grin broadened and he leaned in to whisper to me.

"I'm glad somebody killed him. It saves me the trouble."

"Can I quote you on that?" I asked.

"No, Saxon," he warned. "You can just stay out of my way."

"So much for Anglo-Egyptian friendship!"

Jerry Bruford tugged me away before the argument could develop but my spat with Amir had in fact helped me. It instilled some real aggression into me and made me want to hit back out on the course. I would be playing for myself and for Zuke Everett.

Rutherford Kallgren made a meal of the tragedy. Instead of letting the final round get under way, he made a short, moving speech over the public address system and then decreed one minute's silence in tribute to Zuke. I found his comments morbid. They said more about Kallgren himself than about the murder victim.

Tom Bellinghaus was very much in evidence. His face wore a sad expression that was belied by his jaunty step and his general air of smugness. Zuke Everett attacked the new course and brought it to its knees. He had paid for his temerity and Bellinghaus clearly thought that the price had been a fair one. The question remained whether or not the course architect had exacted payment himself.

Bright sunshine graced the last day's play at the Tournament of Champions. The wind died away to make conditions almost perfect. I was partnered by Bob Tolley, the only other British golfer in the event. Bob had lived and played in America for so long now that his chirpy Cockney accent had all but disappeared beneath a transatlantic drawl. But I didn't mind that. He was still a fellow countryman and I was relieved to have him alongside me.

There had been moments in the past twelve hours when I had been confronted with the fact that I was in a foreign country. They did things very differently there.

"On the tee—Alan Saxon!"

The ovation I got from the crowd around the first tee was quite unexpected. When my name was announced, there was a great communal surge of emotion and applause. I soon realised what had caused it. Without my baseball cap, I looked like Zuke Everett again. In cheering me, the spectators were also showing Zuke what they felt about him. Buoyed up on this tide of good will, I addressed my ball, then swung. My drive went straight down the middle of the fairway.

"Jesus!" said my caddie, deeply impressed.

"There's a lot more where that came from," I promised. "Let's roll!"

My weariness had evaporated now and I was full of ambition. Playing on nervous energy, I tried to emulate Zuke and launch an all-out attack on the course. When they saw what I was doing, the galleries roared their approval and helped to lift my game. Bob Tolley settled for percentage golf and picked his way from hole to hole, but I forsook caution altogether. Advised by Jerry and urged on by the now delirious hordes, I went for my shots with full-blooded commitment.

Inevitably, there were setbacks. I explored the heavy rough, I hit sand, I tested water. But I somehow managed to redeem my mistakes with a series of fine recovery shots.

When I reached the 13th hole, my adrenalin was flowing and my confidence was boundless. It was my last chance to take a bite out of the Bellinghaus wallet and the thought fired me as I stood on the tee. I hit my drive to the right of the lake, crossed the water diagonally with my second shot, then found the green with my third. Producing a long, straight putt, I claimed a stroke off the hole and earned myself a $500 bonus that was very gratifying.

I faltered slightly over the next few holes but staged a minor comeback and finished in style with a birdie that gained me a hero's reception. As the cheers reverberated, Jerry Bruford pumped my arm. On a day when all the odds were against me, I had shot a round of 69 and secured a place on the lower half of the leader board.

As I basked in my triumph, two people sprang to mind.

Zuke Everett, my friend, and Donnelly, my bank manager.

In my own way, I had answered both their demands.

Security men moved in to protect me from the intense media attention that awaited me. After smiling at dozens of cameras and saying a few words into a microphone, I let the security officers bear me off to the relative safety of the locker room.

The tournament was still not over and my own contribution had no real effect on the eventual outcome. Gamil Amir led until the final hole only to see victory snatched away from him by the superior putting of Phil Reiner. The quiet man of the US tour crept up stealthily behind him and slipped past almost unnoticed. It was a very popular win. Amir may have entertained the galleries with his flashy brilliance but the home crowd were nevertheless thrilled when the steady, unsensational golf of Phil Reiner put an American name on the trophy.

It was the next best thing to victory by Zuke Everett.

The ceremony which ended the tournament was every bit as lavish and spectacular as the one which opened it. An orchestra played, there were set speeches, publicity gimmicks were thrown in by the handful. All twenty-nine surviving golfers were lined up in front of the assembled throng and the massed cameras. Like royalty inspecting a guard of honour, Rutherford Kallgren walked along the line and had a brief individual word with each one of us.

"Well played, Al," he said to me. "Great stuff."

"Thank you."

"You were like a second Zuke Everett out there."

He moved on to talk to Bob Tolley and I was left with the haunting aroma of his after-shave in my nostrils.

Kallgren mounted the rostrum, delivered another speech into the microphone, then called for the winner of the inaugural Tournament of Champions to step forward. We joined in the applause as Phil Reiner walked across to the rostrum.

A shapely blonde then emerged from the crowd, wearing little more than a sash which proclaimed her the current Miss California. She was carrying a large, ornate silver trophy and she handed it to Kallgren with a dazzling grin. He in turn presented it to Reiner and they held their handshake so that all the cameras could immortalise the moment.

"What a trophy to have!" observed Bob Tolley beside me.

"I'd prefer Miss California," I confessed. "Much nicer to look at on the mantelpiece and a lot more fun to polish."

Gamil Amir agreed with me. When he went to the rostrum to collect his medal as runner-up, he grabbed the girl playfully and lifted her into the air for the benefit of the cameras. He said something to her as he put her down and she giggled.

"That's what they call Arab oil," noted Bob Tolley.

After the ceremony, we all adjourned to the clubhouse for a champagne buffet and a chance to mingle with the press. Newsmen closed in on me at once but Suzanne Fricker was there to thwart them. She spirited me off to an upstairs room and I was shown into a large office with a glass-topped desk as its central feature.

Rutherford Kallgren was seated behind the desk in a high-backed swivel chair and Tom Bellinghaus stood close to him. They gave me an effusive welcome. The fact that Suzanne stayed with us confirmed her status as a top executive in the Kallgren organisation.

"Sorry to drag you away from the party," said Kallgren. "Just wanted a brief chat with you, Al. How are you feeling now?"

"Pleasantly exhausted," I admitted.

"After the night you must have had, I'm not surprised. Tell me. What's the atmosphere like back at the house?"

"Pretty tense."

"Mrs. Everett?"

"Still in a daze. It knocked her sideways."

"Understandably," he added. "Real shame. Zuke was such a vital part of the golf scene over here." He picked a speck of dust off the sleeve of the coat, then looked up at me. "Do the cops have anything to go on, Al?"

"Not a lot," I said. "The killer was a pro."

"Who could possibly want to set Zuke up?"

"Search me."

"You must have your own theory," he probed.

"I don't," I lied. "Doesn't make sense to me."

"Nor me. Zuke was one of the nicest guys you could meet." He drummed his fingers lightly on the desk. "Did he . . . *say* anything to you?"

"What about?"

"Problems he was having. Fears."

"Not a word," I replied. "All I saw was the same old happy-go-lucky Zuke Everett."

"So he didn't confide in you at all?"

I shook my head.

Kallgren did not improve on closer acquaintance. There was something unnervingly calculating about him and he exuded wealth in a way that was quite offensive. I had struggled to find my niche in the golf world and felt a natural resentment at someone who had bought his way in. As for my theories about Zuke's murder, I was determined to say as little as possible.

When he saw this, Kallgren gave me a bland smile and pulled a long envelope from the inside pocket of his coat. He handed it to me.

"What is it?" I asked.

"Everything we owe you. Appearance money plus winnings. The Kallgren organisation has its faults but we do pay our debts."

"The same goes for me," announced Bellinghaus with forced jollity, taking out a chequebook and a biro. "That birdie of yours at the 13th has earned you another $500."

"Make it payable to Jerry Bruford," I instructed. "It can be the first part of what I owe him. A golfer's best friend is his caddie."

I realised with a start that I was actually solvent again.

Since I'd walked into the office, I was almost $14,000 better off. I could now iron out all my financial problems when I got back home and still have enough left over to cushion myself for a while. From that point of view, the trip to Los Angeles had been a success.

In other ways, however, it was a nightmare.

Bellinghaus handed me the second cheque.

"Thanks," I said. "While I'm here—and while you've

got your chequebook out—I might as well take the money for Helen Everett."

"What money?"

"For that double eagle."

"Aw, now, come on!"

"You just boasted that you pay your debts," I reminded.

"I do. My legitimate debts, that is."

"We all heard what you said on the first day, Mr. Bellinghaus. According to you, the 13th was impregnable. Your offer was $500 for a birdie and $5000 for an eagle."

"Did I mention a *double* eagle?" he challenged.

"No—but only because you thought it was impossible."

"It *was* impossible!" he insisted. "Two freak shots."

"Now, that's unfair!" I retorted, angrily. "Zuke Everett was a pedigree golfer. I watched him play those shots and they weren't freaks. That double eagle deserves some recognition. So pay up!"

"I can't," he taunted. "Zuke isn't here to collect."

"The money should go to his wife."

"I don't remember any mention of next of kin." Bellinghaus turned to Suzanne Fricker. "You're the lawyer, Suzanne. How would I stand in a court of law on this one?"

"It's not a legal matter, Tom," she answered, coolly. "This is a question of conscience."

"My conscience is quite clear," he said, complacently.

"Zuke gets *nothing*!" I exclaimed.

"I'll send a wreath to the funeral."

"Big deal!"

"No need to get so riled up about it, Al," advised Kallgren. "I'd say Tom was within his rights here. Besides, it's not as if that double eagle will ever be forgotten. I'm having a commemorative plaque set up on the 13th tee. Zuke Everett's name will live on."

"Yes, but *he* won't!" I rejoined, vehemently. "It isn't a plaque, Mr. Kallgren—it's a tombstone! That hole helped to kill him. I'm surprised you're not getting full publicity out of it."

"Publicity?"

"Why not go the whole hog and have Zuke's skull stuck

on the flagstick? You could sell plastic replicas of it by way of warning."

"We're not taking this shit from you!" exploded Bellinghaus.

Kallgren raised a manicured hand and the course architect calmed down at once. Controlling his temper, Bellinghaus retreated to the window and gazed out across the green acres of Golden Haze.

There was a long pause.

When Kallgren spoke, his tone was insultingly dismissive.

"Enjoy the party, Al."

Suzanne conducted me out of the office and closed the door behind us. I felt abused. They'd called all the shots.

I'd been interrogated, paid off and kicked out.

On Zuke Everett's behalf, I was now seething with fury.

It strengthened my resolve to track down his killer.

Chapter Four

My mind was in a turmoil. Rage jostled with hatred, then both made way for cold suspicion. I was convinced that the row in the office had a direct bearing on Zuke's death. Both men were involved somehow. Bellinghaus had almost gloated and his motive was self-evident, but Kallgren's position was more complex. He'd put a colossal amount of time, effort and capital into his Tournament of Champions.

Why would he want to besmirch it with a murder?

I reached the bottom of the stairs before I realised that Suzanne Fricker was still with me. I stopped and turned to her.

"Sorry about that, Alan," she said, quietly.

"I asked for it."

"Tom's got a pretty short fuse."

"So I gathered."

"And it's not a wise move to upset Mr. Kallgren."

"Is that what Zuke did?"

"Zuke is immaterial," she replied. "I'm warning *you.*"

"An official caution?"

"Of course not. I'm only speaking as a friend."

She glanced back up the stairs and I could see that she was torn between professional and personal considerations. This Barbie doll had genuine emotions and she wrestled with them openly. Duty to an employer took second place to loyalty to a lover.

"Will you be sticking around for a while, Alan?"

"Oh, yes," I affirmed. "I'm seeing this thing through."

"If there's any way I can help—any way at all—just ask." She took a business card from her pocket and handed it to me. "You can reach me on this number during office hours."

"I'll remember that."

"It's a direct line," she added, sensing my hesitation. "You won't have to go through the switchboard. Nobody will know that we're talking to each other."

"Not even Mr. Kallgren?" I asked, pointedly.

"If you're not happy about it, ring me at home instead. You'll find the number on the back of the card."

I did. It was written in a firm, feminine hand.

"Don't forget, will you?" she pressed.

"No—and thanks."

"Let me help. Please. I owe it to Zuke."

I nodded and slipped the card into my pocket.

Though I tried hard, I still wasn't able to trust Suzanne Fricker. I was getting too many contradictory signals from her and the plastic perfection of her appearance unsettled me. It crossed my mind that she might have been planted on me by Kallgren.

"You're wrong," she insisted, reading my thoughts. "I'm no spy. If Mr. Kallgren knew about this, I'd be in real trouble."

I believed her. She *was* doing it for Zuke.

"Are you going back to the party, Alan?"

"Not on your life," I answered. "I'm going to gather up my things and sneak away! I've got a lot of sleep to catch up on."

"Do you have transport?"

"Clive offered to run me back—Clive Phelps, that is. Golf writer from England. We're old mates." I had second thoughts. "We might not stay old mates if I drag him away from all that free booze. And it'd be cruel to rob him of the chance to invite Miss California back to his hotel room to admire the view."

Suzanne smiled. "He's been beaten to the draw there."

"Gamil Amir?"

"Miss California prefers the Arab stallion. And with respect to your friend, I can't say that I blame her."

"In that case," I decided, "I'll *have* to let Clive stay."

"Why?"

"So that he can drown his sorrows in style. I'll call a taxi."

"Leave it to me," she offered.

"Are you sure?"

"Let Kallgren pay. This is his show."

There was an edge in her tone that bordered on disillusion.

"How did you come to work for him, Suzanne?"

"He asked me."

"Was it as straightforward as that?"

"More or less. He wanted me on the team and he has a habit of getting what he wants." She shrugged. "It was time for a move, anyway. I was getting frustrated in the Special Prosecutions Unit."

"Were you?"

"I'd been there too long, Alan. Seen all the job had to offer. And the delays always used to get to me."

"Delays?"

"Judicial process is a slow business. We'd spend maybe a year or more building up a case only to have it adjourned time and again on some technicality introduced by the defence. I hated having to play a waiting game. I like action."

"Is that what Kallgren offered you?"

"Among other things."

"More money?"

"That, too, of course."

"More scope for your ambition?"

A pause. "Why are we talking about me?" she asked.

"I'm interested, that's all. I get the feeling that you're very ambitious."

"Mr. Kallgren wouldn't employ anyone who wasn't."

"Do you *like* working for him?"

"Most of the time." Her smile was enigmatic. "There'll be a limo waiting outside for you in five minutes."

"Thanks."

When we shook hands, her fingers squeezed mine hard.

"Goodbye, Alan. Keep in touch."

"I will."

Suzanne went off to organise my chauffeur and I made my way to the locker room. I retrieved my golf bag, sought out Jerry Bruford to settle my debts, then went around to the front of the clubhouse.

Phil Reiner was chatting in the foyer with Mrs. Kallgren and her two teenage sons. She had a serene self-satisfaction and the boys had a laid-back eagerness. I wondered if they knew what sort of a man the head of their family really was.

When Phil Reiner saw me, he detached himself with an excuse and came across. His voice had its usual subdued charm and politeness.

"Leaving already, Al?"

"I'm completely shattered."

"I guess you must be. Amazing you were able to play at all today, let alone shoot a round like that. It was terrific."

"You did pretty well yourself, Phil."

"Oh, sure," he replied with easy modesty. "But I'm only a textbook golfer. It's guys like you and Zuke who can set the galleries alight. I envy you that touch of genius."

"Not as much as I envy you that prize money."

"Let's face it, Al," he said, realistically. "Nobody is going to remember this tournament because Phil Reiner won it. What they'll remember is that double eagle. I only made dough—Zuke made history." His eyes glistened behind his gold-framed spectacles. "Lemme tell you something. I'd give every cent of what I earned to have hit those two shots at the 13th!"

His urgency surprised me. I'd never known Phil Reiner speak with such passion before. He really coveted that double eagle.

A Lincoln Continental drew up outside and the driver tooted the horn. We walked across to the vehicle together. My chauffeur got out at once and put my golf bag in the boot.

Phil Reiner and I exchanged a brief handshake.

"See you around, Al."

"Cheers."

"Oh, by the way," he added. "Where was Howie Danzig today? No sign of him anywhere."

"I didn't expect him to be here. Zuke's death poleaxed him. And Howie isn't exactly in the best of health."

"Poor guy. Either way he stood to lose out."

"Either way?"

"If Zuke had lived, I mean." He gave me a farewell slap on the back and opened the car door for me. "Take care of yourself, Al."

"I always do."

I got into the vehicle and he closed the door behind me. He waved as we set off towards the exit, then he went back into the clubhouse to rejoin the celebrations.

As I was driven away from the Kallgren Tournament of Champions, I was assaulted by dozens of questions but the main one arose out of my chat with Phil Reiner. It was like a red hot drill inside my skull.

Why would Howie have lost out if Zuke had lived?

My chauffeur tooted his horn again when we reached the house in Santa Monica and the gates opened electronically. There was another car on the drive, a rather battered Oldsmobile in need of a wash. Its forlorn condition reminded me of Carnoustie and I felt a wistful pang.

I got out, collected my golf bag, tipped my chauffeur and watched him drive away. When I turned to face the front door, I was full of misgivings. Zuke had wanted me to stay on for a few days after the tournament but the situation had altered radically. I sensed that I'd already worn out my welcome and prepared myself for not even being admitted to the house again.

The door opened as soon as I rang the bell. Dominga took one frightened look at me and then scurried off to the kitchen as if fleeing from the risk of contamination.

I stepped into the hall and looked around.

"Helen!" I called. "I'm back!"

There was no answer. If Helen was in the house, she

was choosing to keep out of my way. I was grateful to be spared the embarrassment of meeting her and I had at least been allowed back in. I'd spend one more night there and look for alternative accommodation in the morning.

I closed the front door and headed for my room. Evening shadows gave the corridor a slightly eerie feel. Without Zuke in it, the house was curiously empty and lifeless.

The fatigue which had been threatening me all day now started to claim me for its own. A wave of tiredness splashed over me and I went quite dizzy. I left my bag against a wall and opened the door to my room, intending to go to bed as soon as possible and desperate to say goodnight to the accumulated miseries of the past twenty-four hours.

Then I switched on the light.

The scene which greeted me brought me fully awake again.

My clothes had been torn to shreds and scattered all over the floor. The duvet had been stripped from the bed and the mattress had been hacked unmercifully. Devastation was fairly comprehensive. The furniture had been overturned, the bedside lamp smashed, the mirror broken and the curtains ripped to tatters.

My immediate fear was that my passport had been damaged as well. I knelt down and lifted the lid of my suitcase, which was lying on the rug. Relief surged through me when I saw my passport and travel documents, unharmed. I snatched them up.

Before I could examine them, however, the light went out and there was a rustling sound behind me. The next second, I felt a knee in my back and had a thick, sinewy forearm locked across my throat. The pain was intense. I struggled to get free but it was hopeless. I was up against someone much more powerful. My strength drained away as he applied more pressure on my neck.

The voice was a low snarl of hatred.

"Bastard!"

"Let me go," I gurgled.

"Bastard, bastard, bastard!"

When I tried to protest again, I had no voice. The arm tightened, my head swam and my eyes began to film over. Just before I passed out, I was released and shoved forward hard on to my face.

"Get out!" he ordered. *"Now!"*

I coughed violently and clutched at my burning throat.

"Take all this shit and get out, mister!"

I sneaked a look at him. My attacker was a stocky young man of middle height in T-shirt and jeans. He was largely in shadow but the moonlight was catching the side of his face to reveal swarthy skin, bushy hair and a long, seasoned scar on his left temple.

His tone was rough and uneducated and there was the faint hint of an Hispanic accent. He was positively bristling with anger.

"Hurry up!" he shouted.

"Who are you?" I ventured.

"Hurry."

The kick sent me sprawling and deprived me of any wish to attempt further conversation. I threw my things into the suitcase and snapped it shut. As I tried to go past him, he forced me up against the door jamb and put his face an inch from mine. His breath stank.

"Don't come back!" he warned.

"No."

"Don't fucking come back! Okay?"

"Okay."

"You touch her again, I'll cut your balls off and shove them down your fucking throat!"

He was there on Helen's behalf. I had no wish to let him show his skill with a knife on me. I suspected that Zuke had been the victim of his proficiency with a naked blade.

"Out, mister!"

I was hurled into the corridor. Grabbing my golf bag, I stumbled to the hall and opened the front door. He pushed me through it without ceremony. The gates at the bottom of the drive parted to let me out and then clanged shut behind me.

I'd been evicted by a man in a battered Oldsmobile.

When I glanced back to make a mental note of the car's licence number, I saw a curtain twitch in one of the bedrooms. Dominga was watching my humiliation with the grim satisfaction of someone who'd had a hand in it. I wondered if she'd also had a hand in Zuke's death.

Santa Monica has an abundance of hotel accommodation and I only had to walk a few hundred yards to find what I wanted, but the journey exhausted me. My bag was a ton weight over my shoulder and the handle of my suitcase dug into my fingers.

I checked into a small motel, locked the door and wedged a chair under the handle as an extra precaution. After undressing in slow motion, I fell into bed. Before I could turn out the light, I was asleep.

I slumbered happily for over twelve hours and would probably have stayed there for another twelve if I'd not been interrupted by a loud banging. My head felt like a bass drum that was being pounded in a search for maximum volume. It took me some time to establish that someone was knocking on my door as if trying to batter it down.

Salgado's voice pierced the wood.

"Wake up in there, Saxon! Let us in!"

I opened my eyes and recoiled from the harshness of the light.

"Come on, come on!" he yelled. "What's the matter with you?"

"Hang on!" I croaked.

The banging stopped and the throbbing in my head eased. When I dragged myself out of bed, I realised that I was naked. My pyjamas had been cut to ribbons. Pulling on my trousers I zipped them up and staggered towards the door.

"Get a move on in there!" instructed Salgado.

"Don't shout," I pleaded. "I'm here, I'm here."

I moved the chair and let them in. Victor Salgado was now wearing an even flashier suit that was set off by a vermilion tie. Patch Nelms had on the same clothes he had worn before.

They regarded me with cynical amusement.

"Jesus!" observed Salgado. "You look like something that just crawled off a slab down at the morgue."

"Thanks for the compliment, Lieutenant."

"Why didn't you tell us you moved in here?"

"What?"

"We asked to be kept informed of your movements."

"Oh. Did you?"

"So what's with the change of address?"

"Give me a minute," I said.

I went into the bathroom and filled the washbasin with cold water, plunging my head into it and holding it there for a few seconds. When I dried myself with a towel, I made the mistake of peering in the mirror. Salgado's assessment had been a kind one. The average lodger at a morgue would have more resemblance to a human being than I did.

My face was just a white, distraught blob.

I went back into the room. Nelms had taken the putter from my golf bag and was practising a shot. Salgado was stretched out in an easy chair. He sounded impatient.

"We ain't got all day, Saxon."

"Sorry, Lieutenant."

"Late night?"

"No. An early one, in fact."

"So why here?" he asked. "What was wrong with the Everett house?"

"I thought that Helen—Mrs. Everett—would prefer to be alone."

"Was it your decision to move out or hers?"

"Mine."

"Sure of that?"

"Of course."

"Funny. Not how she remembers it."

"No," added Nelms, pausing in mid-putt. "I rang the house this morning to speak to you. Mrs. Everett said she'd asked you to leave."

"That's not true," I argued.

"The lady seemed pretty certain about it."

Nelms was clearly going to accept her word against mine. He completed his imaginary putt and stood back to admire the result.

"Do you play golf, Sergeant?" I said.

"On my pay? You must be kidding." He dropped the putter into the bag. "Anyway, I think it's a lousy game. Too slow. Too tame. I'll stick with baseball."

"So what happened back at the house?" resumed Salgado.

"Nothing happened, Lieutenant."

"It must have," he urged, "or she wouldn't have thrown you out. What you been up to, Saxon? Trying to get into her pants?"

"No."

"Wouldn't blame you if you had. She's some sexy broad, that Helen Everett. I had a blue veiner just talking to her." His gold tooth sparkled as he gave me a lecherous grin. "You made a grab for the goodies, didn't you?"

"Of course not."

"Okay then. You asked her to gobble your pork and she told you she was strict vegetarian. That how it was?"

"Lieutenant," I explained with a sigh, "it simply wasn't . . . convenient for me to stay there. That's why I moved out."

"So why didn't you tell us?"

"I was going to ring you first thing in the morning."

"First thing in the evening, you mean," complained Salgado. "We hadn't come calling, you'd still be in that goddam bed having wet dreams about Helen Everett." He turned away in disgust. "Aw, for Chrissakes, put on a shirt or something, will you? I feel like I just liberated Belsen."

I reached for my shirt and covered my pale, thin torso. As I did up the buttons, I noticed my suitcase and was relieved that I'd been too tired to open it the previous evening. If they'd seen my hastily packed collection of rags and tatters, they'd have asked some awkward questions about my undignified exit from the house.

Though I had a natural fear of the man who'd almost

throttled me in the guest room, I didn't want to bring the police in on it yet. I liked to fight my own battles. If he really was Zuke's killer, I wanted to get at him first.

I perched on the edge of the bed and brought my hands up to my throbbing temples. Salgado rose to a throwaway sympathy.

"Headache?"

"Fifteen at the last count."

"We'll move this along, then," he decided. "You ever used narcotics on a regular basis?"

"Narcotics?" My surprise was unfeigned.

"Uppers, downers, smack, anything. Illegal substances."

"Never, Lieutenant. That's not my scene."

"Everybody tries a little speed now and then," he said.

"Everybody but me," I replied firmly. "I don't need to get my highs out of a bottle or a needle."

"I thought all you top sports guys had something to turn you on. Give your performance that extra edge."

"What turns me on is golf itself. Pure and simple."

Salgado flicked a glance at Nelms, who took over.

"And Zuke Everett?" he said, casually.

"What about him?"

"Did he use anything?"

"Zuke on drugs?" I shook my head. "I don't think so."

"Why do you say that?"

"Because I knew the man for years. He just wasn't the type. Zuke had enough electricity coursing through his veins as it was. He didn't need to inject any more."

Nelms was sceptical. "That so?"

"Sergeant," I explained, "I stayed with him and his first wife a number of times. We became good friends. I'd have noticed if anything like that had been going on."

"You'd have recognised the signs, huh?"

"Definitely."

"And this time? Staying with his second wife?"

"I saw nothing."

"Then you must've been blind," interjected Salgado. "We got the preliminary lab report on the deceased. Your old buddy had been snorting coke like he was in some sorta race.''

The shock silenced me. Nelms confirmed the facts. ''Another coupla months, he'd have wanted a nose job. Know what that is, don't you? It's when you sniff so much coke it burns through the membrane between your nostrils. You gotta have surgery. There's guys in LA who do that surgery all the time. It pays better than abortions and there's no mess to clean up afterwards.''

''Yeah,'' continued Salgado, ''some dick-heads think that operation is a kinda status symbol. You have a nose job, you're a real junkie.''

I was finding it hard to comprehend.

''Are you certain that Zuke was on cocaine?'' I asked.

Salgado nodded. ''Half this crazy fucking city is doped up to the eyeballs so it don't surprise me that Everett was into glow snow. I did a two-year trick in Narcotics. I seen it all. Lemme give you ten easy ways to spot a guy who's been snorting. One—his eyes . . .''

As the Lieutenant rattled through his list, I realised that Zuke had exhibited all ten symptoms on the night he was murdered. What I'd taken for a golfer's overexcitement after a superlative round was also a drug-induced euphoria. Out of loyalty to a friend, I'd simply refused to recognise the signs for what they were.

The trouble was that there were two Zuke Everetts.

One was the dynamic, talented, gregarious man with a lovely wife, a luxury home in Malibu and an accepted role as the clown prince of the US circuit. The other was a tense, hyperactive, self-willed person who'd dragged me out of bed on my first night there to watch a blue movie in his den.

Zuke Everett was his own best double.

Salgado got up from the chair and scrutinised me.

''Well?''

''You're right,'' I conceded.

''We usually are,'' he asserted. ''Know something? For a cop's kid, you're none too smart.''

''It's hereditary.''

"Let's cut the wisecracks. Tell me about Mrs. Everett."

"Which one? Valmai or Helen?"

"Number two. Now that you learned to pick 'em out, think she might have been on coke as well?"

"No," I said with assurance.

"You don't figure they coulda done it together?"

"Together?"

"Sure. Jazz up their sex life. My experience, a lotta couples like to sniff then screw." He gave a lewd chuckle. "Do it myself. Except it's not coke I sniff. It's pussy perfume."

"Twice as sweet," grunted Nelms.

"Helen Everett was not on drugs," I insisted.

"How d'you know? You share a bedroom with her?"

"No, I didn't, Lieutenant," I retorted. "What's more, her husband didn't seem to either. There was friction between them from the moment I arrived. They had no real togetherness. I'm beginning to think that the only reason I was invited to stay was so that I could act as a buffer between them."

The words came involuntarily but they rang true. My companions obviously thought so as well. Salgado shot his colleague a meaningful look, then heaved a sigh.

"You see what I got here, maybe?"

"What?" I asked.

"Narcotics-related crime. That widens the scope."

He walked to the window and drew back the curtains. Sunlight flooded the room and I closed my eyes against its dazzle. Nelms stepped in closer and took over the questioning.

"Was Zuke Everett a rich man?"

"You've seen the house, Sergeant."

"Mortgage as big as the Empire State. I checked."

"Then look at Zuke's life style. He had to be wealthy to keep that up. I'd say he was very rich."

"And where did it come from?" he pursued. "He had a lousy year on the golf course. Finished well down the money list."

"He had an income apart from his tournament winnings."

"Sponsorship? Endorsements?"

''Zuke was a genuine star,'' I reminded. ''They all wanted to buy that famous grin. I know he had a lean time last year but there were plenty of big pay days on the tour in the past. He must have salted some of it away.''

''Maybe,'' he agreed. ''But there's the minus factor.''

''Minus factor?''

''His divorce.''

''You ever been divorced?'' probed Salgado.

''Yes,'' I admitted. ''As a matter of fact, I have.''

''Expensive?''

''I wouldn't care to go through it again, Lieutenant.''

''Nor me,'' he confided bitterly. ''Slow fucking torture. We got these barracudas over here called divorce lawyers. They get you in a courtroom, they nibble off every bit of you that moves. When I split up with my wife, it cost me an arm, a leg and most of my dick. Divorce? It's legal fucking mutilation!''

''We figure it mighta been the same for Zuke Everett,'' said Nelms. ''His first wife coulda cut one helluva slice out of him.''

''Yeah,'' moaned Salgado. ''Like mine did to me!''

''That how it looked to you, Mr. Saxon?''

But I was not thinking about Valmai Everett. Still less about Mrs. Salgado. Rosemary had just come striding back into my mind. I saw her in that olive green suit she'd bought especially for the court appearance. I flinched from that accusing smile of hers.

It wasn't really *our* divorce: it was Rosemary's. I went along as an interested party and she ended up with everything she wanted.

Our house, our child, a regular pound of my flesh.

She escaped from me and somehow turned me into her prisoner.

''Did Everett *say* anything to you?'' asked Salgado.

I tried to shake her out of my mind but Rosemary owned part of that as well. In perpetuity. She went everywhere with me.

''Did he mention the divorce? Talk about money?''

''No, Lieutenant.''

"There musta been some kind of hint."

"If there was, I missed it."

"You holding out on us again?" he challenged.

"I haven't got the strength."

"Okay, here's the way we see it," he explained. "Everett is a guy with an expensive habit he couldn't afford. Might be the reason he was having trouble getting into his bedroom. He needs the merchandise but he can't come through with the payments. Gets into deep shit. So they send someone to collect. With a stiletto."

"It all turns on the state of his finances," said Nelms.

Salgado was bitter. He had his own Rosemary.

"After a divorce, you *got* no fucking finances!"

"Do you need to bother me with all this? I complained. "If you want to know about Zuke's income, ask Howie Danzig."

"We tried him," replied Salgado. "No dice. He's not answering any questions just now."

"Why not?"

"Because he was rushed to hospital yesterday. Heart attack."

"A bad one," confirmed Nelms. "Doctors are not hopeful."

I felt an uprush of sympathy for Howie. Before the tournament, he was cynical and depressed. After the third round, he was happier than I'd ever seen him and revelled in the celebrations. Then he'd been robbed of his finest player and best asset. Now he was seriously ill in a hospital bed. Howie Danzig would not remember the Kallgren Tournament of Champions with any fondess.

"Have you got anything else to tell us?" demanded Salgado.

"Like what?"

"Like stuff we oughta know. Facts, information, theories."

"Nothing," I said through a yawn. "My only concern right now is how soon I can close those curtains, switch out the light and crawl back between the sheets."

"How long d'you plan on staying here?"

"I've told them to give me a call in a fortnight's time."

"You check out, *we* want to know about it. Comprendo?"

"Oh, I won't be moving just yet," I promised. "I'll be here until the whole matter is cleared up."

"That could take time," he warned. "This is real police work, not something out of a crap TV series. We don't solve a murder in a one-hour episode. So don't expect 'Hill Street Blues.' "

"I never watch the programme, Lieutenant. The only crime series I can bear 'Cagney & Lacey'—and it's not because they work in a police department. I'd watch those two if they had a window-cleaning round." I suppressed the next yawn. "Goodnight."

"We'll be back, Saxon."

"I'll try to look more photogenic by then."

"You think of anything else, get in touch."

"I will," I said without conviction.

They paused at the door. Nelms sounded a grudging note.

"You played well yesterday."

"Thanks. Did you see the highlights on telly?"

"No. I was at the course. Looking around." He seemed peeved. "You shoulda taken up baseball. With a swing like you got, Mr. Saxon, you mighta made a fortune."

"Now he tells me!" I joked.

They went out and shut the door firmly behind them.

Fighting off the urge to collapse on the bed, I crossed to the bathroom, stripped off, steeled myself, then took a cold shower. A shave did wonders for my morale and appearance. After making myself a coffee from one of the sachets provided, I was ready for the first important task of the day.

I rang Clive Phelps at his hotel. My call woke him up.

"I'm not in yet," he mumbled at the other end of the line.

"It's me, Clive."

"Who's me?" he growled.

"Alan."

"Oh, hi!" he said with evident pleasure.

Then he slammed the receiver down.

I dialled the number again and waited a long time before

he consented to answer. His voice sounded marginally less hostile and I could hear him drinking something.

"How did you get on yesterday?" I asked.

"Fine. She left an hour ago."

I was astonished. "Miss California?"

"No," he groaned. "*She* went off with that Egyptian turd. I had to settle for someone a little more downmarket. She works here at the hotel. Not so much Miss California as Miss Rosario."

"Miss *where*?"

"Rosario. It's in Argentina." He became defensive. "I know what you're going to say, Alan, but the Falklands crisis is all over. We've got to build bridges."

"Fair enough," I agreed. "And before you took her to your room to build bridges, did you find anything out?"

"She has a sister who works in a café nearby. Interested?"

"The only thing I'm interested in is that information I asked you to track down for me. Have you got it yet?"

"Of course." There was an ominous pause. "What information?"

"You know damn well!"

"Don't shout," he implored. "I'm in a delicate condition. It was a very long night. Rosario is a big city."

"Three things, Clive," I prompted.

"I remember, I remember. That $10,000 bet. Helen Everett's real name. Valmai's address. Am I right?"

"About the questions, yes. But I want the answers."

"Ah, well, I didn't score so highly there," he confessed. "I did try though, Alan. Honestly. I asked around the press tent. Made a few discreet enquiries elsewhere. Searched high and low."

"But you've come up with nothing."

"Except Valmai's phone number."

"That's a start," I congratulated. "Give it to me."

"I will when I can find it. Hold on." I heard him searching wildly, then he burst into laughter and grabbed the receiver again. "You'll never guess what Miss Rosario left behind in the bed!"

"Tell me another time."

"But it's so funny, Alan."

"Just find that number, please."

"Oh, all right. If that's your attitude . . ."

He put the receiver down and began to search once more. I was kept waiting for several minutes before he was able to read out the number for me. I jotted it down on a slip of paper.

"While we're talking phone numbers, Clive," I said, "make a note of mine, will you?"

"I've got it. Zuke's new house."

"Not any longer. I had to move out."

"Why?"

"It doesn't matter."

"*Why?*" he repeated.

"Helen wanted to be alone. I was in the way."

"That's not the real reason, Saxon."

"It's the only one you're getting."

"So where are you now?"

"A motel in Santa Monica."

He sniggered. "What's her name?"

"Can't you think of anything else but that?"

"Who is she?"

"Clive," I emphasised, "I happen to be on my own."

"Expect me to believe that? *Nobody* stays at a motel alone. It's like going to a brothel and asking for a single room."

"I bow to your superior knowledge."

"Where did you meet her?"

"Listen!" I threatened. "Are you going to take down this number or shall I come over there and tattoo it on your skull?"

He found writing materials and did as I asked.

"I still think there's someone with you," he persisted.

"Two of them, actually," I boasted. "They worked on a shift system all night and they're both sleeping it off now."

"Are you *serious*?"

"Get me the rest of that information," I ordered. "Ring it through as soon as you possibly can."

"But I'm flying to Phoenix tomorrow," he protested.

"So? That gives you the whole of today."

"And what if I can't rustle up the answers today?"

"Miss the plane. Stay here. Stick at it."

"Since when have you been my editor?"

"Since Zuke Everett was murdered in cold blood."

Another pause. "Okay. You'll get your information."

"Thanks, Clive. It's vital."

"Have I ever let you down?"

"Frequently, but I'm prepared to overlook it just this once."

"Cheeky bugger!" he snorted, then he gave me a verbal nudge in the ribs. "Hey, sure you don't want me to fix you up with her sister?"

"Whose sister?"

"Miss Rosario. Try a bit of Argie hospitality."

"Another time."

"She was a right little raver," he recalled with a laugh. "And you know what they say about sisters!"

"I do have other priorities at the moment," I pointed out.

"Let some love into your life, man," he urged.

"Cheerio, Clive."

"It'll do you good."

"I'll wait to hear from you."

I put the receiver down and looked around the room properly for the first time. He was right. It *was* designed for a couple. The double bed was king-sized and positioned alongside a huge wall mirror. A large sofa provided an alternative venue and the generous bath would easily accommodate two bodies. Everything about the place spoke of illicit sex and I wanted a certain person very much.

Katie Billings. The blaze of glory girl.

Reaching for the telephone again, I dialled the number that Clive had given me and braced myself for the inevitable embarrassment. Marriage break-ups of all kinds are traumatic, but it's especially painful if you're the one who is left. I knew that from experience.

Valmai Everett knew it from experience as well. She'd been left high and dry and was entitled to feel bitter about it. Zuke's death would have had a profound effect on her. I just hoped that I could find the right words to say.

She made it easy for me. Valmai was pleased to hear my voice and her tone, though subdued, was friendly. It was only when I asked to see her that the reserve crept in. Excuses tumbled out of her and I had to cut through them to make the arrangement.

"I'll be there this afternoon, Valmai."

Her silence lasted so long that I thought she'd never answer. When it finally came, her murmur was barely audible.

"I'd like that, Alan."

"How do I find you?"

I took down the directions she gave me, then hung up.

It was now mid-morning and there was much to do. I emptied my suitcase and saw that there was nothing worth salvaging. My clothing had been slashed to ribbons. The only consolation was that I'd not been wearing it at the time.

I stuffed what I could into the plastic bag that lined the waste bin and piled the rest beside it. The cleaning staff would no doubt enjoy speculating how the guest in room seven came to have such a tattered wardrobe.

I went to reception and ordered a taxi to take me to the airport in half an hour's time, then I breakfasted in a nearby café and discovered just how hungry I was. Crossing to the small department store on the other side of the road, I bought shirts, socks, underwear, a sweater, a pair of trousers and a jerkin with a zip front. I also fell for a tie with blue chevrons on it.

Back at the motel, I changed into some of my new purchases, then settled down to wait. I reflected on what I needed to ask Valmai Everett. In my opinion, Zuke's second marriage was the crux of it all. It had a destructive effect on his golf and led directly to his murder. Drug abuse was a new factor and the police believed it might be a decisive one, but I wondered if it was a symptom rather than a cause.

One thing was certain. In order to understand the second

marriage, I had to know exactly what went wrong with the first one. That meant winning Valmai's confidence. It could be problematical.

When the taxi arrived, I was whisked off to the airport and had no difficulty securing an early flight to San Francisco. Since there were a mere twenty minutes to wait, I bought a copy of the *Los Angeles Times* and adjourned to the departure lounge.

News of the murder had made the final edition the previous day but the complete story was now on the front page. Under a banner headline was a photograph that made my heart constrict. Zuke was lying on his back in the garden, just as I'd found him. Caught in the glare of a flashbulb, the corpse took on an extra dimension of gruesome horror. When I saw my baseball cap, I had to turn away for a moment.

The report told me nothing I didn't already know. The mention of Alan Saxon was mercifully brief, though I was called upon to utter words that I'd never in fact spoken. Mardie Cutler was quoted as well and described as "resting on medical advice." Howie Danzig's heart attack was given prominence and I was glad to know the name of the hospital where he'd been taken.

Rutherford Kallgren had not missed the opportunity for self-promotion. Heaping praise upon the dead golfer, he argued that his tournament had shown Zuke at the height of his powers. The double eagle, he maintained, was a magnificent response to a magnificent course. When Tom Bellinghaus took over to develop the same theme, I could read no more of the report.

I pulled out the Metro section, which contained the editorial pages. Two obituaries were featured. Pride of place went to a denizen of the Los Angeles Supreme Court ("Former Judge B.V. Strutton Dies at 81"), but Zuke Everett almost matched him for column inches. The inimitable grin was captured in a photograph that belonged to happier days and the obituary itself was satisfyingly fulsome. The only blemish was the reference to Kallgren and Bellinghaus.

Two vultures perched on the man's headstone.

Leafing through the other supplements, I found the sports section and saw that its front page was monopolised by basketball and ice hockey. Golf roundup was tucked away on an inside page between fishing report ("Bass, Catfish Abound in Southland Lakes") and the sailing news ("Joss Wins Battle for Line Honours in Yacht Race to Puerto Vallarta").

The final day's play of the tournament was described in some detail and I was pleased with my one-line mention. Phil Reiner's win over Gamil Amir was portrayed as yet another American triumph in the Middle East and Kallgren was on hand with the predictable quote.

What was far more interesting than the report, however, was the news item that was appended to it. In one crisp and astounding sentence, I learned that Phil Reiner had signed an exclusive sponsorship contract with the Kallgren organisation, which would henceforth be handling all his managerial affairs.

Reiner had sold his soul in the heat of victory.

I tried to work out why I was so shocked.

The flight to San Francisco took just under an hour but I was not aware of any of it. My eyes closed as soon as I settled into my seat and fastened my safety belt. I woke up when we touched down on the runway. After thanking the cabin staff for letting me sleep on undisturbed, I went off into the airport building to rent a car. A whole row of companies tried to solicit my business. I chose the counter that was presided over by a short, vivacious young woman in a smart grey uniform with matching hat. A lapel badge introduced her as Lori Whyte.

She had a good dentist and a cheerleader brightness.

"Welcome to San Francisco, sir."

"Thanks."

"First trip?"

"No, I've been several times."

"Good. How can we help you, sir?"

"I need a car for one day, Lori. A reliable one."

"All our automobiles are totally reliable," she said with beaming assurance. "What did you have in mind?"

"A small one."

"The Chevy Chevette is our most popular subcompact." She indicated the large colour photograph on display. "This is the model right here. Automatic or do you prefer a gear shift?"

"Automatic, please. I need all the help I can get."

"Right, sir. Let's just get the details down."

Lori Whyte handled the paperwork with maximum charm and minimum delay. Unaware that my Access card was already overdrawn, she accepted it without question and treated me as if I'd just bought a Cadillac with hundred-dollar bills.

I would have stood there and basked in the service I was getting had it not been for a sudden realisation that I was being watched. As a tournament golfer who has played in front of spectators all his career, I am used to being on exhibition. But this was different. Here was no golf fan admiring my technique. I was under surveillance.

As casually as I could, I looked all round. There were several people about but none seemed to be showing any interest in me. Whoever was watching knew how to stay concealed.

The lovely Lori handed me a smile with the paperwork.

"You're all set, sir."

"Thanks."

"Have a nice day."

She sounded as if she actually meant it. I liked that.

I was soon climbing behind the driving wheel of a silver Chevy Chevette in a nearby car park. After checking my notes to memorise the directions given by Valmai, I set off.

It was a strange experience to be driving a car again after so many years in a motor caravan. Carnoustie was my home and I adored her but she was a little ponderous on the open road. Being in a small, zippy American automobile made me feel like a married man embarking on his first affair. I was at once guilty and exhilarated, terrified that I'd be found out yet eager to know how far and fast my new vehicle would go.

Valmai's directions were accurate but there was one crucial omission. She forgot to warn me about the traffic. As I left the airport and joined the freeway, I found myself hemmed in, hooted at, carved up and whizzed past on both sides. Average speeds were much slower than on British motorways but I was still unsettled by the random lane-changing of the other vehicles. They all knew where they were going. I spent so much time avoiding them that I couldn't concentrate properly on my own route.

I missed having Carnoustie's solidity around me.

My adultery with the Chevette was a mistake.

San Francisco will always get my vote as the most beautiful city in America. Sophisticated, resourceful and awash with spectacular views, it's a constant delight to the eye and an unashamed act of emotional blackmail. It has an atmosphere all its own and—notwithstanding its polyglot nature—a sense of unity that Los Angeles could never attain.

The best way to see San Francisco is to take your time so that you can savour its idiosyncratic blend of old and new. The worst way—I now discovered—is to leave the freeway by the wrong exit and hare madly through a maze of streets. I knew that the city was built on seven hills but I counted three times that number as I went on an endless rollercoaster ride through a variety of neighbourhoods.

When I crested yet another hill, I saw what I had been searching for—the wide sweep of the bay far below. It was a breathtaking sight and I slowed the car right down to enjoy the panorama. My pleasure was short-lived. A violent clanging sound made me look in my driving mirror. Hurtling towards me was one of the famous cable cars.

Though this quaint mode of transport has many attractions, it also has a serious defect. There is no conventional braking system. It only stops at appointed places. The onus is on other vehicles to get out of its way. I swung quickly to the right; it rattled past with its full complement of passengers.

I was happy to leave my heart in San Francisco but I wanted to take the rest of my anatomy away with me.

When I reached Fisherman's Wharf, I felt confident of my bearings. It was not long before I was queueing to cross the Golden Gate Bridge. The tricky bit, I told myself, was over. Seeing the bridge always excites me but driving over it was a special thrill. With a quickening pulse, I went from San Francisco to Marin County. Almost as soon as I joined the mainland, I took an exit that looped under the highway. It would not be too far now.

Valmai Everett was living at Stinson Beach, a small resort further up the coast. With the massive expanse of the Pacific on its left, the road twisted and turned capriciously for mile after mile, compelling even the most skilful driver to proceed with care. I noted a sign for the Muir Woods National Monument and glimpsed a redwood forest off to my right before I plunged down an incline then slowed to negotiate a hairpin bend.

It was a rugged coastline and the road ran along the top of the cliffs. I was glad to be driving on the side that was further from the edge. A careless driver coming in the opposite direction could easily end up over the unprotected precipice. Valmai had warned me that the route was quite perilous and I now understood what she meant. It was the perfect place for two classes of people. Those favouring scenic beauty. Those favouring suicide.

Stinson Beach was a windswept spot. There was a run of houses, a few shops and a car park whose size suggested a lot of visitors in the warmer weather. I didn't need to look for Valmai's address. She was coming out of the door of a white bungalow as I drove up. Dressed in an anorak, slacks and woolly hat, she had a young Alsatian dog on a lead. I brought the car to a halt immediately and got out.

"Alan!" she welcomed. "Wonderful to see you again!"

"Hello, Valmai."

We embraced and I kissed her on the cheek. She was wearing no make-up and seemed to have put on weight since we'd last met. The dog barked and pawed my legs in a friendly fashion.

"Down, boy!" she ordered, tugging the lead. "I didn't

expect you this early, Alan. I was just taking Louis for his walk."

"Fine. I'll tag along."

"Are you sure? It's pretty cold."

"I could do with some fresh air."

I soon regretted the decision. We cut across the car park, went through a gap in the dunes and came out on the beach. It was like a wind tunnel. The gust was fierce and unremitting. Even when I pulled the zip of my jerkin right up and thrust my hands into its pockets, I was miserably cold.

Valmai unclipped the lead from the Alsatian's collar and he went bounding off across the sand with uncontrolled energy. We had to lean forward at an angle as we walked straight into the icy blast.

"Marvellous place for sailing and wind-surfing," she said.

"Not to mention freezing to death," I muttered.

"What?"

"How long have you been here, Valmai?"

"Six months."

"Why choose this place?"

"It chose itself. I always loved Stinson Beach. Used to come here a lot when I was a kid. We lived in Petaluma."

"Petaluma?"

"Big poultry centre. Nicknamed the World's Egg Basket. That's where I was born and brought up. Right here in Marin County. Petaluma's a comfortable drive away."

"I see. In a sense, you've come home."

"In every sense, Alan."

"What happened to the house in Malibu?"

"It had to go."

We were diverted for a moment by the sight of the dog's antics. He tested the temperature of the water, let out a yelp, then raced back on to dry sand before chasing his tail. Valmai smiled indulgently.

"Crazy animal!"

"Why did you call him Louis?"

"I like the name."

"It suits him."

The wind was buffeting us unmercifully now and my trousers were flapping behind my legs. I began to shiver.

"Must have been a shattering blow for you, Valmai."

"Blow?"

"Zuke's death."

"Oh. Yes."

"I'm dreadfully sorry."

"You needn't be, Alan. It's all over now."

"How did you first hear about it?"

"Please," she insisted. "Zuke belongs to my past. I'd rather not talk about him. Do you mind?"

"No, of course not," I said.

But I did mind. I hadn't come all the way from Los Angeles to be met by a stone wall. Valmai had clearly withdrawn into herself. I would have to bide my time.

We walked for a few hundred yards with Louis charging ahead of us and then doubling back with wild speed. The wind eased slightly and my hair stopped trying to part company with my head. I manufactured small talk and confined it to neutral subjects. Valmai slowly relaxed with me. I was making progress.

Suddenly, I spun round on my heel.

"What's the matter?" she asked.

"Nothing."

"You gave me a start."

"I thought there was somebody behind us."

"Who'd be dumb enough to come on the beach in this weather?"

I joined her laugh but my eyes continued to search. Instinct told me that I was being watched again and I was determined to see who it was this time. But the beach was completely deserted.

"Time to head back now, anyway," she decided.

"Oh, right."

"Come on, Louis!"

In response to her call, the dog abandoned the hole he was digging in the sand. He raced past us in a flurry of legs and tail, then skidded to a halt as he found something worth sniffing.

With the wind at our backs, I felt better at once and the return journey was almost bracing. When we reached the car park, Valmai clipped the lead back on to the collar and Louis chose that moment to relieve himself. We crossed the road and went into the bungalow.

It was a small, attractive, modern building in an excellent state of repair. The living room was bright, cosy and deliciously warm but it was a far cry from the luxury of the Malibu home. I noticed several items of furniture that had survived from the earlier dwelling and many of the ornaments were familiar as well.

There were no photographs of Zuke but he hadn't been entirely banished. Tucked away on a bookshelf, I saw, was a biography of him that had been written a couple of years earlier.

Valmai fed the dog and left him to curl up in his basket in the kitchen. She brought in a tray with coffee and biscuits on it. After gulping down a mouthful, I started to thaw out. Valmai settled down in the easy chair opposite me. Now that she'd taken off her hat and anorak, I could see her properly. The quiet loveliness was still there though it looked a trifle neglected.

"I am sorry, Alan," she volunteered.

"About what?"

"When you called this morning. I gave you a hard time."

"I didn't mind."

"Truth is, I've had a lot of hassle the past twenty-four hours. It's been hell. Phone just hasn't stopped ringing. What with the cops, the newspapers, the TV people . . ." A flash of anger surfaced. "Why pick on me? I'm not even married to the guy anymore!"

I nibbled a biscuit and gave her a minute to calm down.

"Don't you find it a bit lonely here?" I asked.

"With Louis around?"

"I was thinking of human company."

"My mother drives over most weekends," she said with a shrug. "Besides, I like it on my own. Main reason I moved here, in fact. To get away from human company for a while.'' She gave a sardonic smile. ''Not that it turned out that way at first.''

''What do you mean?''

''I guess I was a sitting target.''

''Men?''

''*Married* men. They're a breed apart.'' Bitterness darkened her voice. ''There must have been a dozen or more. All married to good friends of mine. All with the same patter. They just 'happened' to be in San Francisco and thought they'd call in on me. What is it with those guys? They were convinced that I'd be desperate to hop straight in the sack with them. Worse thing was they offered it as a *favour*!''

''I can see why you bought Louis.''

''Present company excepted—men are slobs.''

Helen Everett had said much the same to me. On that point at least, the two women were agreed. Helen had been victimised for her charms and escaped by marrying Zuke. Valmai only became a target when he divorced her. My sympathy went out to both wives.

''I'm surprised you let me through the door,'' I said.

''You're different, Alan. I feel safe with you.''

''I hope that's a compliment.''

Valmai nodded and blew me a kiss.

She finished her coffee, then toyed with the cup for a while before putting it down on the saucer. I could see that she wanted to ask me something and I waited patiently until she was ready.

''How long were you married, Alan?''

''Long enough.''

''Do you still keep in touch?''

''Fitfully.''

''What does she do now?''

''Rosemary? She haunts me.''

''Does she have a job of any kind?''

''That's it,'' I confirmed. ''Spooking me. Full time.''

''So she didn't marry again.''

I laughed. ''No man is brave enough to take her on,

Valmai. In her own sweet way, Rosemary is a daunting prospect. She embodies all that's wrong with the English class system."

"And what about you?" she enquired. "Have you never thought about a second marriage?"

"I've *thought* about it. Yes."

"But that's as far as it went, by the sound of it. Why?"

"Once bitten."

"I know the feeling," she murmured.

"Also," I stressed, "there's Lynette to consider. I don't know why but I hate the thought of her having a stepmother."

"I can understand that."

"Lynette is very special to me and I have to share her as it is. I don't want to fit another person into the equation. Permanently, that is. I get on well with my daughter the way things are."

"How often do you see her?"

"That's the problem. Not often enough."

"Tell me about it."

I talked freely and found myself confiding things that I'd never even been able to mention to anyone else. Valmai was attentive and sympathetic throughout. She prompted me gently and drew the whole story out in the most painless way.

There was an immediate bonus.

In telling her about the break-up of my marriage, I was helping her to confront her own. As I recalled some of my battles with Rosemary, she in turn began to make comments about her difficulties with Zuke.

I was at last getting behind her defences.

"Did it hurt, Alan?" she wondered.

"What?"

"When she walked out on you."

"I was in a complete daze for almost a year."

She looked at me soulfully for a long time, then pulled her knees right up so that she could wrap her arms around her legs. Huddled in the chair, she spoke softly about her own problems.

"We always wanted children. Zuke couldn't wait to be a

father. But it wasn't to be. We tried for years and never gave up hope." She paused and bit her lip. "It was me. I had every kind of test imaginable and some of them were pretty humiliating, I can tell you. But I went through with it all because I believed that we'd make it in the end. And we did. Almost." A sad smile appeared. "Did you know that I became pregnant, Alan?"

"No. When was this?"

"Over eighteen months ago. We were knocked out by it. Zuke was so frightened that something might go wrong that he sent me back home to Petaluma whenever he went off to play in a tournament. Mom took care of me. She was even more nervous about it than Zuke. Talk about being wrapped up in cotton wool." Valmai paused. "Everything was fine and dandy until the last month. And then . . ."

The memory seemed to make her shrink. Her head dropped to her knees, her arms tightened and her shoulders hunched. A woman I had always admired for her serenity was now a mass of tensions.

"And then?" I coaxed.

"The baby died," she said, simply. "I went for one of my regular check-ups and the doctor couldn't hear its heart beating. It was dead. There was nothing they could do about it."

"It must have been terrible for you," I consoled.

"That wasn't the end of it," she whispered, recalling an added torment. "They told me it would be better if I went to term. So I did. I carried a dead thing around inside me for another three weeks. It was torture, Alan. I don't know how I got through it."

"You're a martyr," I soothed, leaning across to pat her on the shoulder. "What an ordeal to face! How did Zuke react?"

A hardness crept into her eyes and her voice.

"That was the start of all the trouble."

"Trouble?"

"I went into a depression straight after," she explained. "It went on for months. I hardly knew one day from the next. When I finally came out of it, most of the damage had been done."

"What damage?"

"Money worries, arguments with Howie, loss of form, the other women . . . When Zuke did something, he did it big. There was I, needing love and comfort and I find myself in the middle of a crisis."

"You mentioned money worries."

"I don't know all the details," she admitted. "I was kept out of it. What I do know is that Zuke never could handle his finances properly. Easy come, easy go—that was him. Howie had some terrific rows with him over money. I'd hear them yelling at each other." A note of despair was sounded. "Then it affected his golf. That was it."

She offered a hand and I held it comfortingly in my own.

"Did Zuke blame you about the baby?" I asked.

"Yes."

"But that's so unfair, Valmai."

"He got to be like that. Towards the end."

"And the other women?" I said, quietly.

"It wounded me at first," she replied wearily, "but I soon got used to it. I *had* to. I didn't mind as long as he was discreet about it. He was looking for something that I couldn't give him any longer so, okay, let him get on with it!" The weariness increased. "Then he met Helen Ramirez. I couldn't compete with that."

"You can from where I'm sitting," I reassured.

"He was infatuated, Alan. He just wouldn't listen." She sat up and used a fist to bang the arm of the chair. "I hate him, I hate him! So don't ask me to feel sorry that he's dead because I don't care. It's nothing to do with me any more. He's not mine."

Her face was at war with her words. For all her denials, I could see in her eyes that she still loved him in some ways. Zuke had betrayed her but he had not wiped out everything there'd been between them. I felt that there was something she ought to know.

"On the day that he played that incredible round of golf," I informed her, "Zuke filled his den with photographs of you. He did wrong by you, Valmai, and he knew it. On his last day, he turned to you for help—not to Helen."

"I know, Alan."

"How?" I asked in astonishment.

"You promise not to tell anyone?"

"Of course."

"The cops mustn't know. It's none of their damn business."

"Don't worry," I assured. "I'm getting to be quite expert at hiding things from Lieutenant Salgado."

She perched on the edge of the chair and regarded me.

"Zuke rang me that same morning."

"Before the third round?"

"Yes," she confirmed. "It was a real shock. I hadn't spoken to him in ages and suddenly his voice is on the end of the line from Santa Monica."

"What did he want?"

"He wanted me to wish him good luck."

"Did you?"

"Yes."

"It worked, Valmai."

"Only on the golf course."

Silent tears trickled down her cheeks and her body sagged. I offered to take her in my arms but she waved me away and controlled herself at once. After drying her tears, she got up to inspect her face in the mirror. She spoke over her shoulder.

"Who killed him, Alan?"

"That's what I'm trying to find out."

"Have I said anything that's been of any help?"

"Lots. Thanks."

"Know the real reason I tried to stop you coming here?"

"What?"

"The resemblance. I didn't want to be reminded of Zuke again." She turned round. "But I'm glad you came now."

"Me too. There's one last thing," I said, getting to my feet. "Did Zuke take drugs of any kind when he was living with you?"

She stiffened at once. "No, he didn't!"

"Are you certain of that, Valmai?"

"Absolutely certain," she retorted, vehemently.

"Look, I didn't mean to offend you," I apologised.

"I'll give you the answer I gave to Lieutenant Salgado. Our marriage had its problems but there was nothing like *that* going on. When he was with me, Zuke never touched narcotics."

She was back on the defensive again. My visit was over.

I handed her the card I'd picked up at the motel and asked her to contact me there if she should think of anything else. Valmai had already told me far more than she'd intended but I sensed that she was still holding back something important. It was no use trying to pressurize her. If I backed off and gave her time to reflect, she might volunteer the information in her own good time.

I made departure noises and she ushered me to the front door. The Alsatian came padding out of the kitchen to lick my hand by way of farewell. I gave him an affectionate pat.

Valmai held the dog's collar as I opened the door.

"It was a boy," she said.

"A boy?"

"Our baby. The one that died. We were going to name it after my father, you see." Her sad smile returned. "He's called Louis."

I glanced down at the dog. It wagged its tail.

"Safe journey," wished Valmai.

I kissed her on the cheek before striding away.

Louis barked his own kind of goodbye.

Chapter Five

As soon as I drove out of Stinson Beach, I knew that I was being followed. At the airport and during the walk with Valmai, there had just been an unpleasant sensation. This time I had visual evidence as well. Rounding a sharp bend, I slowed the Chevette down and kept an eye on my mirror. A big blue car cruised into sight, then checked its speed when it saw me up ahead.

Trailed from the airport. Watched on the beach. Shadowed on my return journey. I felt annoyed and apprehensive. My instinct was to stop and confront whoever was on my tail but I remembered that discretion was the better part of valour.

I elected to make a run for it.

Gradually accelerating as I drew away from the next bend, I soon lost the blue car from my driving mirror. I went as fast as I dared along the coast road, screaming around the curves, racing along the straighter sections and flirting more than once with the edge of the precipice. Far below me, the Pacific rolled in with mild-mannered turbulence.

After a couple of miles I was convinced that I had shaken off my pursuer, so I reduced speed slightly. The headlong dash was proving to be a test of nerve as well as driving ability. Since I am used to trundling along in a motor caravan, the strain began to tell. I slowed, I relaxed, I played safe.

It proved to be a costly error.

My driving mirror was suddenly filled with a blue car that was powering its way towards me. I pressed my foot down on the accelerator but had no chance against its superior pace. As yet another bend loomed up ahead, the blue car pulled out and eased up alongside me. In the split second I allowed myself to look across at him, I saw that the driver was a swarthy young man with thick, black hair. He was alone, sitting well forward and staring grimly through the windscreen.

The blue car sailed past me and cut across my path at the critical moment. I braked fiercely to avoid collision, swung to the right and sent a small avalanche of stones over the side of the cliff. While the other vehicle straightened to glide around the bend, I fought hard to control the skid and prayed that I would stop before I ran out of road.

The Chevy Chevette squealed in pain as its tyres burned their way across the hard surface. We swung crazily from side to side and then turned right around as we screeched to a juddering halt immediately before the bend. Only half the vehicle was now on a solid foundation. The rest of it jutted out in space and I was held there with it.

When I tried to move, the car rocked precariously. The slightest change of balance could send it over the edge. I cursed the fact that it was a left-hand drive. In a British car, I would have been sitting above solid rock. As it was, there was nothing but fresh air below me.

Not daring to budge an inch, I pressed my hand down on the horn and kept it there. Minutes passed before I saw another vehicle coming towards me from Stinson Beach. It was a pickup truck and it halted a dozen or more yards away.

A big, brawny man in overalls came running over. He peered through the windscreen to assess the extent of my plight.

"Holy shit!"

"Have you got a rope or something?" I pleaded.

"Just hold on there."

I had a further agonising wait while he rummaged in the

back of his truck. He reappeared and waved a long steel pole at me.

"Open this window," he ordered.

"I daren't move."

"Then you got problems, buddy," he warned. "You don't move, you don't live. Now, come on, will you?"

Resting the steel bar on top of the Chevette, he pressed down with his full weight. The car steadied a little and the fractional improvement encouraged me to try doing as he said. I released my safety belt and eased myself sideways with excruciating slowness. When I was in a leaning Tower of Pisa position, I reached out gingerly for the handle of the window. I wound it at a snail's pace; the glass inched down.

"Get a move on," he said, impatiently.

"Almost there."

"Make sure it's right down."

"I will." The final turn was completed. "It's done."

"Okay," he explained. "Here's what we're gonna do. I pass in the bar and you take a good grip with both hands. Right? Then I pull you through the window. Keep your legs clear of the steering wheel or you'll get dragged back if she goes over the edge. We only got one shot at this, buddy, so let's make it a good one."

"I'm ready."

"I sure as hell hope that *I* am."

With one hand still pressing down on the car, he used the other to pass the bar in through the window. I gripped it firmly and brought my legs up slowly so that they were across the driving seat. When the bar was jerked through the window, I intended to go with it.

"What d'ya say?" he called.

"Ready and waiting at this end!"

"Okay—let's go for it!"

He brought his other hand down to grab hold of the bar, then heaved backwards with all his force. As I was pulled towards the open window, I put my feet against the door behind me to gain extra thrust. The balance altered dramatically. Before I was properly clear, the car rocked violently and plunged over the side of the cliff.

I took a blow on my leg and hit the ground with a thud.

But I was safe.

The Chevy Chevette, meanwhile, somersaulted through the air until it landed on the jagged rocks below. There was a loud explosion as it burst into flames. I thanked the man profusely. We stood on the lip of the precipice and watched the inferno.

My companion gave a genial chuckle.

"One thing, buddy," he observed, slipping an arm consolingly around my shoulders. "You'd have had a great view on the way down."

A police car and a fire engine arrived on the scene about twenty minutes later. I had to give a lengthy statement and convince the police that my injury—a bruised thigh—did not merit a hospital visit. Editing the facts carefully, I made it all sound more like an accident than a deliberate attempt on my life. I supplied no details about the driver of the blue car. He was on my personal wanted list.

Gazing down at the charred wreck, I was grateful that Lori Whyte had persuaded me to take out comprehensive insurance. I had enough on my plate without having to worry about a massive bill from the car hire company.

In spite of my protests, the police insisted on driving me out to the airport. I sat in the back of their car like a villain on his way to trial. There was no thrill as I crossed the Golden Gate Bridge this time. I simply gave a shudder when I saw the notorious island prison.

Alcatraz was my father's spiritual home.

It symbolised his view on law and order. The bleak rock was now only a tourist attraction but the sight of it still brought his voice echoing back. When I was growing up in suburban Leicester, my father ran his own private Alcatraz.

I was its sole inmate.

I closed my eyes for the rest of the journey and tried to concentrate on more immediate concerns. It seemed clear to me that I'd been followed from Los Angeles. My sleep during the flight had prevented my noticing anything and I was far too preoccupied with the traffic as I drove through San Francisco.

Unless I was mistaken, the man in the blue car was also the proud owner of a battered Oldsmobile. I'd met him once before in the guest room of a Santa Monica house. The forward position of the car seat suggested that he was not very tall and his frame had been sturdy. Had I seen his other profile, I believed, there would have been a scar on the temple.

But why had he gone to such lengths to kill me? He could have snapped my neck in two at our first meeting if he'd been intent on murder. Why release me if it put him to the trouble of coming after me again? The answer was patent.

I was getting too close for comfort.

Somebody was afraid that I'd find out the truth in the end. Unless I was stopped. The road to Stinson Beach had been the ideal place in which to dispose of me. The man had seized his opportunity. It was deeply alarming but there was one aspect that was heartening.

I must be on the right track.

When we got to the airport, I went straight off to find Lori Whyte to apologise for what had happened to her company's vehicle. She took it on the chin and came back with her cheerleader smile.

"Don't let it worry you, sir."

"Then you're not upset?"

"Course not."

"That's a relief."

"We're bound to lose an automobile from time to time," she said, airily. "That's the way it goes. Anyway, a Chevy Chevette can be replaced. We're just glad we didn't lose a customer over that cliff."

"So am I, Lori."

She laughed and asked for a more detailed account of the accident. I gave her the revised version in which the would-be killer was only a man in a hurry who probably didn't even realise the danger he left me in as he whizzed past.

Lori heard me out with polite attention.

"There was no need for you to say sorry," she added. "Not as if it was *my* automobile. It was the company's and they got hundreds."

"I was afraid you might get into trouble because you were the person who rented it out to me."

"Oh, the company doesn't work like that," she said with a giggle. "Just as well. First month I was here, I hired out a Camaro that got stolen and used in a bank robbery. What about that, huh?"

"You must have some kind of jinx."

"Yeah. Could be."

I paused. "Actually, Lori," I continued more seriously, "there was another reason for coming to see you. I wanted to ask you a favour."

"A favour?"

She was expecting me to make a pass at her and her tone warned me that I'd be wasting my time. My request was quite different. It struck me that a man with a battered Oldsmobile in Los Angeles was unlikely to have a shining new car on standby at San Francisco airport. In all probability, he'd rented the vehicle. When I described the blue car to Lori, she identified it at once.

"That was a Pontiac Grand Am."

"Do you have any in your fleet?"

"No, sir."

"Then who does?"

"Avis—and a few of the others." She pointed to the Avis counter on the opposite side of the hall. "See that one on the right? That's a Grand Am."

"And that's my boy!" I confirmed, looking at the photograph.

"There you go, then. Ask around."

I leaned on the counter and tried to sound exhausted.

"Lori," I confided, "I've had one hell of an afternoon. I don't suppose you could help me out? Apart from anything else, those girls know you. They might not like a total stranger trying to pump them." I offered a tired grin. "I'd be eternally grateful."

"I'm not supposed to leave my position, sir."

"Go on. I'll mind the shop."

She weighed me up, glanced around, then nodded.

"Wait here. I won't be long."

"Ask what the man looked like, will you?" I instructed.

Lori Whyte came out from behind the counter and I had my first view of her legs. They were short but attractively slender and they permitted her a quite bewitching gait.

When she had no luck at the Avis counter, she moved on to another but she drew a blank there as well. The third girl seemed to know something and showed Lori a list but the latter shook her head. At the fourth port of call, she had more success.

My hopes rose as I watched her in earnest conversation with a grinning young man who worked for National Car Rental. He consulted his records, then wrote on a pad, tore off the sheet and handed it to her. Lori thanked him and headed back towards me. The young man studied her legs with frank enthusiasm.

"Well?" I asked, eagerly.

She went back behind her counter before she spoke.

"I hope you know what this cost me, sir."

"Cost you?"

"That guy on National is not supposed to divulge booking information to anyone—least of all to a competitor." She threw a contemptuous glance at him. "Just so happens that the jerk has been trying to date me ever since he got the job."

I was touched. "And you made the supreme sacrifice for *me*?"

"I agreed to have a drink with him when I'm through here." She grimaced. "I sure hope it was worth it."

"What did you get?"

"A blue Grand Am was rented to a man who came in on the same PSA flight as you. He called from LA Airport to have it standing by for him." She passed the slip of paper to me. "He was Mexican. Gave his name as Mr. Gomez and that address. Oh, and he paid in cash. That's unusual in our business. Everybody has plastic these days. The

National parking lot called over an hour ago to say that the automobile had been returned and was available for rental again.''

''That's marvellous, Lori! Did your friend say anything about the man's appearance?''

''Only that he was in his twenties. Medium height, solid build. Wearing a brown jacket and a hat. That's all I got.''

''It's more than enough.''

''I'll remember that when I'm having a drink with that jerk over there.'' Her smile blossomed again. ''As long as we give customer satisfaction, sir. That's what counts.''

''Lori Whyte,'' I declared. ''I love you.''

I bent over the counter to kiss her, then waved my farewell. As I limped past National Car Rental, I was pleased to see that I'd wiped the grin off the young man's face. He and Lori would now have something to talk about in the bar.

I went back upstairs and headed for the PSA desk. The woman on duty was very obliging. When I asked after my friend, Mr. Gomez, she punched up the information on her computer. Gomez had flown back to Los Angeles on the previous flight.

Quiet elation stirred. I was making progress.

Gomez was my man. The name was probably a false one—hence the absence of a credit card—and the address also fictitious, but I now knew for certain that I'd been followed from Los Angeles by a professional killer. He was Mexican and already had three victims.

Zuke Everett. My clothing. A silver Chevy Chevette.

I felt pleased. When I went to the bookstall to get some post cards, I even bought one for my father. A splendid view of Alcatraz.

It was my turn to get back at *him*.

It was late evening before I returned to the motel. A message from Clive Phelps was waiting for me and I dialled his number as soon as I went back to my room. When the hotel switchboard put me through, Clive answered at once in breathless tones.

"Hold on, will you—because I can't!"

He dropped the receiver and I heard it bang against something hard. I was then treated to some fairly appalling noises. Clive Phelps was not alone. I had no wish to listen to a miniature radio play about his private life and so I put my own receiver down on the bedside table.

It was minutes before I heard him yelling down the line.

"Saxon! Where are you? Come back—all is forgiven!"

I crossed over to the telephone and picked it up.

"How did you know it was me?" I said.

"Because I asked you to give me a bell."

"Supposing I'd been your wife?"

"Then we'd never have had the three kids."

"You know what I mean, Clive," I clarified. "Supposing it had been your wife ringing up out of the blue?"

"We've been married a long time, Alan. She's got more sense than to make random phone calls when I'm far away in a foreign hotel room." I heard him draw deeply on a post-coital cheroot. "Anyway, sorry I was engaged when you called. Miss Rosario is a chambermaid here. She'd just popped in to turn down my bed."

"I hate to come between a man and his bridge-building."

"And what a bridge!" he boasted. "Sydney Harbour stuff."

"Could we move on to important matters?" I requested.

"You want her sister's phone number, after all?"

"No, Clive. I want some action."

"Then you should have been here five minutes ago."

"Who placed that bet on Zuke Everett?" I demanded.

"Not so fast. Let's take the easy one first."

"The easy one?"

"Got a pencil handy? Helen Everett—or Helen Ramirez, to use her stage name—was born in Monterrey. Her real name was Veronica Quiroga." He spelled the surname for me and I wrote it down. "By all accounts, the woman has been around in a big way. She's left a lot of smiles among the male population here. Then she married Zuke. You know the rest."

"Not quite," I muttered. "Anything else?"

"Only that she's hot for golf writers," he added, knowledgeably. "And there's a mole on her right tit."

I knew for a fact that there wasn't a single blemish on her body but I didn't challenge his claim. He couldn't be expected to understand what had occurred between Helen and me on the night that her husband was murdered. Clive lived in a world of sudden pounces and sordid conquests. It made him judge everyone by his own standards.

"What about the bet?" I asked.

"Don't mention that bloody thing!" he groaned. "You owe me a mint, Alan. I spent a fortune to get the name you wanted."

"And what was it?"

"Sit tight and listen," he ordered. "I'm not going to be cheated out of my full moan. I chased around for *hours*!"

"But you got there in the end?"

"I'm coming to that." He puffed at his cheroot again and I heard him exhale the smoke. "First problem—tracking down the bookie. That cost me a packet, for a start. He was called Agonistes. Tiny little polecat of a man with the kind of suit that I couldn't even afford to hire. As for booze!" Clive gave a hollow laugh. "He made me look like a temperance freak. Did everything but swim in the bloody stuff. When I asked him about the bet, he told me that all his transactions were strictly confidential. A bottle later, he agreed to drop the 'strictly' but stuck by the 'confidential.' Halfway through the third bottle, he said he'd whisper a name in my ear. You can imagine what his breath was like by that stage. He almost singed my lughole off!"

"What was the name?" I pressed.

"Gary Posner."

I shrugged. "Means nothing to me."

"Nor to me. Until I did some more charging round, that is."

"And?"

"I finally caught up with him. Gary Posner is a businessman. Makes sportswear. Quite successful at it, judging by the size of his office. Gorgeous secretary. One of those tall, slinky birds with nice hips. I could see that she liked me."

"Tell me about Posner," I insisted.

"Who? Oh, yes." He paused to take a swig of something, then belched mildly. "At first he denied all knowledge of the bet. Apparently, the law's been round there so he's had a bellyful of answering questions. I had to calm him down and win him over with my celebrated silver tongue. Gary Posner placed that bet for a friend of his." Clive chuckled with glee. "You'll never guess who that friend is."

It came to me at once and I blurted it out.

"Zuke Everett."

He was wounded. "You knew all the bloody time!"

"I didn't, Clive. Honestly."

"I could have saved myself all that slog!"

"It was pure intuition."

"Bollocks!"

Clive had another drink to soothe his hurt feelings. I'd robbed him of his major revelation and he was upset. It was some time before he consented to tell me what else he'd learned.

"Here's something you *didn't* know, Mastermind," he announced. "Over the past year, Zuke made a habit of it."

"Betting on himself?"

"Betting on himself—and losing."

"How much?"

"Thousands. Posner wouldn't put a figure on it."

"Where does *he* fit into all this?"

"Posner and Zuke were partners," he explained. "Zuke had a stake in the business until last year. He asked Posner to buy him out when he was desperate for cash. Seems to be a recurring theme."

"What does?" I said.

"Zuke's shortage of the ready. He cut back on a lot of other business interests as well. Must have been in real straits."

"That's the picture I've been getting, Clive."

"Then, of course, there's Howie Danzig," he reminded.

"Yes, he was closely involved in all Zuke's financial affairs."

"According to Posner, the two of them had some ding-dong battles. Zuke became so irresponsible. It nearly drove poor Howie round the twist." He heaved a sigh. "Christ! What could be worse than managing a professional bloody golfer?"

"Being one."

He laughed. "Fair comment."

"Any word on Howie, by the way?"

"I contacted the hospital earlier. He's still in intensive care. They described his condition as stable, which is their euphemism for consistently bad." He took another drink but spared me the belch this time. "Report concluded. Over and out."

"Thanks, Clive. You did well."

"So what's new?" he boasted. His tone became reflective. "One thing about old Zuke, though. The man had guts."

"What do you mean?"

"Look at the situation he was in, Alan. On his uppers, fighting with his manager, struggling to find his form. Then, after two very ordinary rounds of golf, what does he go and do?"

"Put $10,000 on himself to win the tournament."

"Yes," he added. "Then Zuke went out and shot a fabulous round of 64. That takes nerve. You have to admire him."

"Oh, I do," I attested. "Very much."

There was a brief silence in tribute to Zuke's memory.

"Anyway," resumed Clive chirpily, "what did *you* do today?"

"Went to San Francisco."

"That's not fair," he protested. "While I'm doing the donkey work here, you go off sightseeing."

"I went to visit a friend. Valmai Everett."

"Ah. That's different. Tell all."

I gave him a short account of what had happened and told him the truth about the attempt on my life. His manner changed at once.

"Why didn't you say all that to the police, you idiot?"

"You know how I feel about men in uniform."

"For God's sake, Alan! Someone is trying to kill you."

"I'd worked that out for myself."

"You need protection," he urged.

"Why?"

"Because he may have another crack at you."

"Not if I'm surrounded by a cordon of police."

Clive gulped. "You're not actually *inviting* attack?"

"I'll be ready for him next time," I promised.

"Don't be stupid, man. You're dealing with a pro here. He could pick you off at any time."

"He hasn't managed it so far," I pointed out. "Besides, a pro doesn't take chances. I'm safe as long as I'm with other people."

"Look what happened to Zuke."

"I'm not likely to forget that in a hurry."

There was another silence as Clive considered the situation.

"Do you know what I'd do in your position?" he said.

"What?"

"Head for home on the next available plane."

"I'm not running away," I asserted.

"See it in the nature of a tactical withdrawal."

"Sorry, Clive. It's not my style."

"What *is* your style—being forced over a cliff?"

"I survived."

"Alan," he argued, "as long as you stay, you're a target."

"So?"

"Sooner or later, the killer will get you."

"Not if I get him first," I countered.

"But you have no idea who he is."

"I'm not that far off and he knows it. If I wasn't breathing down his neck, why would he bother with me at all?"

"I still say that you should cut and run," he advised.

"Not a chance."

"Be sensible, Alan."

He murdered Zuke and he had a go at me," I said. "I've

simply got to stay. I want to nail him, Clive. And I want to nail whoever's behind him pulling the strings."

"Who do you think that is?" he asked.

"I'm not certain yet," I admitted. "But I will be soon. When I've got all the information I need. Talking of which, I want you to find out something else for me."

"I can't," he complained. "I'm flying off to Arizona."

"Not until tomorrow. That's a long way off yet."

"I do expect some time to eat, drink and be merry, you know."

"Not to mention your bridge-building commitments."

"Exactly."

"The night is young," I argued. "With luck and a following wind, you should be able to fit it all in."

"I intend to," he vowed with a cackle.

"Clive, *please*. Could we just forget about your Argentinian handmaiden for a moment? This is important."

"Go on. I'm listening."

"There are two things I want you to do for me."

"Organise your funeral and choose the hymns."

"Find out all you can about Rutherford Kallgren."

"Are you joking?" he gasped. "That could take weeks. Months. Kallgren is head of a multinational corporation, which means that he belongs to the Millionaire Crooks Brigade. Those blokes know how to cover their tracks."

"What I need is the story of his involvement in golf. When did it start and why? How did he come to team up with Bellinghaus? What are his plans for the future? Talk to your American colleagues, Clive. Dig up the dirt."

"There's plenty of that," he conceded. "Kallgren is about as popular among my fellow-scribes as AIDS."

"While you're collecting horror stories about him, ask about Phil Reiner as well. That's the second thing I need to know. Why has Reiner signed up with the Kallgren organisation?"

"Answer's obvious. Reiner wants a licence to print money every time he swings his club."

"There's more to it than that, Clive."

"Then the person to tackle about it is the resident harpie."

"Who?"

"Suzanne Fricker. She deals with all the contracts."

I realised with a start that he was right. Suzanne Fricker must have been instrumental in finalising everything. Tucked away in my wallet was her business card and an invitation to ring her. It was time to see if her offer of help was genuine.

"I'll handle her, Clive," I decided.

"Wear rubber gloves," he advised. "She likes it sanitised."

"You concentrate on Reiner himself. Try to speak to him."

"No point, Alan. He never gives interviews. Full stop."

"What happened to that celebrated silver tongue of yours?"

"I'm saving it for Miss Rosario tonight," he said. "Phil Reiner is the Invisible Man of golf. When he won the tournament, all he gave us was a brief, noncommittal chat. I mean, I've heard of people playing their cards close to their chest. He plays them behind his sodding back!"

"Do your best, Clive. That's all I ask."

"Why am I still friends with you?" he protested.

"Because I give you all the peach assignments," I soothed. "Right. Let's get organised. What time is your flight tomorrow?"

"Ten-thirty in the morning."

"I'll join you for breakfast at your hotel."

"You can't, Alan."

"Why not?"

"I'm spoken for. Miss Rosario and I planned to have breakfast in bed tomorrow. She's got a most individual way of serving warm croissants. All I have to do is lean forward and nibble."

"Eight o'clock," I ordered. "In the dining room."

"You're blowing up my bloody bridge!"

"If you're not waiting for me at a table," I warned, "I'll come up to your room and show you *my* individual way of serving warm croissants. And you won't be able to lean forward and nibble *these*."

"I refuse to be intimidated."

"Goodbye, Clive. You've got work to do."

"Don't hang up on me," he bleated. "You haven't told me your last request yet."

"Last request?"

"Yes. I don't want to introduce a ghoulish note but Alan Saxon does happen to be on some hit man's top ten list. There's an even chance that you won't make it for breakfast tomorrow."

"Thanks for the boost to my morale."

"Just so that I know," he continued. "Where would you like me to scatter your ashes? St. Andrews?"

"Carnoustie."

"The golf course or the motor caravan?"

"A handful over each."

I put the receiver down and made myself a cup of coffee. As I sipped at it, I went through the list of suspects in my mind. All of them remained possibilities. Kallgren. Bellinghaus. Gamil Amir. A new name kept suggesting itself, though I could not understand why.

Phil Reiner. The man of secrets.

I took out the business card and telephoned a number. Suzanne Fricker answered almost immediately in a crisp voice.

"Hello."

"Suzanne? It's Alan Saxon here."

"Alan!" There was surprise in her tone. "Nice of you to call."

"You did say that you'd give me a spot of help."

"Oh, I will. Just tell me what I can do."

"It's that item in the paper. Phil Reiner joining the Kallgren organisation. Were you involved in that?"

"Yes, I was," she said guardedly.

"Could you tell me a bit more about it, please?"

"Well . . ."

I could hear her wrestling with divided loyalties.

"It's important," I pressed. "I wouldn't ask you otherwise."

There was further hesitation before she came to a decision.

"Do you have any free time tonight?"

"Plenty of it, Suzanne."

"Is there some place we could meet? I don't really want to discuss this over the phone."

''Suits me.''

''Have you eaten yet?''

''No.''

''Hungry?''

''Starving,'' I confessed.

''Why don't I rustle up some supper here?'' she volunteered.

''I don't want to put you to any trouble.''

''No trouble, Alan. Besides, it'll be more private.'' Her business voice took over. ''A limo will pick you up in an hour. The driver will know where to bring you. Where are you now? Zuke's house?''

''A motel not far away.''

I gave her the name and address, then she hung up.

As the bath was running, I stripped off and examined my injured thigh. A large, dark bruise acted as a vivid memento of my last contact with the Chevy Chevette. I lowered myself into the water and relaxed. Other aches and pains announced themselves. I soaked them thoroughly.

When I had dressed and shaved, I spent some time writing the post cards I bought in San Francisco. Lynette, as ever, came first. I'd already sent her a view of Santa Monica Beach and I followed it up with an aerial shot of the Golden Gate Bridge.

Katie Billings was next. My first card to her had featured Disneyland and she now got a colour photograph of a cable car rolling up the steep gradient of Hyde Street with the bay behind it. I addressed the post card to Miss Blaze of Glory and suffered another pang.

Winter in St. Albans seemed like paradise lost now.

Alcatraz glowered up at me. I was still trying to think up a suitably crushing message for my father (''Desirable residence to let—bring your own prisoners'') when the telephone rang. The tense voice of Mardie Cutler filled my ear.

''Alan? Is that you?''

''Yes.''

''Thank God!'' she gabbled. ''Mardie here. Been trying to get hold of you all evening. I called Helen but she said you'd moved out for some reason and I simply had to speak to you so in the end I tried that Lieutenant Salgado and he gave me your number. Thing is—''

''Mardie,'' I interrupted, gently. ''Take it easy, will you?''

''What?''

''Where's the fire?''

''Sorry,'' she said with a nervous laugh. ''I guess I'm a bit overwrought. Well, who wouldn't be in my position? It was *awful*!''

When I eventually calmed her down, she told me that her apartment had been broken into earlier that day. Among the things stolen were her address book and hi fi equipment, both essential to her job. She was experiencing the usual feelings of invasion. Afraid to spend the night alone, she'd asked a girlfriend to move in with her.

''I simply must talk to someone about it, Alan.''

''The break-in?''

''That—and something else. You're the only person I can tell.''

I knew at once that she wanted to talk about Zuke.

We arranged to meet on the following day. Mardie suggested a small hotel as the venue and I promised to be there. She was almost pathetically grateful. I'd saved her from a sleepless night.

Valmai. Helen. Suzanne. Mardie.

Four women in the life of Zuke Everett.

I had the firm conviction that one of them could lead me to the man who'd been responsible for his death.

Suzanne Fricker's apartment was quite enormous. It was on the eighth floor of a luxury block not far from Sunset Boulevard and it commanded a stunning view of nighttime Hollywood. The main room had a three-piece suite of genuine leather, a huge coffee table surmounted by a stoneware lamp, a desk, swivel chair and filing cabinets, well-stocked bookshelves, a television, an elaborate hi fi system and a dining area that was set on a raised platform. In one corner, I noted, were an exercise bicycle and a multi-gym. Contemporary paintings and ornaments abounded.

''Good of you to come at such short notice, Alan.''

"It was kind of you to invite me."

"I was hoping you'd get in touch."

Suzanne Fricker offered her hand and I took it. Her manner was at once formal but friendly and it matched the atmosphere of her apartment. The lighting was subdued but I was still able to see and admire her deep pink sheath dress with its plunging V-neckline. Two round, bronzed breasts were in view separated by a large golden coin that hung from a chain around her neck.

She saw my interest and fingered the coin with a smile.

"It's an eagle. The old $10 piece."

"Every woman has her price," I joked.

"I never thought of it like that," she replied, crossing to the drinks cabinet. "I opened a bottle of sparkling wine, by the way. I hope that's okay."

"Fine by me."

"California's best."

Suzanne lifted the bottle from its ice bucket, uncorked it with a pop, then filled two long-stemmed glasses with dancing bubbles. She sauntered back across the thick-pile carpet and handed me my drink.

"Thanks," I said. "Cheers."

"To Zuke," she insisted.

"To Zuke."

We clinked our glasses and sipped the wine. It was good.

"Supper's just about ready if you'd like to come over and take a seat," she invited. I followed her to the dining area. "Don't expect anything special, mind. I keep my cooking simple. From the ice-box to the microwave."

She went off into the kitchen and I sat down at the oval table. It was set for a three-course meal. Cutlery, condiments, table mats and linen napkins were of the highest quality. A thick, scented candle burned in the middle of the polished mahogany.

Memories of my last night with Katie Billings came surging into my mind. Our meal on that occasion had consisted of pizzas and Sauternes in the bedroom. The window had given us the inspiring view of Carnoustie standing out in the snow and doing its best to upset the neighbours. Katie had been my kind of woman.

With Suzanne Fricker, I might be out of my depth.

"Chilled melon," she announced, bringing in the first course.

"My favourite starter."

She unloaded the things from the tray, then sat down opposite me. Almost immediately, a telephone rang on her desk. Cursing under her breath, she got up and went across to answer it.

Her caller got very short shrift.

"Yeah, who is it?" she asked. "Oh, hi there, Candice . . . Listen, sweetie, I'm in the middle of a meeting right now. Can I call you back? . . . Thanks. Speak to you later."

When she put down the receiver, she unplugged the telephone and switched on the answering machine. I noticed that there was a second telephone on the desk, a flashy red model with gold digits on it.

Suzanne returned to the table with an apologetic shrug.

"Sorry about that, Alan. We won't be disturbed again."

"What's the red phone? The hot line?"

"You could call it that."

"White House or Pentagon?"

"Mr. Kallgren. He had it put in when I started work for him. It's his private line to me so that he can be sure of getting through. When I use that phone, I talk business."

"And which one are *we* going to talk on?" I wondered.

She looked me in the eye. "The open line."

"I appreciate that."

When I started eating, I realised just how hungry I was. Apart from a couple of biscuits with Valmai and some light refreshments on the flight back, I hadn't touched anything since mid-morning. Suzanne noted my appetite and served me with a second slice of melon.

The main course consisted of steak, sautéed potatoes, broccoli and peas. A rich sauce full of aromatic herbs disproved her claim to have relied entirely on the microwave oven. We switched to a full-bodied red wine and the conversation became more serious.

"Okay," challenged Suzanne. "How can I help you?"

"Let's start with Phil Reiner."

"He signed on the dotted line. We own him now."

"Could you give me some background to that?" I said.

"Of course," she answered, readily. "The negotiations went on for three or four months. Phil never rushes into decisions. It took time to persuade him that he'd be better off with the Kallgren organisation, but he came round in the end."

"Were you involved in the negotiations with him?"

"No, Alan. It was someone else's job to track him down and trap him. I simply drew up the contracts to keep him safely caged in."

"Is that what he is, Suzanne—caged in?"

"It was a figure of speech."

"Why did Kallgren choose *him*?"

"Because Phil has a lot going for him," she argued. "He's your handsome, clean-cut, clean-living American golfer who's a credit to the game. One of the good guys. He may be a bit shy but that'll change when Mr. Kallgren starts to promote him."

"I thought Reiner was under contract to someone else."

"He was."

"Kallgren buy him off?"

"He took over the whole company," she revealed, pouring more wine into both our glasses. "This hasn't been released to the press yet but, as of today, Mr. Kallgren owns DLZ Management of New York City, Chicago and Los Angeles."

I saw the implications. "But they have other players on their books apart from Reiner."

"Eleven of them," she confirmed. "They've all been offered the opportunity to come and shelter under the Kallgren umbrella."

"Who else is he after?"

Her gaze faltered for the first time. She drank deeply from her glass, then ran a long finger slowly around the rim. Her silver nail varnish glistened in the light of the candle and the coin that dangled from her neck was a blur of shimmering gold.

"There are limits, Alan," she whispered.

I raised my own glass. "To Zuke Everett!" I toasted.

Her eyes flashed and she sat up. Checking the retort she was about to make, she glanced down at her watch instead. When she looked across at me, her gaze was steady again.

"At this time tomorrow night," she confided, "Mr. Kallgren and I will be dining at the Beverly Wilshire with Gamil Amir."

"Thanks, Suzanne. I needed to know that."

"What else do you need to know?"

"Tell me about Tom Bellinghaus."

She laughed. "That horny old bastard!"

Suzanne talked openly about the course architect. She didn't like him and had fended him off more than once. I knew that Bellinghaus was obsessional. He now emerged as dishonest, deeply ambitous, and skilled in the politics of business. If Golden Haze became a success, he stood to make millions of dollars in the long run.

I helped Suzanne to clear the things away and carried a tray into her large and meticulously clean kitchen. We had lemon sorbet for dessert and followed it with cheese and biscuits. I suddenly found that we had finished the red wine and moved on to liqueurs.

The languid mood helped me to ask the next question.

"Did Zuke come here often, Suzanne?"

She nodded and gave a wistful smile.

"How did you first meet him?" I said.

"At a party thrown by Mr. Kallgren. About five months ago."

"So it was after his marriage to Helen?"

"Oh, yes. The honeymoon period was over by then. Problems were surfacing." She stared into the flame of the candle. "The party was a gigantic publicity exercise for Golden Haze. Hundreds turned up. Zuke was there on his own. His wife refused to come at the last moment and his manager had no time for Mr. Kallgren. Zuke and I took one look at each other and that was it."

"Some enchanted evening."

"Just about. Corny as hell, maybe, but so what?"

"Not enough of it about," I observed.

"There were speeches, of course, and then Tom took over. The Bellinghaus Road Show."

"I'm glad I missed that."

"He'd made this video of Golden Haze and we all had to watch it while he gave a running commentary. The lights were down and I was standing at the back. Then I felt a hand slip into mine. It was Zuke. We sneaked out and came back here."

Her eyes moistened and she blinked to stem the tears. I warmed to her. Suzanne Fricker was proving to be unique. Alone of the Barbie doll range, she'd had a heart implant.

"You see," she continued, "I have this trouble with men."

"Fighting them off."

"Quite the reverse, Alan."

"I don't believe it."

"Oh, come on. Just look at me."

"Terrific view from here," I heard myself saying.

She took my hand and squeezed it gratefully. In the glow of the candlelight, she looked almost beautiful. A synthetic illusion. I kept hold of her hand as she talked on.

"Most guys run a mile when they see me. I know what they think. Suzanne Fricker has got ball-breaker written all over her. Who wants to lay a mega-bitch like that?" Her tone hardened. "Oh, there are plenty of dirty old men like Tom Bellinghaus who'll make a grab at anything that moves and I also get the weirdos who can't resist taking a crack at me in order to put me in my place. I even had one guy who told me he could only screw women who earned more than he did—then he was surprised when I invited him to stick it up his own ass!" She took a deep breath, then smiled. "You see my problem, Alan. Real men are in short supply. That's what made Zuke special. He wasn't like the rest of those jerks. He knew about love." She leaned in closer to me. "That's my story. What's yours?"

"I'm still trying to live it down."

"Old wounds?"

"Something like that."

She gazed deep into my eyes and I found myself kissing her hand. Though I'd been wary of her at our first meeting, I was now drawn to her. Suzanne had confided in me. She'd shown me her weaknesses and touched on one of mine in doing so.

"Would you like anything else?" she asked softly.

"What's on the menu?"

"Come and find out."

The bedroom had a formal luxury to it. Subtle tones of white and pink complemented each other everywhere. The carpet was ankle deep. The bed was a four-poster with a billowing canopy.

Naked apart from the coin around her neck, she lay in the middle of the duvet with me and searched my body with her fingers. Her kiss had an urgency to which I responded at once. Suzanne held nothing back. The four-poster shook violently.

Suzanne Fricker was a proficient lover. She seemed to be going through an established routine and there was a slightly functional quality about it all, but I didn't mind that in the least. Earlier that day, I'd almost driven over the side of a cliff in a Chevy Chevette. It was wonderful to be alive and I could think of no better way to celebrate the fact. It gave my ego a tremendous boost.

When it was all over, I lay on top of her in a state of mild exhaustion. The gold coin had been pressed hard between us and I saw that it had left its imprint on both of us.

"A double eagle," I noted.

Suzanne eased me off her, then reached out to the bedside table and handed me a box of tissues. She vanished into the bathroom and I heard the shower running. When she finally emerged, she was wearing a pink bathrobe and mules. Her manner was briskly affectionate.

"Get dressed. I'll make some coffee."

Zuke Everett might have brought love into her life but he'd taught her nothing about afterglow. I felt used. Hurt.

While I was drinking my coffee, she rang for a limousine. It soon arrived. She took me to the door and slid back the bolts.

"I'm glad you called," she said.

"Can I ask you a personal question?"

"Of course."

"Was it because I reminded you of Zuke?"

She kissed me on the cheek. "That, too."

I went out into the hallway and she locked the door behind me. After making love to Helen Everett, I'd felt guilty and ashamed. This time, it was different. There was pleasure, surprise and a degree of wounded pride. I couldn't fathom Suzanne. It worried me.

The limousine was waiting to take me back to the motel. When I reached the privacy of my own room again, something occurred to me for the first time.

I'd been seduced.

Clive Phelps had never looked worse. When he lowered himself on to the seat beside me, I had grave doubts that he would ever get out of it. His skin was sallow, his eyes bloodshot, his moustache drooping sadly. His crumpled suit and general air of listlessness completed the impression of a man who'd spent a very long night on a very short park bench.

While I ate a hearty breakfast, all that he could face was a cup of black coffee. The first sip made him grimace.

"As bad as that?" I asked.

"Yes," he croaked. "I'm just not up to it any more, Alan."

"What happened?"

"I tried to build one bridge too many."

He groped in his pocket and brought out a packet of cheroots. I took them from him and stuffed them back in his pocket. He moaned.

"No, Clive. Not while I'm eating."

"I'll expire without a smoke."

"I promise to catch you as you fall."

"You're a sadist," he accused.

"Sadism is better than pollution."

He forced himself to try the coffee again. After one more taste, he spooned in extra sugar and stirred. I got down to business.

"Right," I announced. "Spill the beans."

"I feel like spilling the contents of my stomach," he warned.

"Save that for your encore. Give me the facts first."

"Can't you manage a little human bloody sympathy?"

"Wait your turn in the queue behind Zuke Everett."

"Sorry. I asked for that."

"So how did you get on last night?"

"Very slowly."

"What's the word on Kallgren?"

"Less than flattering," he replied. "The consensus of opinion is that he's the biggest shit in the history of the arsehole—and that's only what his friends call him. He's smooth, slimy and too fucking successful by half. Kallgren is a bloated capitalist who's been on an F-plan diet. He's into every damn thing."

"Including golf."

"That started some years ago," he said, pulling a notepad from his pocket and flicking to the right page. "Someone told him what the commercial potentialities of the game were and he moved in fast. He bought a stake in club manufacture, golfwear, accessories, the lot. And being Kallgren, of course, he had to have his own course."

"Golden Haze."

"That's when Tom Bellinghaus came on the scene. He's very much the rogue elephant among course architects and you can see why. Most of his work has been outside the States and it's needled him. He's a prophet who wants to be accepted in his own country. Golden Haze was his big chance. Bellinghaus wanted to design a course that was good enough to host a US Open."

"No danger of that, I hope."

"Not at the moment. The USPGA have been very wise so far. They know the kind of man Kallgren is. They've refused to commit themselves to including his Tournament of Champions on their circuit. Bellinghaus is none too pleased about that. He feels rejected.''

''My heart bleeds for him,'' I said with measured irony.

Clive took out his cheroots again and pleaded silently.

''No,'' I decreed.

''Just one?''

''I'm still eating my breakfast.''

''Alan, I'm gasping.''

''Self-denial is good for the soul. Now, put those filthy things away before I get angry.'' They disappeared grudgingly into his pocket. ''Any joy with Phil Reiner?''

''None. Wouldn't even take my calls.''

''Where's he staying?''

''The Bel Air Hotel. At Kallgren's expense.''

''Mm. Nice place.''

''Very nice,'' he agreed. ''I almost screwed one of the waitresses there last year. Italian piece with earrings the size of strap-hangers on the London underground.'' A tired grin split his pallid face. ''She ran too fast for me.''

''Is Reiner playing in the Phoenix Open?''

''No,'' he reported. ''He's staying here to get adjusted to his new management. Or maladjusted, as the case may be. The mystery man is a Kallgren golfer now.''

''He may not be the only one.''

I told him about the takeover of DLZ Management, a company which represented sportsmen from many fields. I also mentioned the dinner engagement that Kallgren had that evening with Gamil Amir.

Clive was in no way surprised by the intelligence.

''All fits in with what I heard. Kallgren's been on the sniff for ages. He's what one of my American colleagues calls an ambitious fucking sonofabitch. Remember Harold Smith?''

''The boxing promoter?''

''That's the one,'' he confirmed. ''When they finally nabbed him, he was on the verge of taking over the entire sport. Kallgren is trying to do the same thing with golf.''

''Wasn't Smith involved in computer embezzlement?'' I recalled.

"To the tune of more than $20 million, old son. Right here in Los Angeles. He had a contact inside Wells Fargo Bank who worked out the perfect fiddle. They got away with it for years and Smith was able to build himself a boxing empire."

"The police caught up with him in the end, though."

"Only because he'd been breaking the law."

"I don't follow."

"That's what makes Rutherford Kallgren so much more dangerous than Harold Smith. He's moving into golf *legally*. It's his own bloody money, not something he's embezzled from a bank."

"Fair point," I conceded.

"Smith was an out-and-out con man but everyone loved him. He was the last of the big spenders—drugs, women, racehorses, you name it. Kallgren's the opposite. A legit businessman but everyone loathes him. And one of the reasons is that he's too good to be true. The façade is marvellous. Devoted family man, dynamic tycoon, patriotic American."

"And what's behind the façade?"

"A monomaniac who wants to buy up the game of golf. Over the last year, he's approached several players and waved his chequebook under their noses. Fortunately, they all turned him down."

"Phil Reiner didn't. Why was that?"

He sighed. "That's the great enigma, Alan."

"How ever did Kallgren tempt Reiner into his camp?"

"Only one answer, to my mind."

"Money?"

"Big money."

"I wonder."

"Kallgren made him an offer he couldn't refuse."

It sounded plausible but I was still unconvinced.

Clive finished his coffee and rallied enough to demolish a piece of toast. We chatted until it was time for him to go up to his room to pack. He remembered that he would be leaving something behind at the hotel and he sought to pass it on to a friend.

"Are you still determined to stay on?"

"I have to, Clive."

"Then why don't I introduce you to Miss Rosario?"

"Waste of time."

"You don't like building bridges?"

"I hate warm croissants."

A taxi took us both to the airport and I helped him in with his luggage. Issuing a string of dire warnings against my staying, Clive urged me to hop on the next plane to England while I could. I waved him off, then went to hire myself another car. After the disaster with the Chevy Chevette, I chose a Honda this time. I drove away with one eye scanning the mirror.

I was not being followed.

The hospital was vast and it took me some while to locate the wing of it in which Howie Danzig was being looked after. Uniformed bustle surrounded me. The place was ultra-modern and expensive.

A soundless lift took me up to the fifth floor, where I stepped out into a wide, gleaming corridor. The nurse on duty at the desk told me that Howie was only receiving visits from close relatives and she didn't even pretend to believe my story that I was a favourite nephew who had flown the Atlantic to be at my uncle's bedside. I tried the plain truth instead and it eventually bore fruit. She allowed me five minutes with the patient.

I hoped that it was going to be enough.

The room was small, featureless and full of medical equipment. Howie was propped up in bed and connected to some bottles by plastic tubes. He looked older, smaller and lay quite motionless. His watery eyes flicked in my direction as I entered.

"Hello, Howie," I said. "Are they looking after you?"

"Al . . ." His voice was weak and hoarse. "I'm fine."

I brought a chair to sit beside the bed and leaned in.

"Howie, I need some help," I explained.

"Help?"

"To find the man who murdered Zuke."

"Told the cops . . ."

"I want to ask you a few questions."

" . . . all I know . . ."

"Zuke had financial problems, didn't he?" He nodded his head very slightly. "How bad were they?"

"Bad."

"Could he have gone bankrupt?" Another slight nod. "Why did he marry Helen Ramirez?"

"Ha!" His contempt was muted but very evident. "She . . . made him."

"Did you know he was on drugs?"

There was a pause. "Next question . . ."

"That means you did," I deduced. "When did it start?"

"Told the cops . . ."

"Was it *before* he married Helen—or after?"

"Man's dead, Al . . ."

"It was before, wasn't it?"

"Who cares?"

"Did Valmai know about it?"

"Valmai?" The name brought a semblance of a smile to his face. "She was . . . lovely. Valmai understood about . . . his golf. He won. With her . . . he won. We all won . . ."

"I saw Valmai yesterday," I said. "She sends her love."

"Saw her?" Another smile tried to break through.

"I flew up to San Francisco. She lives at Stinson Beach. Valmai was very sorry to hear that you were in hospital. She asked to be remembered to you, Howie."

"Thanks."

"We talked about the good times."

"Valmai was lovely . . ."

"She knew, didn't she? About the drugs."

"Great golf . . ."

"Valmai knew."

"We won. We all won . . ."

The watery eyes flickered as they looked at me, then he nodded his head almost imperceptibly. My guess had been correct. Valmai Everett had lied to me. She had denied that Zuke had taken drugs. I wondered if she had lied to me about anything else.

Howie Danzig was fading fast. The effort of speaking even for such a brief time had taxed him and he was about to drift off to sleep. I wanted one more answer before I left the room. I shook his arm gently until his lids fluttered open. He needed a moment to identify me.

"Al . . ."

"I'm still here, Howie."

"Tired."

"Yes, I know. I won't keep you, I promise."

"Told the cops . . ."

"One last question. That's all."

"Tired."

"What sort of contract did you have with Zuke?"

"Sleep."

"Howie, can you hear me?" I whispered. "What sort of contract?"

But his eyes had closed again and his breathing had become more regular. I waited for a full minute but he didn't stir. Howie had gone beyond me. I put the chair back, then came to take one final look at the manager. He seemed terribly frail now.

"Goodbye, Howie," I said, quietly.

His hand twitched and then inched forward over the sheet. I reached down to take it. With the last of his strength, he squeezed my fingers. His hand went limp.

Howie had answered my question after all. He and Zuke Everett had never had a written contract. It was all done on a handshake.

It was typical of both of them.

Chapter Six

When I left the hospital car park, I drove straight back to Santa Monica. It was time to return to Zuke's house. Caution had been keeping me away but I now swept it aside. I had to confront Helen Everett. There was certain information that only she could provide and I was determined to coax it out of her. I hadn't forgotten the threat made by my attacker. It gave me an additional reason to go back.

The house looked rather jaded against the dark sky. It needed fine weather to set it off and the sunshine had disappeared. Outside and inside. The drive was empty. No battered Oldsmobile this time. I stopped at the gates and sounded my horn. After a few seconds, they opened to admit me. I came to a halt, then got out.

Dominga opened the door and alarm filled her eyes when she saw me. I was ready with a Spanish greeting for her.

"*Buenos días.*"

"*Mil rayos!*" she exclaimed.

I put my palm against the door as she tried to slam it in my face. Pushing it open again, I stepped into the hall. Dominga looked up at me with a mixture of fear and hatred.

"*Fuera de aquí!*" she shouted.

"I want to see Mrs. Everett," I insisted.

"*Vaya al diablo!*"

Another Spanish voice quelled her at once.

"*Basta!*"

Helen Everett was standing in the doorway to the living room. She nodded towards the kitchen and Dominga scuttled off. Wearing a white blouse with a full red skirt, Helen was as arresting as ever. She put her hands on her hips and struck her Katy Jurado pose.

"Good morning," I began. "It's me."

"We have nothing to say to each other."

"I think we do."

"Please, Alan. I don't want to speak to you."

"At least give me the chance to say I'm sorry."

"Sorry?"

"The other night," I reminded her. "You came into my room."

Embarrassment made her shrug and avert her gaze.

"It was . . . not your fault," she muttered.

"You certainly made me feel as if it was."

"Forget the whole thing."

"I can't do that."

"Look," she blazed, "I don't wish to talk about it!"

"We have to, Helen. And you know why."

There was a long silence. Her embarrassment deepened and her hands played nervously at her skirt. When she tried to speak, her mouth could not produce words and she turned away. I crossed over to her and stood behind her.

"I'd like an explanation," I said, quietly.

"Go away."

"Who was he?"

"Just leave me alone."

"Helen," I demanded, grabbing her by the shoulders and spinning her round to face me, "what's going on here? That madman cut all my things to ribbons and then jumped on me. Now, who is he?"

"I don't know."

"Tell me!"

"It was nothing to do with me—I swear it!" She broke away and moved to the front door. "Please go. For your own sake."

"Not until you've given me some answers."

"Alan—"

"What are you hiding from me?"

"Nothing."

"He murdered your husband—doesn't that *matter* to you?"

The accusation in my voice was like a blow across her face and she reeled. Tears of pain and recrimination came in a flood and she brought her fists up to the side of her head. Dominga came out of the kitchen to see what all the commotion was about. Her eyes were dark with venom as they fixed on me.

I tried to console Helen but she pushed my arms away. With mascara running freely to disfigure her face, she took refuge in her native language.

"Váyase!"

"Listen—"

"Salga de aquí!"

"I didn't mean to—"

"Dése usted prisa!" she ordered.

"Por Dios!" added Dominga.

I gestured an apology and went out through the door.

"Stay away from me," begged Helen, "or he'll kill you."

"Tell the police about him," I urged.

"I can't!"

It was not the first time she'd closed a door in my face.

I went back to the car and got in. The gates opened before I even started up the engine. As I drove out through them, I did not need to look behind me. I knew that Dominga would be watching.

I swung left on to the main road and headed towards the motel. After a hundred yards or so, however, I saw something which caused me to slow to a halt. A chauffeur-driven Mercedes had passed me on the other side of the road. Seated in the rear of the vehicle was a man I thought I recognised. I watched in my wing mirror as the car reduced speed and stopped outside the Everett house. A blast on the horn caused the gates to open and the Mercedes rolled on through them.

I drove on a short distance until I could pull off the road and leave the Honda beside a parking meter. A narrow stretch of grass ran along the front, interspersed with park benches and broken up by clusters of palms and other trees. It was an attractive place to promenade in the sun and offered a majestic view of Santa Monica beach far below. The Pacific was restless.

Using the trees as cover, I made my way back up the road until I could see into the drive of the house. The chauffeur was waiting in the Mercedes. His passenger had clearly been invited in. I checked my watch. It was over a quarter of an hour before the visitor came out again. Helen Everett stood at the door with him. Her make-up had been restored now and she'd regained her composure. When the man took her hand and kissed it, she even released a smile.

He got into the car and it surged through the gate as they parted. I stepped back behind a thick palm tree as the Mercedes went past, but I peeped round in time to see the face of the passenger. It was wearing a grin of self-congratulation.

I hadn't been mistaken about his identity.

It was Gamil Amir.

The hotel was in downtown Los Angeles and I had some difficulty finding it at first. It was located in a quiet street and looked more like a private house than a hotel. Large, solid, double-fronted and perhaps a century old, the place had a faintly English feel to it. When I climbed the steps and went in, I found myself walking over an Oriental carpet in a hallway that was full of antiques. It was a refreshing change from the aggressive modernity of the rest of the city.

It was early evening. Mardie Cutler was waiting for me in the bar, a small room with the same atmosphere of vanished elegance. She leapt out of her seat and clutched at me.

"Hey, I'm so glad you've come, Alan!"

"Sorry I'm late. Got lost."

"Lemme buy you a drink."

"This one's on me," I overruled. "What is it?"

"Vodka," she confessed.

We were soon sitting at the table with our drinks. There was only one other couple in the room and they were examining a large menu. Mardie had promised that the place would be quiet.

"Look at me," she said, holding up her glass. "I've touched nothing but orange juice for two years and now I'm on this. Got through a coupla bottles since . . ." She took a quick sip to steady herself. "Gee, I'm so relieved you got here, Alan."

Mardie Cutler was no longer the lithe, happy girl who had met me at the airport with a kiss. She was strained and haunted. Her loose-fitting white dress had a rope belt and one hand twisted it incessantly.

"What exactly is the trouble?" I asked.

"Everything."

"Take it from the top."

"Been a nightmare."

"In what way?"

"Zuke, the robbery, the man . . . I just can't take it, Alan."

I put a soothing hand on her arm. She was trembling.

"Day after it happened," she recalled, "I just lay on the bed and cried my heart out. The doctor gave me some pills but they didn't do much good. There's no pill gonna bring Zuke back, is there?"

"No, Mardie. I'm afraid not."

"Yesterday was pretty much the same. I'd cancelled my whole schedule again—hell, I was in no fit state to dance around to music! Then—about this time, I guess—I went out to the drugstore. All I took was my purse. I was only gone fifteen, twenty minutes. When I got back . . ."

"The break-in had occurred."

"I nearly threw up, Alan. I was so shocked."

"How did they get in?"

"Through the front door," she said, chewing her lip. "That was the terrifying thing. No forced entry. They musta had skeleton keys or something. It don't exactly make you feel safe when you know someone can get in that *easy*."

"Did they damage the place at all? Vandalise it?"

"No, but I knew they'd been in there just the same. It hits you right in the gut. It's like you're being spied on."

"And they took more or less everything of value?"

"None of it's worth very much except the hi fi. That was my livelihood they walked off with. Without the hi fi, I don't dance. And the address book had all my clients' numbers in it and a record of my work over the past few years."

"Presumably the sound system's insured?"

"Oh, sure, but that's not the point. They're trying to get at me—and it hasn't stopped there." She drained her glass before she spoke. "I think I was followed."

"Today?"

"On my way here," she said. "This guy in a Lincoln, he tailed me all the way down Figueroa Street. Turned off when I did. Drove on past when I pulled into that parking lot around the corner."

"Did you get a look at him, Mardie?"

"I didn't dare." She gave a nervous laugh. "Could be wrong, of course. State I'm in, I imagine all kinda things. But it was creepy."

"I'm sure."

There was a lengthy pause. She toyed with her rope belt.

"Another drink?" I offered.

"No thanks but lemme get you one."

"I'm fine."

Another pause opened up. Mardie was finding it hard to talk about the subject that had really brought us together that evening. I tried to provide her with a short-cut.

"How long did it go on?" I asked, tactfully. "You and Zuke."

Her surprise was tinged with pleasure. She sounded grateful.

"How did you know?"

"The signs were fairly obvious, Mardie."

"Oh." She was worried.

"You're a busy young woman with her own business to run," I pointed out. "You wouldn't take time off to meet me at the airport unless you wanted to do someone a big favour."

"I'd have done anything for him," she said, simply.

"How long did it last?"

"Three months. Almost to the day. Three months, then he was . . ." She shook her head to dismiss the tears and took the opportunity to talk about the fond memories. "We used to come here, Alan. Our secret hotel. Mostly out-of-town guests, so it's very private. Nobody would recognise Zuke here. We were just . . . two more people in the bar."

Mardie talked with an amalgam of pride and guilt, wanting me to know the story, yet fearing some kind of moral disapproval. She had liked Zuke instantly. Their relationship had stayed on a jokey level at first, then she arrived one morning to lead Helen in a workout and found that she was not there. Zuke was supposed to have rung Mardie and told her that his wife could not make the session because of an urgent dental appointment.

Conveniently, he forgot to pass on the message.

"Since I was there, he said, I might as well have the workout with him." She giggled. "He was so funny, jumping about with nothing on but a pair of tennis shorts. We laughed and laughed. Then he tripped and fell to the floor. I bent down to help him up." Her eyes sparkled. "That was the first time. The music kept on playing. It was fantastic."

Three other women had told me about Zuke Everett. In each case he had emerged as a warm, generous, effervescent man with a positive attitude to life. Mardie painted substantially the same portrait but she added some darker tones as well. Zuke came over as a tormented person who was trying desperately to cope with the fact that his second marriage had been a resounding mistake.

"That's why I didn't feel bad about it in front of Helen, you see," explained Mardie. "I was helping her as much as Zuke. I was sorta keeping their marriage together."

"How much did Helen know?"

"As much as she wanted to, I guess."

"And why did she stop sleeping with him?" I wondered.

"He wouldn't say—but it hurt him deeply." Her face clouded. "You must think I'm a real bitch."

"Why?"

"Going off with Zuke behind her back."

"I'm not making any value judgements," I assured her. "The fact is that you kept him afloat during a very testing time. I'd say he was lucky to know Mardie Cutler."

She brightened. "Thanks, Alan. I was only a small part of his life, maybe, but it was enough for me. I just felt great when I was around him."

"So I noticed."

"Then *this* had to happen. Just as he was getting on top."

"On top?"

"Yeah," she confided. "Zuke told me that this tournament would change everything. He stood to make a heap of money. Reckoned that all his problems would disappear."

"Did he say where the money was coming from?" I pressed.

"No. From winning, I guess."

"Was there any mention of betting on himself?"

"He joked about it—that was all."

"But his debts seem to have been enormous," I observed. "How on earth could he hope to pay them all off?"

Before I could pursue the subject, we were interrupted by the sound of a small bell tinkling away for all it was worth. Mardie giggled and sat up excitedly.

"It's the Magic Show."

"The what?"

"There's this crazy old guy runs the hotel. He puts on the Magic Show once a week. Man, he's really off the wall!"

The bell tinkled on and came into the room with a strange sprightly figure in top hat and tails. He was short, dapper and overflowing with geniality. His white moustache and side-whiskers put him in his sixties but he was patently still a child at heart.

"Time for the Magic Show, everyone!" he announced.

He doffed his top hat and made an elaborate bow.

"Good evening, Mr. Smith," he said to me, shaking my hand.

"Good evening," I replied, then saw I was holding an egg.

"Do you like them soft-boiled or hard-boiled, sir?"

"Soft."

"Then this one is no use to you. It was laid by my rubber duck."

He reclaimed the egg and bounced it on the floor like a ball. Pretending to swallow it whole, he pulled a face, gulped loudly, then pranced out ringing his little bell.

The other couple left the bar with a chuckle. There was an amiable eccentricity about the old man that compelled attention. He was part and parcel of the hotel's quirky character.

"Zuke and I always tried to make it on Magic Show night."

"That good, is it?"

"No. It's silly. But it used to make us laugh."

"Do you want to give it a whirl now?" I suggested. "We could both do with a laugh."

"I'd love to see it just once more."

"Then let's go."

I escorted her out of the bar and along a corridor.

"By the way," she warned, "he calls everyone Mr. Smith."

"Even the women?"

"They're always Mrs. Smith," she said with a giggle. "If you run a hotel, you only get to meet Mr. and Mrs. Smith. Get it?"

The Magic Show was held in a large, gracious room at the back of the building. Its walls were covered in tapestries and its floor was strewn with Oriental rugs. A magnificent old grand piano stood in one corner while another was occupied by a tall, antique grandfather clock with no hands on its face.

A low stage had been built against one wall and a black velvet curtain ran along the back of it. Various accessories of the magician's art were set out, including two tall cabinets that stood on castors.

The centre of the room was taken up by ten or more small, round tables and residents had taken their places at most of them. We found a table for ourselves and sat down. There was an atmosphere of warm anticipation that was hard to resist.

Lighting was subdued to give a gentle glow. Two spotlights focussed on the stage itself and the piano was lit by a standard lamp. A cadaverous waiter passed among us with a tray bearing champagne in long, fluted glasses. I bought two as he stopped at our table. Mardie giggled as we clinked our glasses.

We were both going to enjoy the Magic Show to the full.

"Ladies and gentlemen . . ."

The magician had mounted the stage to begin his act.

He got a spontaneous round of applause. He thanked us all individually, rattling off our names as his head moved from table to table with lightning speed.

"Thank you, Mr. and Mrs. Smith, Smith, Smith, Smith, Smith, Smith, Smith, Smith, Smith, Smith, Smith." He beamed all over us. "Allow me to introduce myself. I am Charles Fenton Cornelius, your host in this delightful hotel and your humble servant in this Magic Show." He repeated his elaborate bow to more applause. "First, I require the services of an assistant and I call upon Benjamin Reed Cornelius to fulfil that role here tonight."

"It's a ghost," whispered Mardie in my ear.

"A *what*?"

"This is the bit that always got Zuke."

"Is Benjamin Reed Cornelius here?" he boomed.

A deep silence. The residents glanced around uneasily.

"Give him a little time," advised the magician. "He's been dead for over sixty years." There was a rustle of laughter. "Maybe I should have told you that Benjamin Reed Cornelius, who happened to be my great-grandfather, built this hotel before the turn of the century." He pointed to the grand piano. "He died on that very stool, ladies and gentlemen—playing his last waltz."

"Watch the clock," hissed Mardie.

"Why?"

"You'll see."

"He's here!" declared the magician. "The old gimp has come back. All we have to do is find him. Everybody quiet now!" He cupped his hands and called. "Great-grandfather, where are you?"

The clock started to chime furiously and several people reacted with a shout of surprise. Then one of the tapestries began to twitch about. On another wall, a bell pull went vigorously up and down.

"He'll settle down in a moment," promised the magician.

The curtain behind him began to shake and then the whole room seemed to be alive with chiming and twitching and unexplained movement of inanimate objects. Mardie giggled happily all the way through it.

Suddenly, some chords were played on the piano.

"He made it," said the magician. "We can begin."

Though there was nobody within three feet of the piano, its keys moved again as some scales were played at speed.

"Stop showing off, Great-grandfather," scolded our host. "Now then, ladies and gentlemen, here is your chance to match your musical skills against Benjamin Reed Cornelius. Try to find a tune that he can't play. Shout'em out loud and clear."

" 'Beautiful Dreamer,' " came the first offer.

"Thank you, Mr. Smith."

The piano played the first few bars of the song and drew gasps of amazement. Other challenges were called out and they were all met. Unseen fingers played their way through nursery rhymes, folk songs and modern ballads. Inevitably, a comedian in the audience had to try to call the pianist's bluff.

"Okay, Benny, boy," he yelled. "Lemme hear what you can do with Rachmaninov's Piano Concerto Number 2 in D Major."

"He doesn't play that," said the magician.

"See?" boasted the man. "I caught old Benny out."

"You caught yourself out, Mr. Smith," rejoined our host

with a smirk of triumph. ''Rachmaninov's Piano Concerto Number 2 happens to be in C Minor.'' He pointed to the grand piano again. ''It's all yours, Great-grandfather. Take it away.''

The familiar opening chords boomed out and the audience clapped in approval. Mocked by his friends, the comedian had the grace to join in the applause.

''There's always some clever dick like that,'' noted Mardie.

''How does it work?'' I wondered.

''I don't know.''

''The piano must be wired up in some way.''

''Stop trying to figure it out,'' she counselled. ''Just go with it, Alan. It's much more fun to believe it really is a ghost.''

I took her advice and surrendered to the occasion. The Magic Show was simple, old-fashioned, harmless enjoyment. Our host kept up a light, comical patter as he went through a range of conjuring tricks. There was an endearing amateurism to the whole thing that I loved. Charles Fenton Cornelius certainly put his own stamp on the hotel. The most I had elicited from the manager of my Santa Monica motel was a surly ''Good morning.'' The Magic Show was much more user-friendly.

What added to the general amusement was the fact that the magician made no attempt to disguise the mechanics of his tricks. When he demonstrated his vanishing act, for instance, he put a member of the audience into one of the cabinets, wheeled it up against the velvet curtains and gave it a hard smack. We all heard a panel fall open at the back of the cabinet and saw the curtains part as his assistant slipped out through them.

Mardie was completely carried away. Though she had seen the show many times before, it had never staled for her because it was an integral part of her love affair. Its familiarity was its joy to her. As she giggled and clapped her way through the performance, she was reliving the happy times she had spent there with Zuke Everett.

Once again I was doing duty as his double.

She now got her chance to take part in the Magic Show.

"For my final trick, ladies and gentlemen," announced the magician, stepping to the front of the stage, "I require the assistance of a young woman of nervous disposition. And I believe I see the very person sitting right there."

He indicated Mardie, who shrank back with a laugh.

"No, not me. I couldn't!"

"Go on," I encouraged.

"Come on, Mrs. Smith," insisted our host, descending from the stage to take her hand. "Everybody thinks you're the ideal person."

Taking the hint, the audience joined in with shouts of approval. Still making token protests, Mardie allowed herself to be led up on to the stage and put into the other cabinet. It was painted rather like a Chinese screen and had a series of narrow slits in it. Mardie was locked inside but her face showed through a hole and her hands poked out through two smaller holes.

The magician crossed to the table and held up one of a number of wide-bladed swords. He sliced an apple in two as proof of the razor sharpness of the cutting edge, then dropped the sword on to its point. It embedded itself into the wood and quivered to and fro.

"Help!" cried Mardie. "Lemme outa here."

"Relax," soothed the magician. "If anything goes wrong, I'll offer you a job playing duets with my great-grandfather."

He gave the cabinet a twist and it made one revolution. With Mardie's tense face staring out at us, he inserted the first sword into a slit in one side and pushed. The point came out through a slit on the other side of the cabinet.

"Hey," said Mardie in delight. "I didn't feel a thing."

"There you are, Mr. Smith," argued the magician, leering pleasantly at me. "We'll soon have your wife back in one piece." He inserted the next sword into a second slit on one side of the cabinet. Once again its point appeared through the opposite wall. He cupped Mardie's chin in his hand. "This is your better half, Mr. Smith." He changed his mind and pointed at the area below the two swords. "Or maybe that is."

More swords and more jokes followed and the trick

reached its climax. Taking the broadest blade yet, the magician placed it against a chest-high slit in the front of the cabinet. Mardie looked down and grinned. When the sword was rammed home, however, her grin disappeared. There was a twitch in the velvet curtains at precisely the moment that the magician plunged in his blade.

Mardie's face tightened in anguish and her scream echoed around the room. Some of the audience thought it was all part of the act and they clapped, but I saw the terror in her eyes before they snapped shut. Leaping up onto the stage, I pushed the magician aside and swung the cabinet around. The point of the sword had come out through the slit at the back, but another weapon had been thrust into it.

I shuddered when I saw the handle of a stiletto.

By the time I'd grabbed for the lock and wrenched open the cabinet, the back of her white dress was one huge, ugly, red stain. Shock and revulsion spread through the room. Other screams were heard.

Mardie Cutler's words were curiously prophetic.

She'd watched the Magic Show just one more time.

Police headquarters were located in a vast, modern building of ferro-concrete and double-glazing. Its exterior had a stark purpose about it that kicked hard at the tripwires of my phobias. After one look at the place, I decided not to risk a second. The atmosphere inside had the same brutal impersonality that I find on all police premises. American versions of my father glared up at me as I walked past. They obviously worked on the same principle that he did.

I was presumed guilty until proven so.

After only a minute of it, I mentally tore up the post card of Alcatraz. The joke no longer seemed very funny. Taken in for some routine questioning, I still felt that I was in custody.

The interview room was small, frugal, unimaginative.

A desk, three chairs, a telephone, a wastepaper bin, a metal ashtray. The walls were bare and the view of Los Angeles through the window seemed distant.

Lieutenant Victor Salgado and Sergeant Patch Nelms

had no talent for hiding their displeasure. They grilled me remorselessly as they took my statement and they let me know exactly what they felt about my visit to California.

Salgado was particularly trenchant.

"Next time you get an invite to come here—stay away!"

"Thanks for putting out the welcome mat, Lieutenant."

"You're as fucking welcome as a boil on the dick," he said with warm disgust. "I mean, look at your record in one fucking week, will you? A guy starts kidding around in his garden with you and he gets bumped off. You take a broad to some crummy hotel and she ends up on a slab as well. Keep this up, we're gonna need a new subdivision here. Saxon-related homicides."

"None of it was deliberate," I argued.

"Exactly. You did it all without fucking trying."

"Lieutenant—"

"Put your mind to it, you could cover the whole city with stiffs."

"There's no need to exaggerate."

"Don't you tell me what to do, scumbag!" he snarled. "You're on my fucking territory now. *I* call the shots."

Before he could call any more, the telephone rang and he snatched it up viciously, keeping his eyes fixed on me all the time.

"Salgado!" he barked, then his tone mellowed. "Oh, hi, Captain . . . Yeah, sure . . . Okay, I'll come up right away." He put the receiver down. "The Captain wants to keep tabs. Won't be long, Patch."

"Right."

"See if *you* can drill some sense into this guy."

Salgado stalked out of the room and shut the door behind him. Patch Nelms appraised me with dark brown eyes and drummed out a tune on the desk with the flat of his hand. He got up from his chair and paced around the narrow confines of the room as if trying to think of something to say.

When his question came, it caught me unawares.

"Ever met a girl name of Lori Whyte?"

"Lori Whyte?"

"Car rental. San Francisco airport."

"I do believe I did."

"Why didn't you mention it to us?"

"Sergeant," I reasoned, "I can't be expected to tell you about every pretty girl I meet. It would cramp my style unnecessarily and take you away from more important work."

He sat on the edge of the desk and gazed down at me. His neutral expression was almost as unsettling as Salgado's open dislike. He let his fingers tap out another melody on the wood.

"You think *all* cops are dumb?"

"Quite frankly, I try not to think about them at all."

"What happens if someone steals your golf clubs?"

"I buy a new set."

"You don't call a cop?"

"My father has spent the past twenty years trying to steal my golf clubs," I told him. "Except that he doesn't make a grab at them and run. His technique is much more subtle than that. Psychological theft. All in the mind." I crossed my legs and folded my arms. "That's why I'd never call a policeman."

"Lori Whyte said you were a nice guy."

"You've spoken to her?"

"She sent her best wishes."

"Thanks."

"So did Valmai Everett."

Nelms had been doing his homework. He was thorough. I'd underestimated him and came to have a grudging respect as he talked on.

"You flew up there to see Mrs. Everett and pump her for what you could get out of her about the deceased." He corrected himself. "About *one* of the deceased. Though Mardie Cutler was alive when you left San Francisco. Still be alive today if it wasn't for you."

"Me?"

"You're the one they're after," he explained. "Not some girl who takes aerobics sessions. *She* wasn't trying to do our job for us. That's your pitch. If you'd gone over that cliff with the car, they wouldn't have needed to waste another stiletto."

His argument was sound and it didn't make me feel any better about myself. At the same time, I was going to admit as little as I could. Mardie's death had given me further cause to press on. I was not going to hand over to the police everything that I had struggled to find out. They had their way. I was sticking to mine.

"I was involved in an unfortunate accident, that's all."

"Unfortunate for Mardie Cutler."

"It was not deliberate, Sergeant."

"I pulled the report. Don't believe a word of it."

"I was *there*."

"So was the blue Grand Am."

He saw my discomfiture and grinned. Picking up the ashtray, he played with it until he bent it out of shape, then set it down on the desk again. Having kept me waiting, he offered some elucidation.

"They got some smart cops up there," he noted with pleasure. "One of them plays golf. He was in the squad room when the report of your 'accident' came in. Recognised your name, put two and two together, gave us a call. We took it from there."

"And what did you decide, Sergeant?"

"You were followed, Mr. Saxon. Probably by the same guy who killed Zuke Everett. Looks like he can handle an automobile just as well as a stiletto. Cops up there went over that Grand Am with a microscope. Nothing. He don't leave traces."

"It was an accident," I maintained. "With no witnesses."

"Just you and him."

"That's right."

"You stick by that?"

"To the letter."

Anger showed. "Didn't your father teach you *anything*?"

"Yes, Sergeant. He told me not to speak to strange men."

Nelms stood up in surprise, then let out a rich chuckle,

allowing big white teeth to come briefly into view. He sat down beside me to continue his questioning.

"What about Stinson Beach?"

"Can't recommend it. Too blowy."

"Why were you there?"

"Valmai is a very dear friend of mine," I insisted. "I didn't go to pump her for information, as you just claimed. It was purely a social visit."

His scepticism was intact. "I get it. You go the best part of five hundred miles so you could take the dog for a walk."

"Louis was an optional extra."

"I called her earlier today, Mr. Saxon. She says that you wanted to talk about her marriage."

"I talked about my own as well. We compared ruins."

"Then you drove back to San Francisco and had this . . . slight accident on the way." I nodded and he rubbed his hand across his chin. "That kid at National Car Rental. Bright cookie. Spoke to him, too."

"You seem to have rung everyone but the dog."

"He gave us a description of Mr. Gomez that tallies with the one we got from that clerk at the hotel. The clerk remembers seeing a man—Hispanic, medium height, solid build, twenties—wandering into the lobby this afternoon."

My interest quickened. "This afternoon?"

"When he missed you in the Grand Am, he decided to take out Mardie Cutler with a stiletto."

"But why?" I demanded. "Why did he pick on *her*?"

"I aim to ask him that myself," he promised. "Right now, all I know is this. We're looking for a mean Mex who carries a blade."

"What's happened to Mexicans?" I complained. "In my day, they were easy-going characters who sat around in the sun all day wearing those funny hats."

"You been watching too many old movies," Salgado cut in.

I hadn't heard the door open. He was standing there with a buff folder in his hand. My last remark had not endeared me to him.

"My old man was born in Mexico City," he said. "Only time I ever saw the bastard wear a sombrero was on holiday in Texas. You got any other racial hang-ups we oughta sort out before we go any further?"

I remained silent. He threw the folder on to the desk as he went to sit behind it. Nelms seemed to know what was going on.

"Narcotics?"

"Report came through," said the other, sourly.

"Big zero?"

"They got off their asses for once and managed to track down Zuke Everett's source. Slime-ball named Vincent. No problems with money. Everett liked the best stuff and he always paid for it in cash."

"So much for drug-related crime," I said cheerfully.

Salgado glared at me with improved distaste.

"Open your mouth again when nobody asks," he warned, "I crap in it." He swung his eyes to Nelms. "How far you got?"

"San Francisco."

"Told him about her apartment?"

"Not yet."

"Show him."

The sergeant thrust a hand into his coat pocket and brought out a tiny, rounded, silver object. When he dropped it into the ashtray, it bonded to the metal. He frowned his question at me.

"Some kind of magnet, obviously," I answered.

"It's a bug," he explained. "We found it during our search of Mardie Cutler's flat. Stuck to a steel lamp near the phone. We figure it was planted during the break-in."

Salgado reclaimed the bugging device to play with it.

"Much easier and quicker than a phone-tap," he said. "All you gotta do is stay within range and you hear everything the girl says and does. They knew she called you and fixed up that meeting this evening. So they were able to check out the hotel first."

I was baffled. Mardie Cutler may have been involved with Zuke but she still seemed an unlikely target for a killer. What could be achieved by her death? And why go to such trouble to monitor her movements? She was quite harmless.

Salgado saw my consternation and shook his head.

"We don't know for sure either," he admitted, "but here's the way it coulda been. You start pretending you're a private dick and stumble on to something. They try to waste you. Mardie has some information that's vital to you and they gotta stop her passing it on."

"But she didn't *give* me that information, Lieutenant."

"So you say."

"She didn't, honestly," I returned with passion. "All she wanted to talk about was what happened to Zuke."

"Okay," he conceded. "There's another angle."

"I can't see it."

"Maybe the poor kid didn't *know* she was sitting on something big. They were afraid it might just slip out when she was with you. Too big a risk. So they bring in the stiletto boy. Same one who got Zuke Everett, we reckon. He checks the hotel this afternoon, follows her there this evening and—zap!"

"But he couldn't know that Mardie would be involved in the Magic Show," I responded. "It happened on the spur of the moment."

"So? He took his chance. Just like he did in the Everett garden." Salgado dropped the bugging device back into the ashtray and rested his hand on the desk as he leaned forward. "He knows how to wait and watch. That room was pretty dark. He coulda been tucked away at the back and nobody woulda known. All they were interested in was watching that old guy do his parlour tricks. The girl goes in the cabinet. He knows he can get round the back of that curtain. So he joins in the act."

Patch Nelms listened impassively to his superior. I had the feeling that he didn't entirely agree with the theory being put forward. Salgado waved a hand and gave him his chance to come in.

"Could be there's another wrinkle," he suggested. "They're

worried about something the girl can tell to Mr. Saxon. If they hit him, then Mardie Cutler is no problem.''

My disquiet grew. ''So the killer was there to pick off me or her,'' I said. ''Whichever he could get at first.''

''That's the way I read it,'' agreed Nelms.

''Adds up,'' decided Salgado.

My mind was a hornet's nest. I felt guilty and deeply upset over Mardie's death. A new dimension of fear was brought in. I'd been a possible target. If I'd been locked in the magic cabinet, it would be *my* next of kin they were trying to track down.

''Remember Yankee Stadium?'' asked Nelms.

''What?''

''Your baseball cap.''

''Oh, yes.''

''What happened when a guy goes to the plate?''

I shrugged. ''He tried to hit the ball.''

''Supposing he don't?''

''Three misses and he was out.''

''That's the rule here, Mr. Saxon,'' he said, solemnly. ''You've been lucky twice so far. Not the next time.'' He held up a finger each time he mentioned a number. ''Strike one—near Stinson Beach. Strike two—that hotel this evening. With me? This is baseball now, not golf. Three strikes—and you're dead!''

The impact of his words made me shiver.

Salgado reinforced the message in his own manner.

''You wanna stay alive, you use your fucking head,'' he ordered. ''You wanna do it your way, Alan Saxon is the next fucking blood donor. Now, what's it gonna be? Ready to trade?''

''Trade?''

''You help us—we save you.''

''I *have* helped you, Lieutenant.''

''Yeah,'' he sneered. ''Like you helped that traffic cop up in Marin County. You piss around with the facts.'' He banged a fist on the desk. ''I want this bimbo, Saxon. I got two homicides and an attempted to cuff round his fucking wrists. They're leaning on me upstairs. They need results.

So I'm gonna lean on you." He got to his feet with dramatic suddenness. "Stop screwing round and tell us every fucking thing you know!"

"What else is there to tell?" I said evasively.

"Let's start with Valmai Everett."

"Skip all that shit about walking the dog," advised Nelms. "You went there to pump her, didn't you?"

"Yes," I confessed. "But I got nothing. Valmai would only talk about the good times. It's the way she wants to remember him. As far as she's concerned, Zuke died the day he walked out on her. When I mentioned drugs, she got quite angry and denied there'd been any of that while they were married. I was more or less asked to leave."

Salgado found my amended story more convincing.

"And the trip back?"

"It *could* have been deliberate, Lieutenant."

"It fucking was."

"I couldn't be sure. It all happened so fast."

"We all know when someone tries to kill us," he insisted. "Why didn't you come clean with that traffic cop?"

"Have *you* ever been hanging over a precipice in a car?" I challenged. "It doesn't do much for your peace of mind, I can tell you. I was shaking like a leaf. Allow for some confusion."

"Confusion cleared by the time you got to the airport," noted Nelms. "That guy didn't try to bump you off, why get Lori Whyte to help you trace him? He didn't tail you from LA, how come he rented a car from the airport himself?"

I conceded his argument with a sigh and a nod.

"Let's move on to Howie Danzig," suggested Salgado. "We know you paid him a visit. What did you get there?"

"Nothing, Lieutenant. He can hardly talk."

"What did you expect to get?"

"I wanted to see how much he knew about Zuke's private life."

"That brings us to Mardie Cutler."

"You've just spent hours getting a full statement from me on that score," I promised. "I gave you all the details—

even down to Benjamin Reed Cornelius and his magic piano."

"She called you to ask for help."

"Yes."

"Why you?"

"She trusted me."

"The girl was scared, why didn't she come to us?"

"Mardie wanted a shoulder to cry on," I replied. "With all your many virtues, Lieutenant, you could never set up in the sympathy business."

Patch Nelms permitted a sly grin to steal across his face. His superior quelled it with a poisonous glance, then turned back to me. He sat down again as he spoke.

"Okay. Gimme the names."

"Names?"

"On your list," he said. "We want the mad Mex with the stiletto but we also want whoever pays his wages. You been sniffing round long enough to get some idea who that might be. Gimme the names."

I looked from one to the other. Patch Nelms watched me coolly and there was enmity in Salgado's gaze. If I didn't make some show of co-operation, I might be in police headquarters all night. Claustrophobia was already giving me pins and needles.

"I think you should take a close look at Kallgren," I volunteered.

"We have. Who else?"

"Tom Bellinghaus."

"We got him, too."

"Gamil Amir."

"That the Arab guy with the vagabond dick?"

"He had some kind of feud with Zuke," I reported. "I saw them clash in the locker room. Amir made a threat. And he wasn't exactly grief-stricken when Zuke was killed."

"We'll follow it up. Anyone else?"

"One more."

"Shoot."

"Phil Reiner."

"Didn't he win the tournament?"

"Only after Zuke dropped out."

"You think there's a connection?"

"It's just a hunch," I admitted. "There's something very odd about his tie-up with the Kallgren organisation."

"Odd?"

"He's the last golfer I'd have expected to sign up like that."

"Then why did he?"

"I'd love to find out," I said. "I don't think Phil Reiner was directly responsible for Zuke's death, but he's implicated somehow. I get these strong vibrations."

"Yeah, so do I," he confided. "Every night. Main reason my wife ran out on me. Couldn't stand living with a sex maniac."

"That's my list, Lieutenant."

"Kallgren. Bellinghaus. Amir. Reiner."

"In that order."

"We came up with someone else as well," he announced.

"Who?"

"Helen Everett."

"Helen? But that's ridiculous," I protested.

"We don't think so."

"Why could she possibly want to kill her husband?"

"Women often try to murder their husbands," he observed, drily. "We got dozens of cases on file. Women can be violent fucking creatures when they're riled. Look at my wife—once threw a fucking meat cleaver at me." He flashed me a smile. "Yours ever do anything vicious to you?"

"Yes. She married me."

He went off into peals of laughter and banged the desk.

"I like that, I like that."

Nelms remained impassive. I waited till Salgado calmed down.

"Coming back to Helen," I said. "You're way off beam there."

"She sure don't act like any widow I ever saw," he resumed. "When we interviewed her, she looked so guilty she was shaking all over."

"Zuke meant everything to her."

"Then why didn't she sleep with the poor mutt?"

"Lieutenant—"

"Maybe she knew he was getting it up with Mardie Cutler. There's your motive—jealousy." Sarcasm crept in. "We Mexicans are a hot-blooded race, Saxon. All that lying around in the sun."

"Helen did not set up the murder," I insisted.

"She coulda caused it, though," commented Nelms.

"Patch has been checking her out," explained Salgado. "Seems that she's run with some pretty fast company. Last guy she lived with, he wasn't too pleased about her moving out to get married. Tried to stop her any way he could."

"We're still looking for him," added Nelms.

"She's in this up to her neck," decided the Lieutenant. "I know when a person's hiding something. Then there's that housekeeper of hers. Dominga. I talked to her in Spanish." Sarcasm resurfaced. "Wore my sombrero just to let her know I was a true Mex."

"What did she say?" I asked.

"That's our business," he said. "Tell you this, though. That little lady wasn't any too fond of Mr. Zuke Everett. She's the only person so far who believes he got what he deserved."

It accorded with my own view of the housekeeper. I saw her face again, watching me as I stood outside Helen's bedroom. She had a real capacity for hatred.

Salgado yawned, then sat back in his chair with his hands behind his head. He regarded me through hooded eyes, then made up his mind.

"I oughta book you for impeding a police investigation."

"Blame my father."

"Scram!"

"I can go?" I said with relief.

"We got all we can use tonight," he affirmed. "From here on in, Orgaz can take over."

"Who?"

"Orgaz. One of my men. And no jokes about his name.

He's very sensitive about it. You call him 'orgasm,' you won't have one for a helluva long time." He grinned at my bewilderment. "We're putting a man on you, Saxon. Care and protection."

"But I don't want any protection!" I retorted.

"It's not for you," he corrected. "It's for me. I want to safeguard my reputation around here. You get yourself stabbed as well, I look bad. Orgaz goes with you. He's booked into the motel. Two rooms down from yours."

"Lieutenant, this is quite unnecessary."

"He's waiting downstairs for you. Good cop."

I checked myself from saying that that was a contradiction in terms and resigned myself to the inevitable. Salgado didn't only want to keep me alive. He wanted me under surveillance so that I wouldn't find the killer before he did. In a way, it was a compliment.

I stood up and threw Salgado a farewell in raw Spanish. "*Buenas noches.*"

"Hasta la fucking vista!"

Nelms took me out and guided me towards the exit.

"Almost forgot. Message from Lori Whyte."

I was pleased. "For me?"

"Guy from National wasn't such a jerk. They made out good. Had a drink, took in a movie. Seeing him again tonight."

I was curiously reassured.

But for me, the couple might never have got together. After all the incidental damage I seemed to have caused, it was nice to know that I could bring a little joy into someone's life.

During the drive back to Santa Monica, I tried to ignore the detective in the car behind me and concentrate on the gruesome events of the evening. Mardie Cutler's death had rocked me even more than Zuke's. She'd been in my care at the time. I felt responsible.

Locked in the cabinet, the girl had been such a defenceless victim and I was haunted by the sound of her final, ear-splitting scream of terror. One savage thrust from a stiletto had put her beyond the reach of any magic.

My interrogation at police headquarters had been harrowing but it had thrown up a lot of new information. Salgado's theory about Mardie appealed to me. I sensed that she did know something vital that she might unwittingly have passed on to me. It was to do with her ambiguous role in the Everett household. As I wondered how she had first met Helen, another picture popped into my mind.

My first day in California. Just after my arrival at the house. Mardie Cutler telephoning a client to apologise for being late. Holding a small, leather-bound object in her hand.

The stolen address book. That was the crucial factor.

Somewhere in her little book was a name that would connect everything up. A name that linked Mardie with Helen. A name that led to a professional killer with two murders to his credit already.

The break-in at her flat had a twin purpose. To plant the bugging device and to steal the address book so that it wouldn't come into our hands after her death. The theft of the other items from the apartment, including the hi fi equipment, was a decoy.

Without realising it, Mardie knew the name of the person behind it all and she had to be stopped before she let that name slip out. The manner of her death had been callously ironic. She'd been a young, happy, laughing victim, caught up in the middle of a dangerous situation with knives threatening her from all directions.

Symbolically, she was stabbed in the back.

I was so convinced by my deductions that I beeped my horn in celebration. Orgaz immediately pulled up beside me to see what the problem was. I waved him back behind me, then went through it all again in my mind.

The motel was in Broadway but parking was limited, so I left my Honda in the indoor car park around the corner in 2nd Street. It provided free overnight parking and Orgaz took advantage of the offer as well. He was a big, dark, shambling man around my own age and his new grey suit gave him the look of a businessman who'd just arrived from Mexico City. I had no wish to strike up any kind of friendship with him and he seemed content to carry out his orders with taciturn efficiency. It was a minor consolation.

He took me to my room and waited until I was safely inside before he went off to his own. The relief of being alone again was tempered by the fact that an armed detective was stationed so near. For a brief moment, I was thrown back to my boyhood in Leicester. Sharing my nights with a policeman. Never free. My father sleeping in the next bedroom. Dreaming of arrests.

A faint noise brought me back to the present at once.

I was not alone, after all. There was someone in the bathroom. Its door was closed and its light was off, but the whisper of sound had alerted me. The sensible thing would have been to fetch Orgaz as quickly as possible, but I had been pushed too far to be interested in sensible solutions.

Two friends of mine had been murdered while in my company. Someone had to be called to account. If that someone was now lurking in my bathroom to attack me, I wanted my chance to strike back. Trying to move as casually as possible, I switched on the television, then used its sound as a cover when I drew my putter from my golf bag. I kept my eye on the bathroom door throughout, but it did not move.

Evidently, he was waiting for me to go in.

I found enough courage to whistle and pottered around the room to make the sort of noises he would expect. I pulled the curtains closed with a swish, turned on the bedside lamp and flung back the duvet. Then I strode towards the bathroom door.

Turning the handle, I stepped sharply back and pushed the door open with the putter. The man made his leap but there was nobody there to take its impact. As soon as he came into view, I swung the club and caught him a glancing blow on the head. It both stunned and enraged him. Hurling himself out of the bathroom, he grappled with me in the middle of the room and forced me to the floor. The putter dropped to the carpet just out of my reach.

It was the same young man.

Swarthy, medium height, stocky build.

The scar was a livid streak on his left temple.

"I told you to leave her alone!" he hissed.

There was no stiletto for me. I was going to be strangled with his bare hands. Sitting on top of me, he got a grip on my throat and began to apply pressure. He was powerful and determined but I was not just fighting for my own life. I was struggling to avenge two deaths as well and it lent me extra strength.

Grabbing his wrists, I slowly eased them away from my neck. Then, with a supreme effort, I turned sideways and brought one thigh up to dislodge him. He rolled off me and hit the television hard, sending it crashing over. Picture and sound were murdered as the plug was snatched out of the power point.

I was on my feet at once but he came at me again, diving for my legs with a yell of fury. Jerking my knee up hard, I hit him under the chin and saw his eyes glaze for an instant. But he was not finished yet. He got up and circled me menacingly, cursing to himself and looking for the chance to pounce.

When he made his lunge, I was ready for him. Moving to one side, I grabbed his arms and pulled violently to help him on his way. With the added impetus, he shot across the room and went headfirst into the huge wall mirror, causing it to explode into a delta of ugly cracks. Blood poured from his scalp but it only served to goad him on to further efforts.

But I was armed again now. Having snatched up the putter, I held it out to prod him away. He made a wild grab at it, then threw himself straight at me. I was too quick for him again. Evading his tackle, I lashed out with the club and smashed his shin. He pitched to the floor with a cry of pain.

I raised the putter to strike but got no further.

The door burst open and Orgaz came charging into the

room with a gun in his hand. Sizing up the situation at a glance, he aimed the revolver at the prostrate figure and barked his command.

"Police! Don't move!"

He pulled out handcuffs, secured the man's wrists behind his back, then turned him over with his foot so that his blood-stained face was glaring up at us. Still keeping the gun pointed at my attacker, Orgaz turned to me with a baffled expression.

"Why didn't you call me?"

"Do I look as if I needed help?"

He reached for the telephone, summoned assistance, then went to stand over the cowering figure. The excitement of our success made him laugh out loud. He put a hand inside the man's coat and pulled out a wallet. Flicking it open, he studied the name on the driving licence, then handed it across to me.

When I read the name myself, I quailed inwardly.

Angel Quiroga.

He was not the man who'd stabbed Zuke Everett and Mardie Cutler. He had not tried to force me over a cliff near Stinson Beach. The real killer was still at liberty.

He had a double.

Angel Quiroga.

Helen Everett's last word to her husband came back to me.

"Angel."

The young man was her brother.

Chapter Seven

Police procedure once again came between me and my sleep. It was hours before I finally got to bed. Orgaz knew his job. As well as having a talent for kicking in motel room doors, he was well versed in the art of pacifying an irate management. In view of the damage, disturbance and bloodstains on the carpet, they were entitled to feel aggrieved. After Orgaz had smoothed their ruffled feathers, however, they came to shower me with abject apologies and moved me to a better room.

Set against his virtues, Orgaz had two major defects.

He was a policeman. And he was still there.

I lay on the bed and tried to untangle it all in my mind. Angel Quiroga was engaged in some private battle of his own. He was in no way involved in the murders of Zuke and Mardie. Fuelled by some inner passion, he'd been set on to me by Dominga and seemed to believe that he was somehow defending his sister's honour.

When I'd met him in the guest room at the Everett house, I'd seen him in the half-dark. The next time I encountered him—or so I thought—was when he drew up alongside me in a blue Pontiac Grand Am. My brief glimpse of him had shown me his right profile and I'd assumed there was a scar on his left temple.

My third sighting had been in the half-dark of a young man's memory. In recalling Mr. Gomez, the clerk at the National Car Rental desk had given a good general description of Angel Quiroga. There'd been no mention of a facial scar but I put this down to the fact that Gomez had been wearing a hat.

Further corroboration had come from the receptionist at a downtown hotel. The man who had familiarised himself with the place on the afternoon before the Magic Show had also sounded temptingly like Quiroga. I'd been so eager to believe that one and the same man was responsible for all the violence that I'd never even stopped to consider there might be two of them.

A professional hit man and a crazed younger brother.

Helen's strange behaviour was now explained. As she stood over Zuke's dead body in the garden, she feared that her brother was the murderer and she guiltily shielded him during the interview with Salgado and Nelms. When she knew that his only crime was an assault on me and my clothing, she still felt obliged to protect her younger brother. I ended up feeling sorry for both of them.

Veronica Quiroga. Helen Ramirez. Helen Everett.

Raped. Exploited. Widowed.

She had not had much luck with any of her names.

Sleep continued to stalk me but refused to move in for the kill. I was physically exhausted and emotionally drained. I was also psychologically shattered. After all my efforts, I'd still not found the man I was after. There were two of them. I'd got the easy one.

Golf summed up my dilemma. I felt as if I'd driven superbly from the tee to drop my ball in the very heart of the green. When I got to it, however, I found that someone had moved the hole another two hundred yards away. I had to emulate Zuke Everett and hit an even better second shot that landed right in the cup.

I needed my own double eagle.

Sleep took mercy on me and smothered me into oblivion.

I rose early and dived into a restorative bath. While I was making a coffee, Orgaz arrived to see what my plans were. I told him that I would be staying at the motel for a while to make some telephone calls. He welcomed the news and saw the chance to breakfast at the nearby restaurant. I waved him off and locked the door.

It was time to search for Mardie Cutler's address book. The simplest way to find the name I wanted was to contact Helen but I suspected that she might not wish to speak to me after my dealings with her brother. I was right. As soon as she heard my voice, she hung up. Silence has its own eloquence.

Only one option remained. Since I didn't have the address book, I had to recreate it painstakingly name by name. When Mardie dashed away from the Everett house on the first day of my visit, she'd been going on to a client called Mrs. Hahn. I grabbed the first massive volume of the telephone directory and thumbed through it.

There were dozens of Hahns. In my crude panic, I thought that they had poured in from all over America to colonise the city and to make my job an ordeal. I could be on the telephone all day. Then I recalled what Mardie had said about Mrs. Hahn. She was not a woman who could be cancelled. That suggested an imperious female, which in turn meant that she had money.

Going through the list, I pencilled out all the names with addresses in the poorer neighbourhoods. I concentrated my attack on areas like Beverly Hills, Hollywood, Burbank and Santa Monica itself. I struck oil at the fourteenth attempt. Mardie's client lived in the exclusive luxury of Laurel Canyon.

Mrs. Hahn had been shocked to learn of the girl's death and immediately converted the tragedy into a personal setback. How would she manage now that Mardie was unable to fulfil her twice-weekly commitments? Murder was such an inconvenience. I let her parade her selfishness for a while, then asked her if she knew any other clients of the dead girl. Mrs. Hahn gave me two names and numbers.

I was rolling.

It was slow, grinding work and I had to listen to all kinds of monologues, moans and expressions of sympathy, but each new call produced fresh clients. The address book was starting to fill up again. It was a Mrs. Joan Rysdale of Bel Air who supplied the vital name.

"Oh, I've known Mardie for over a year, Mr. Saxon."

"How did you first meet her?" I asked.

"Through my best friend," she said, cheerfully. "Greta was always talking about this wonderful girl who took her for fitness classes."

"Greta?"

"Yeah, that's right. Greta Kallgren."

I had established a link at last.

Greta Kallgren was the lean, handsome woman with a blue rinse whom I'd seen at the party before the tournament. Through his wife's desire to stay young and supple, Mardie Cutler was connected with Rutherford Kallgren. Her death no longer seemed a random act of malice.

My speculations were interrupted by a knock on the door. I was wary. It was not Orgaz. He always called out my name. I crossed to the door and spoke through it.

"Who is it?"

"It's me, Alan," replied a familiar voice. "Valmai."

I let her in at once and we embraced. Looking pale and anxious, she clasped my hands and squeezed them tightly.

"What on earth are you doing here?" I asked.

"I came as soon as I heard the news this morning."

"News?"

"That girl's murder. Leading on from Zuke's death." Her concern for me was touching. "I saw the report of your automobile accident as well. I feel dreadful about it, Alan."

"I lived to fight another day."

"No thanks to me. You might have been killed."

Valmai's conscience was troubling her. She admitted that she'd kept several things back from me at Stinson Beach because they'd been too painful to disclose and because she hadn't wanted to tarnish Zuke's memory. Now that she realised the danger I was in, she was ready to tell me everything if it would help to save me.

I was moved. Valmai had flown all the way down from San Francisco in order to be with me. What she had to say could not be imparted over a telephone. I guessed at its highly private nature.

Since I'd had no breakfast, I took her out to the restaurant for a mid-morning brunch. I said nothing to Orgaz about my departure from the motel but he sensed it at once. As we sat in the window of the restaurant, I saw him waiting in his car across the road.

Valmai's tension slowly eased. I did not rush her.

"How's Louis?"

"Fine. I left him with a neighbour."

"I'm surprised you didn't saddle him and ride to Los Angeles."

She smiled. "Yeah, he is pretty energetic, isn't he?"

"I didn't even know you liked dogs," I remarked.

"Neither did I till I was on my own."

She picked at her food. I could see her gathering strength to embark on what she'd come to say. I tried to make it easy for her.

"It's to do with the baby, isn't it?"

"Yes."

"Zuke took it badly."

"Very badly."

"He'd waited all that time for a child," I said, quietly. "When it was stillborn, he just went to pieces. Am I right?"

Setting her knife and fork aside, she looked up at me.

"He became impotent."

I could find no words to break the silence that ensued.

"It finished us," she continued.

As she explained what had happened, I saw why she'd been so reticent before. In talking about Zuke's problem, she had to relive her own humiliation and disillusion. He'd blamed his wife entirely. In losing the baby, she'd robbed him of his manhood.

"Didn't he seek medical advice?" I asked.

"He tried everything, Alan. His shrink told him that it was just a psychological block. All he had to do was to be patient." Her bitterness deepened. "Not Zuke. He couldn't wait. It was getting to his game, you see. I was the reason for that as well."

"How did he make that out?"

"You know the kind of player he was," she recalled. "A power golfer. Real swashbuckler. When he couldn't cut it any more, he turned on me. Said it was my fault he'd lost his balls out on the course."

"That's a terrible thing to say."

"There was much worse."

"How long did it go on?"

"Months," she replied. "Then he came home drunk one night and told me there was someone else. In fact, there'd been a few. Much *younger* women. He could do it with them. That proved it was all me."

"It proved nothing of the kind, Valmai," I assured her.

"Zuke believed it did and that's what counted." She shrugged helplessly. "I was all washed up."

"What about drugs?" I probed, gently.

She nodded. "That was the other nice surprise I got."

"Cocaine?"

"He tried everything, Alan. Pot, acid, amphetamines, barbiturates. Then he found coke and that was the one for him. He used to snort it with some of his lady friends. Boasted how much it improved his performance in the sack." Her face puckered in distress. "I loved that man for years but he made me sick to my stomach at the end."

"Did Howie realise what was going on?"

"Oh, yes. He threatened to walk out if Zuke didn't kick his habit and pull himself together. The stuff Zuke was on, it came very expensive. It was burning a big hole in our capital and Zuke wasn't winning. Sometimes he'd fly two thousand miles to play a tournament and not even make enough to pay for the air fare. Some of his sponsors were getting edgy. They like success."

"What about Helen?" I asked.

"She was welcome to him," said Valmai, sharply. "Zuke was a mess when he left me. Quite frankly, that woman deserved a medal for taking him on."

"Helen must have known he was on drugs, surely?"

"No, Alan. That's what made her special, according to Zuke. He didn't need anything when he was around her.

She was a drug in herself. He told me . . ." She chewed her lip and looked down at the tablecloth. "He told me that she'd given him his balls back."

I tried to absorb all that she'd divulged and relate it to the man I'd known. It put everything into a new perspective. Simply talking to me about it had been an endurance test for Valmai and I didn't wish to make her suffer any further.

"Does any of that help?" she said, hopefully.

"It explains a lot," I thanked. "But it only takes me up to the point where you two broke up. I need to know about his second marriage. Why things went wrong there."

"Have you tried talking to her?"

"She won't let me anywhere near her, Valmai."

"Why not?"

When I told her about Angel Quiroga, she reacted with surprise. It became astonishment when I explained about Zuke and Mardie Cutler. She thought it over for a while, then got up from the table.

"Let's go see her right now," she insisted.

"Helen?"

"What's to stop us?"

"I wouldn't even get into the house."

"Yes, you will," she promised. "You're with me."

I admired her courage more than ever. Helen Everett symbolised all the things that she'd lost and Valmai had every reason to stay well clear. A confrontation with Helen was bound to be painful to her in dozens of subtle ways. For my sake, she was ready to go through with it all. I gave her a soft kiss of gratitude on the cheek.

I paid the bill and we set off. Since the house was within walking distance, there was no need to take the car. Orgáz tailed us discreetly. When we reached our destination, Valmai stopped to appraise the house. There was a quiet satisfaction in her gaze. It did not compete with the Malibu home.

The gates were open and the battered Oldsmobile was on the drive. Evidently, the brother had parked it there before paying his courtesy call on me at the motel. As memories stirred, I was glad that Angel Quiroga was now in police custody.

Helen answered the door herself. Anger at seeing me was mixed with curiosity at seeing Valmai. Nothing was said. It slowly dawned on her who her female visitor must be.

The two wives assessed each other without malice.

"You'd better come in," said Helen.

We went into the living room.

Helen was wearing a silk housecoat and fur slippers. Her hair was unkept, she had no make-up on and she was pulling on a cigarette for comfort. I adjudged that the news about her brother had given her a bad night. She was self-conscious about the fact that she did not look at her best and it made her tone defensive.

"What can I do for you?"

Valmai went straight in with impressive purpose.

"We need some help," she announced bluntly. "Two people have been murdered already, Helen. Unless you can do your share, Alan is going to be the next victim. I think we've had enough killing. So do you."

Helen stubbed the cigarette out in an ashtray, then sat up.

"What would you like to know?"

"Some of this may be rather personal," I warned.

"Ask your questions," she invited, calmly.

"Why did the marriage go sour?"

It rocked her slightly but she soon recovered.

"Lots of reasons," she confided, thrusting her hands into the pockets of her housecoat. "Before we got married, Zuke was everything I'd ever wanted. Afterwards . . . it was so different. None of his promises came true. He couldn't afford them. Also . . ."

She drew back from what she was going to say and folded her arms. Then she seemed to go off into a private reverie. I exchanged a glance with Valmai, then tried to prompt Helen.

"Also?"

She remained in her trance. Miles away. Valmai reached her.

"Was it because of the baby?" she challenged.

Helen was flattered. "How did you know about that?"

"Was it?" pressed Valmai.

"Maybe."

"Did he keep on about it?"

"Maybe."

"*Did* he?"

The words came out of Helen in a torrent of recrimination.

"Yes, he did," she protested. "Zuke talked about nothing else on our honeymoon. We must have a baby, must have a baby. I wanted children, yes, but not yet. I wasn't even ready to think about it for five years at least. My career comes first. I have to keep my figure. But Zuke just wouldn't understand. He kept on and on and on. We must have a baby soon, he said. It's the only way to prove I'm a man. It's the only way to show we have a real marriage."

Out of the corner of my eye, I saw Valmai wince.

"In the end," continued Helen, "I couldn't stand it any more. It was there between us whenever we got close." She took a deep breath. "So I stopped being his wife. In that sense."

Veronica Quiroga had chosen the wrong name. She was not really Helen Ramirez in *High Noon.* She was playing the Grace Kelly part of the wife who turns her back on her husband in his hour of need.

Zuke Everett had been completely beleaguered.

Do not forsake me, O my darling.

"I want to ask you about Mardie," I said.

"Oh God!" murmured Helen, putting a hand to her throat. "That poor girl. Why did they have to kill her?"

"Where did you meet her?"

"What?" She was in a daze.

"Mardie. Who introduced her to you?"

"I saw it on TV last night. It was horrible." She tried to focus on me. "You ask me something?"

"Who introduced Mardie Cutler to you?"

"Mrs. Kallgren."

"When?"

"Not long after we moved in, I guess," she decided. "Zuke went to this big party Mr. Kallgren threw and came home with a dinner invite. I was thrilled. We went to this mansion in Fremont Place. I've never seen such a beautiful house. Like a palace."

"Who was there?"

"That was the funny thing. I'd expected a lot of people. But it was only us, Mr. and Mrs. Kallgren and this woman who works for him. Suzanne Fricker. Something to do with contracts."

"Yes, I've met Suzanne," I said.

"The meal was delicious. Served on silver."

"How did Mardie's name come up?"

"Mrs. Kallgren was asking me about my work. How I kept in shape. Then she went on to say she had this fantastic girl who gave her fitness classes. Mardie Cutler."

"Go on."

"I can't quite remember how it happened but I agreed to meet Mardie and try a session with her. That Suzanne woman knew Mardie as well. Recommended her. She turned out great. Until . . ."

She buried her face in both hands to cope with the grief.

Valmai looked at me, then reached out to put an arm around her.

"How did Zuke get on with Mardie," she asked, gently.

"He liked her."

"Was that all?"

Helen's hands went down and she was quite composed.

"It's all I needed to know. The rest was up to them."

Valmai studied her carefully for a minute, then spoke with muted sympathy. The natural enmity she felt towards Helen seemed to be fading away.

"Why did you marry him?"

"Because he was the only man who asked me."

"There has to be a better reason than that, Helen."

"Zuke was kind to me. He took me seriously. I loved him."

"You must have known you were taking on a few problems."

"Oh, yes," agreed Helen with a sigh. "But they didn't seem to matter. You knew my story, you would understand. I came from a poor country to a rich one. All my life, I wanted to marry someone here. To be an American citizen."

Valmai nodded and sat back in her chair. I took over.

"That party at the Kallgrens'."

"Yes?"

"Did Howie Danzig know about it?"

"Of course not," replied Helen. "Zuke made me promise never to tell him. Howie didn't like Mr. Kallgren at all."

I knew why the Everetts had been invited to dinner. It was the last piece of evidence that I needed. I gestured to Valmai and we both stood up to go.

"Thanks, Helen," I said. "You've been a great help."

She got to her feet and seized my arm impulsively.

"I owe you an apology, Alan. For my brother."

"Blood is thicker than water," I offered.

"I tried to stop him but he wouldn't listen. Angel is loco sometimes. He frightens me. That's why I wouldn't speak to you when you called yesterday. But Dominga told him you'd been here."

"Is he always that impetuous?" I asked wryly.

"You know what happened when we crossed the border," she reminded. "Those bandits. Find the pretty one. When Angel tried to save me, they knocked him to the ground. He still carries the scar on his head." A spasm of pain shot through her and she trembled. "There is a scar *inside* his head as well. Because of that day, he cannot bear any man to touch me."

"Not even your husband?" I said.

"No. He thinks they all want to defile me." She shook her head and sighed. "There were other men but I lied to him about those. With Zuke, it was different. You cannot hide a marriage. Angel went mad. He threatened to kill Zuke. At the start, I thought he had." She released my arm and stood back. "I'm sorry for what he did to you, Alan.

He's my brother and I love him but he is in the right place now. Angel needs to be locked away. Someplace where they can help him."

I thanked her again and we turned to go into the hall. Helen came after us and said nothing until the front door was open. Then she offered a hand to Valmai. There was an awkward pause. Valmai then shook the hand and leaned in to kiss Helen on the cheek.

"Would you like to stay for a little?" invited Helen.

Valmai considered. "Please. I'd like that."

The two wives had found something in common. It was time to leave them alone together. One last thought nagged at me. A smiling visitor kissing Helen's hand.

"Gamil Amir called yesterday," I said. "I saw him as I left."

"That's right."

"What did he want?'

"He said he'd come to pay his respects." A smile brushed across her face. "Then he asked me if I'd have dinner with him next time he was in Los Angeles. I told him I'd wait and see."

"You should have introduced him to your brother," I suggested with a wicked grin. "He might have had second thoughts."

I gave them each a farewell kiss and arranged to meet Valmai later on. Then I hurried out and down the drive. The battered Oldsmobile seemed like a fitting memorial to Angel Quiroga.

I was in such a rush to get back to my own car that I completely forgot about Orgaz. My sole purpose was to reach Kallgren as soon as possible. His wife had not just casually mentioned Mardie's name in the course of a dinner party. The girl had been planted in the Everett household deliberately. She had been used by Kallgren and then disposed of before anyone could learn the truth.

Zuke would only have been invited to dinner for one reason. I was not surprised that he had kept it secret from his manager. As I thought about Howie Danzig, lying critically ill in hospital, I felt even more urgency and broke into a trot.

I was puffing slightly when I reached the car park but I didn't slow down. The Honda was on the second level and I ran quickly up the ramp. My vehicle stood in shadow. Another car and a van were nearby. I fumbled for my keys but I didn't need them.

Before I could take my hand out of my pocket, I was pushed hard against the side of the Honda and held there while a cloth was pressed over my nose and mouth. By the time I realised what was happening, it was too late to struggle. Red hot needles sped up my nostrils and jabbed my brain. My eyeballs were on fire. My throat was smouldering.

The nightmare started immediately.

My father had bought Alcatraz and installed me as its only guest. I was in a tiny punishment cell from which all light was banished. It was foul-smelling and oppressively warm. Noise assailed my ears from all directions. Something pummelled my body.

A small grille opened in the door. I had visitors.

Rosemary peered in at me through the bars and clicked her tongue in severe disapproval. Then Lynette's face appeared as well. My daughter had been brought to see her father in his moment of maximum distress. She tried to put a hand through the bars to reach me.

I lunged towards her and banged my head on the steel door. My father's laugh reverberated around the cell. Another face came into view. It was my bank manager. Donnelly. He watched me with a cold smile, then slammed the grille shut to blot out the light.

The whole cell now seemed to contract and revolve. It picked up speed and hurtled through the air until it landed in the sea with a huge splash. Water rushed in to engulf me. When I tried to swim, I found that my hands were tied. When I tried to speak, salt water gushed into my lungs. I was drowning.

My head started to clear with painful slowness.

The first thing I noticed was the water. It was beneath

me. I wasn't drowning. I was in some kind of small yacht. An engine came to life and its subdued roar matched the throbbing of my skull. I opened an eye but it was filmed over and I could see almost nothing.

My hands *were* tied behind my back. Another thick rope held my body tight against the chair in which I was sitting. I opened a second eye and the blurred vision improved. I saw that I was in the cabin of the craft. It was well-appointed and tailored for comfort. Two bunks were set against one wall. A long, upholstered seat stood opposite. There was a small desk and I was in the armchair behind it. Desk and chair were screwed firmly to the floor. The telephone and answering machine on the surface of the desk were also held in place.

I tested the ropes with a heave but my bonds held tight.

I could still taste the chemical that had overpowered me.

As my brain started to function again, I tried to work out what had happened. My attacker had been waiting for me. While I was still unconscious, he'd driven me away in the van or the car that had been parked near the Honda. I opted for the car. The man would have known that Orgaz was lurking outside and a van was much more likely to arouse a detective's suspicion. I'd been smuggled out in the boot of a car.

It was no wonder I'd had a nightmare about being locked up in a confined space. All my neuroses had been touched off.

There was a clock on the cabin wall. I had a rough idea what time I'd left the Everett house and got back to the car park. Allowing a margin for error, I estimated that the longest I could've been unconscious was half an hour. Probably less.

We couldn't have driven all that far from Santa Monica.

The note of the engine quickened and water swished beneath us. We were on the move. Through one of the portholes, I saw that we were easing past a forest of masts and rigging. There seemed to be no end to the vista.

It gave me our location. Marina del Rey.

The largest man-made small-craft harbour in the world.

Just south of Venice, the harbour is a magnet for devotees of sailing and deep-sea fishing. Zuke had once shown me around it on one of my previous visits. I forgot how many thousands of craft he told me were moored there.

Marina del Rey was within easy reach of Santa Monica.

I was going on a pleasure cruise. Even in its befuddled state, my mind told me that I wouldn't be coming back. In a frenzy of anger, I strained against the ropes but they held firm. There was no way that I could break free.

Only one hope remained. To summon help.

My hands and body were tied but my legs were not. If I could somehow use them to reach the telephone, I might have a slim chance of raising the alarm. I set about my task with a zeal that was tinged with unashamed panic.

The first problem was to remove my shoe and a sock.

A shoe alone would not suffice. I had to press a single number on the digital display and a thick sock would make that difficult. What was needed was an unencumbered big toe.

My shoe flicked off easily but I soon realised that I'd have to shed the other in order to dislodge my sock. Curling one set of toes inside the top of the other sock, I pushed and jiggled for all I was worth. Over-eagerness told against me. I felt perspiration trickle down my neck. Pausing for a rest, I schooled myself to be more patient, then started again. The sock slowly gave way to my persistence and rolled off. The whole operation had taken several minutes.

I lifted my knee as high as I could and got the heel of my bare foot on to the desk. A new challenge presented itself. The telephone had not been designed for use by the big toe of someone who was tied in a chair. I was at the wrong angle. Struggling against my bonds, I bent over sidewards so that my leg could twist over. My foot was now parallel with the top of the desk.

The rope was biting into my flesh and every movement was a separate agony but I forced myself on. It was all to no avail. The telephone was a few vital inches out of reach. Panting from my exertions, I throbbed all over with pain. Despair began to nibble at me. My hope had been stillborn.

Then I noticed the answering machine.

It couldn't save me but it might help to clarify something. If I switched it on and played back some of its messages, I might learn who owned the yacht and who, therefore, had ordered my abduction. To have my suspicions confirmed would be a small but important consolation.

The answering machine was closer than the telephone but it still posed problems. Because it was further to the left, I had to use the other foot. This meant removing a second sock, but I went through the ritual once more and another big toe was soon ready to go to work. I got my left foot up on to the desk, angled it over so that it was parallel with the top, then moved it gingerly towards the machine.

A downward jab of the toe depressed a button and a light showed that the answerphone was now on. I hit another button and activated the replay tape. There was an electronic bleep, then a man's voice was heard.

"Returning your call. I agree. This deserves some kind of celebration. I suggest the same place as before. Now that it's all signed and sealed, we ought to formalise things by—"

He was cut dead in mid-sentence.

A stocky figure had come into the cabin, seen what I was doing and dived at the desk to switch the machine off. He swung an arm to knock my foot off the desk and the blow was felt in every part of my body. To ensure that I had no further fun with my big toe, he unplugged both the telephone and the answering machine.

My contact with the outside world had gone.

The man stood over me and glowered. He was in his twenties. Hispanic, swarthy, medium height, chunky build. Close to, he didn't really look like Angel Quiroga but there were definite similarities. Both men had the same manic glare.

We'd met before. I'd seen him through the window of his Pontiac Grand Am on the road from Stinson Beach. I'd viewed his handiwork in a Santa Monica garden and at a

Magic Show in a downtown hotel. I'd felt his crushing strength in a car park. To assist my identification, he pulled out a stiletto from beneath his coat and held its point an inch from my eye.

Fear made me stiffen as he turned the blade in his hand. His lips drew back to reveal uneven teeth. He enjoyed my suffering for a few minutes, then laid the point of the knife against the side of my head before running it right down my cheek in a soft caress.

A visible shudder went right through me.

"You're dead," he growled.

"Why didn't you just stab me in that car park?"

"I have orders."

"Who from?"

"To make you disappear."

"Mr. Kallgren?"

"For good."

"It's him, isn't it?" I pressed.

He crossed to the cabin door, then thought of a joke.

"Don't bother to put your shoes back on."

"My shoes?"

"You won't be needing them where you're going."

His cruel laugh went back up on deck.

I was left in a welter of apprehension but my thoughts were not entirely concerned with my own immediate fate. The voice on the answering machine kept coming back to echo in my ears.

I'd recognised it at once.

It was Phil Reiner.

The next half an hour was a race between hope and despair. Still held fast in the chair, I did my best to persuade myself that I would somehow be rescued. Orgaz would certainly have reported my disappearance by now and they would be out looking for me. They might even have traced the car which took me to Marina del Rey.

Depression set in when I considered the hopelessness of their job. Searching for a small yacht among the thousands in the harbour would be like finding a very small needle in a very large haystack. The police had no idea in which direction we'd sailed. After half an hour we must be well clear of Santa Monica Bay. One more speck on the vastness of the Pacific.

As I began to surrender to the notion that death was almost inevitable, I sensed what form it would take and I blenched. Zuke and Mardie had died in a gruesome manner but there'd been a merciful swiftness about their despatch. It was all over in a flash. They'd been the unsuspecting victims of opportunist murders. Both had been stabbed during moments of relative happiness.

My case was different. I had to endure the torture of the wait. Whoever had given the command wanted me to suffer. There would be no stiletto this time. No dead body to help the police with their enquiries. Just a few brief bubbles on the surface of the water.

While a hired killer was about his business, Rutherford Kallgren would be sitting in the comfort of his office waiting for a phone call to tell him that Alan Saxon had been eliminated as well.

The address book of his crimes would vanish with me.

My thoughts strayed to the people I'd be leaving behind. Lynette would be destroyed. Her relationship with her father had been sustained over the years by infrequent meetings, irregular letters and impromptu phone calls but there was a wealth of unspoken love that bonded us together. I wished I'd rung her since I'd been in California. All that she'd have to remember me by were a view of Santa Monica Beach and an aerial shot of the Golden Gate Bridge.

Post cards from a man in a hurry to get killed.

Rosemary would be shaken by my death as well—I would be out of her reach at last. Clive Phelps, of course, wouldn't forget me. He'd write the obituary of a lifetime in his newspaper and then go out and get himself gloriously drunk.

Katie Billings would be sad. I'd warmed up a cold winter for her and shared a lot of happiness in her cul-de-sac. Donnelly, I suspected, would not hear the news for some time. He'd go on sending me hate mail about my financial shortcomings.

Then there was Carnoustie. I'd left her in a garage to be serviced and refurbished while I was away. I had a vision of her wasting away in the corner of the forecourt, a faithful animal that has lost its master and has no wish to outlive him.

Noises sliced through my morbid introspection. The engine slowed down, then cut out. Waves lapped as we began to drift on the tide. Heavy footsteps descended from above.

The man who came into the cabin was tall, wiry and middle-aged. He had the look of a sailor about him and wore a full beard. Tucked into his belt was an automatic pistol. Without saying a word, he untied the rope that bound me to the chair. Pulling out the gun, he jabbed it against me to indicate that I should rise.

My hands were still tied behind my back and my feet were bare. My head was pounding, my muscles aching and my stomach knotted. I was hardly in a fit state to meet my Maker.

I went up the narrow staircase, out on to the deck. Bright sunshine threw dazzling patterns on to the green water. Blue sky stretched all around us. There wasn't another craft in sight.

The swarthy young man was in the stern, resting on one knee. When I saw what he was doing, my lungs broke out in armed rebellion against me. There were three large buckets on the deck, each filled with solid concrete. He was patiently threading a chain through the handles. Evidently, it would be wound around me as well.

It was not an appealing way to take my leave of the world. I wondered if I was to be shot first. Or would they simply rely on three buckets of cement and the law of gravity?

I was pushed into the stern and made to stand by the rail. The chain made an ugly, rasping noise as it was twisted once more around the handles and I tensed myself to feel its weighted coldness against my skin.

Then another sound intruded. A helicopter.

Both men reacted in surprise and I clutched my opportunity with tied hands. As the sailor turned away to look upward, I put my foot in the small of his back and pushed hard. Before the young man could grab me, I dived overboard into the surging water, kicking hard with my feet and trying to stay submerged for as long as possible.

The sailor was vindictive. As soon as I surfaced, he fired vengefully at me and the bullets sent up tiny waves all around me. I went under again and used my legs to go even further from the yacht. The water was less than warm and the current was strong but I had no quibble to make. An unscheduled dip with my hands tied was a big advance on a downward plunge with three buckets of cement.

More shots were fired when I came back up for air but they were all off-target. I heard the engine start up again and was caught in the wake as the propeller churned the water. At first I thought they were beating a hasty retreat. When I floated on my back and stole a glance at the yacht, however, I saw that my executioners had decided on a more effective way to kill me.

Taking the craft in a wide circle, they brought it back with the clear intention of slicing right into me. I had no defence against them except another dive in the hope that I could get beneath the hull. My sodden clothes were an added handicap. They restricted my movements and clung coldly to my body. Even in a swimming costume, it would not be easy to avoid the approaching yacht. Dressed and unable to use my hands, I was going to need a lot of luck and determination. Timing would be crucial.

I lifted my head to watch the craft bearing down on me. Its prow was high in the water as it cleaved its way forward at top speed. Creating a white spray, it closed in on its target. I waited until the last possible moment and then dived, kicking frantically with my bare feet to send myself down. The hull raked past me with only inches to spare and the propeller all but touched me. Turbulence was overwhelming and I lost all control. I simply held my breath, closed my eyes and waited until I eventually bobbed back to the surface.

The effort had taken virtually all my strength and I knew that I could not repeat the manoeuvre. As the yacht turned in a circle for a second attack, I steeled myself for the impact. All I could do was to float on the surface. I was, literally, a sitting duck.

My enemies were not able to take advantage.

When the craft was forty yards or more from me, shots rang out in earnest. The helicopter had its own firepower. It was coming in fast and the two men decided to put self-preservation before the minor chore of killing me. Veering off to the right, they took the yacht in a mad dash across the open sea.

The waves created by the sudden change of direction swamped me and sent me under. I came up spluttering to find that the helicopter was now hovering above me. There was a splat as a self-inflating rubber dinghy landed in the water nearby; then a man was winched down on a cable. When he got into the dinghy, it was a matter of seconds before he'd paddled to me and hauled me out of the drink. A sharp knife cut through the rope that held my hands and I rubbed at the pain in my wrists.

I'd swallowed more than my fair share of the Pacific Ocean but I was still able to gurgle my thanks. It was the first time in my life that I'd been glad to see a policeman.

As soon as the man was safely in the dinghy, the helicopter had swung away to give chase and I wondered if we were going to have to paddle all the way back to Marina del Rey. My question was soon answered. Two high-powered police launches appeared on the horizon. While one turned off in the direction taken by the yacht, the other headed towards us with shrill urgency. It reduced its speed when it got close and floated alongside.

Patch Nelms reached over to lift me bodily into the stern of the craft. My rescuer climbed aboard as well and secured his dinghy. I lay on the deck like the day's catch, dripping all over and with just enough vestigial strength to twitch. As the launch set off again, Victor Salgado looked at me with undiluted amusement.

"Well done!"

"What for, Lieutenant?" I murmured.

"Leading us right to 'em."

"Is that what I did?"

"Sort of," he explained. "Orgaz got the number of the automobile that took you away from that car lot. We traced it to Marina del Rey. Checked on all the craft that'd set sail. One of 'em belonged to Rutherford Fucking Kallgren."

"Kallgren?"

"Yeah. Vain bastard. Puts his insignia on every goddam thing he owns. Probably had it tattoed on his wife's ass so he's got something to look at when she goes down on him." He chuckled at his own joke. "His vanity saved you. That yacht was not only flying the Kallgren flag. Had his fucking logo painted on the top of it. Dozens of boats had seen it. We got a fix and came running."

"How you feeling?" asked Nelms.

"Wet."

"You did great."

"Thanks."

"Know something?" added Salgado.

"What, Lieutenant?"

"We'll make a fucking cop outa you yet."

The threat was enough to send me into a dead faint.

Orgaz worked his wonders with the management yet again. When I walked barefoot into the motel with a blanket wrapped around my still soaking clothes, he soothed them with a few words and guided me to my room. I unlocked the door, then held Orgaz back as he tried to follow me in.

"I like my privacy," I insisted.

"Lieutenant says I gotta stick close."

"I need a shower."

"You take a leak, I'm supposed to hold it for you."

"Give me fifteen minutes."

"Okay," he agreed reluctantly. "But I'll be right here."

He sat on the floor and leaned against the jamb.

I locked the door after me, then went straight to the bathroom to run a shower. After stripping and sluicing myself off, I towelled thoroughly and put on the clothes I'd worn on the last day of the tournament. Since my only surviving footwear was still on the yacht, I had to remove the studs from my golf shoes and put those on.

I checked the time. Seven minutes before Orgaz started tapping at the door. It was enough to give me a head start. I opened the window as quietly as possible and stepped through it. Keeping low past the other windows, I made it to the road, then sprinted to the indoor car park. Fortunately, the ignition key had survived my dip in the Pacific.

I got into the Honda and drove away.

The yacht had been overhauled by the police and the two men taken into custody. Salgado and Nelms had gone off to interview Kallgren and I'd been asked to change before being taken back to headquarters by Orgaz. But I refused to be cut out of the action altogether. There was one person I was determined to confront myself.

Phil Reiner. The quiet man was going to hear noise.

Somehow he was connected with the death of Zuke Everett, the murder of Mardie Cutler and the attempted drowning of Alan Saxon. I wanted to get to him before the police. He was mine.

The Bel Air Hotel is situated in a residential neighbourhood that translates into block after block of superb mansions. I went down Stone Canyon Road, then turned into the hotel car park. As I hurried away from the Honda, I noted the leisured elegance about the place, with its feel of a country villa. It was very stylish.

Clive Phelps had given the Bel Air a five-star rating on the strength of one of its waitresses but it was important to me because of one of its guests. Phil Reiner. Staying there while his new lord and master was footing the bill. Living on blood money.

When I got to the desk, the receptionist told me that Reiner was in his room. Spurning the lift, I went up the carpeted stairs as fast as my tired legs would carry me. On the second floor, I turned down a wide corridor and strode quickly along until I found the room that I was after.

I knocked firmly on the door. There was no reply. I knocked much harder and called out.

"Reiner! Open up!"

A surprised voice came at me through the timber.

"Who is it?"

"Alan Saxon. I want to speak to you."

"It's not convenient just now, Al."

"Let me in."

"I'll come down to the lobby in a while."

"Let me in!" I demanded, banging on the door.

"Take it easy!"

"Well, hurry up in there!"

"Okay, okay," he appeased. "I'm coming."

The door was unlocked, then opened six inches. Phil Reiner peered tentatively around it. He was wearing a bathrobe and had a towel around his neck. I'd never seen him without his gold-framed spectacles before. He seemed much younger.

"I was taking a bath," he explained.

"I've just taken one myself. In the Pacific."

I pushed past him and walked into the middle of the room. Its size and opulence were striking. It made my own accommodation look like a broom cupboard with social pretensions.

"What the hell is this?" he asked angrily.

"I'm sure you can guess, Phil."

"Alan, you'd better have a damn good reason for forcing your way in here."

"Try this for size. Kallgren tried to have me killed today. He hired two men to take me out on his yacht and help me to explore the ocean bed with a bucket of cement in each hand."

"You're out of your skull!"

"While I was in the cabin on Kallgren's yacht, I heard your dulcet tones on the answering machine." The information startled him. "Am I still out of my skull?"

"No," he admitted. "I did ring Mr. Kallgren a couple of

days ago when he was out sailing. But only to fix up dinner.''

''A celebration, you said.''

''Well, yes.''

''What were you celebrating? Zuke Everett's murder?''

''I find that remark in very bad taste!''

''I wasn't too struck with a remark of *yours*, Phil.''

''Mine?''

''On the last day of the tournament. Just as I was leaving Golden Haze. You told me that Howie Danzig would have lost out even if Zuke had lived.''

''So?''

''That proved you were in on the whole thing.''

''What whole thing? This is crazy!''

''You knew that Zuke was all set to join the Kallgren stable, didn't you? That's why his manager would have lost out. Zuke'd had secret negotiations and was about to sell out. Then he did something that was quite unforgivable.''

''Go on.''

''He changed his mind. After that marvellous third round, Zuke decided that he could *play* his way out of trouble, after all. Given the chance. But he wasn't, was he?''

''Get to the point, Alan.''

''The police thought at first that he might have been murdered by mistake. That the killer was really after me. It was dark and we do look alike. But Zuke was definitely the target that night in his garden. He had to be punished for obeying his instincts.''

''Instincts?''

''When it came to the crunch, Zuke just *couldn't* sell his soul to a man like Kallgren. His instincts were against it. So would mine have been. Zuke and I were similar in that respect as well, you see. We both loved the game for its own sake and loathed the idea of the sharks moving in on it.''

''Kallgren is not a shark,'' he said defensively.

''Why did *you* team up with him, Phil?''

''That's my business.''

''You're in this up to your neck, aren't you? I bet you

couldn't believe your luck when Zuke was snuffed out. Just in time to let you romp home to win that tournament."

"That's one hell of an accusation!" he protested.

"Oh, I can do a lot better than that."

"I think it's time you left, Alan."

"Shall I tell you how I see it?" I persisted. "Zuke Everett told Kallgren what he could do with his offer and that's why he got himself killed."

A smooth voice behind me took my breath away.

"I hope you have a very good lawyer, Mr. Saxon."

Rutherford Kallgren had come in from the bathroom. He was wearing a dressing gown. In that single moment of recognition, all sorts of things were explained. About Phil Reiner and his excessive love of privacy. About Kallgren and his meticulousness. I now understood why the golfer had signed up with his new management.

It all came as a complete shock to me and I was left with egg on my face. Kallgren walked over to stand in front of me.

"Let's take it from the top, shall we?" he said, calmly.

My rage cut straight through my embarrassment.

"You planted Mardie Cutler on Zuke."

"I went along with the idea," he conceded, easily. "Why not? It was useful to have someone in the house keeping tabs on him. All's fair in love and business."

"Even murder?"

"Believe it or not, I do draw the line at that."

"Then what happened to Zuke and Mardie—a suicide pact?"

"You're way out of line here!" urged Reiner.

Kallgren was placid. "Let him finish, Phil."

"When Zuke pulled out of his deal, you had him killed. Because Mardie was an integral part of it all, she had to be removed as well. Today it was my turn."

Rutherford Kallgren subjected me to his sardonic gaze. When he finally spoke, there was a subdued fury in his modulated voice.

"I have my blemishes, Mr. Saxon," he confessed. "Which of us doesn't? But I do *not* shit on my own doorstep. I spent years dreaming about Golden Haze and more years building it. Do you think I wanted a dead body lying all over my inaugural tournament? Do you imagine that Tom Bellinghaus enjoyed having blood on those nice new greens of his? Zuke Everett was a fool. I offered him a great deal and he reneged on it. That might've hurt me but it didn't make me kill him."

It sounded uncomfortably convincing. He rolled on.

"As for Mardie Cutler, my wife adored that girl. Greta was heartbroken when she heard the news. Okay, Mardie was useful to us. Indirectly. Where's the harm in that? But she was also a friend of my wife. I was not involved in her death in any way."

"What about today?" I challenged.

"Today?"

"Those men on your yacht."

"I'll be most interested to know who they are," he returned. "As Phil told you, I was on my yacht a couple of days ago but I haven't been near it since. As a matter of fact, it was on loan."

"On loan?"

"To one of my senior executives."

The name sprang from my lips at once.

"Suzanne Fricker?"

"She asked if she could have the use of it."

Evidence which had consistently pointed to Kallgren now transferred to her and was far more damning. She had motive, means and opportunity. Suzanne Fricker was the person behind it all.

A Barbie doll with a killer instinct.

"Would you get the hell out of my room now!" said Reiner.

I shuffled my feet and hunched my shoulders in token apology. Having gone into the room with guns blazing, all I'd managed to do was to inflict a few wounds on myself. I'd disturbed them during an intimate moment to level wild charges at them. They were both deeply angry.

I shielded my embarrassment behind a long silence and

drifted towards the door. The two of them stared impassively at me. Kallgren then took control with aplomb.

"I think we should forget what happened in this room."

"Fair enough," I agreed.

"Alan Saxon never actually came here."

The bargain was struck. In exchange for my discretion, I was being spared any legal repercussions. My stupidity would remain hidden from public gaze and so would their relationship.

"For the record," Kallgren added. "My wife does know."

"Know what?" I asked, blankly.

He nodded his approval. I would say nothing.

"Goodbye, Al," said Reiner.

"Goodbye, Mr. Saxon. Catch an early plane home, won't you?"

I went swiftly out of the room and pulled the door behind me. The egg on my face had thickened now but I didn't mind that. I now had overwhelming proof that Suzanne Fricker was the real murderer.

She had chosen the buckets of cement for me.

I used a public telephone at the hotel to try her office number. Her secretary told me that she was at home, then gave me some advice on how I could best drive there from the Bel Air Hotel. I was on the move immediately. With no time to appreciate the beautiful gardens, I ran to the Honda, jumped in and accelerated away. The drive to her apartment block gave me time to compose my thoughts.

Suzanne had been clever. To divert suspicion from herself, she'd pretended to help me. Having ordered Zuke's death, she told me that she'd loved him. On the day she tried to have me forced over a cliff, she'd even taken me into her bed.

It was a chilling memory.

There was another advantage in befriending me. It enabled her to see just how close I was getting to the truth. When she realised that I'd press on with my investigations to the bitter end, she gave the command to have me removed. I was appalled by the ease with which I'd been misled.

When I reached her apartment block, I pressed her bell and spoke to her over the intercom. For someone who'd never expected to hear my voice again, she reacted with impassive control and asked if I was alone. I told her that I'd come back with the police if she'd prefer that. Suzanne invited me up.

The buzzer sounded and the door opened. I was in.

She was coolness itself. When she let me into her apartment, she behaved with calm politeness. I noted the suitcase standing outside the bedroom door and there were other signs of imminent departure.

"Making a run for it, are we?" I observed.

"I'm taking a few days' vacation, that's all."

"I think they'll give you a longer holiday than that. What's the sentence for first-degree murder in California?"

"Is that supposed to be a joke, Alan?"

"The police have arrested your two chums."

"I really do have to be on my way."

"Kallgren is wondering why his yacht has been impounded."

"If you'll excuse me, please . . ."

She tried to cross to the suitcase but I blocked her way.

"Do you always sleep with men before you have them killed? Is that your turn-on? Is that why Zuke and I got lucky?"

I stopped her hand as she went to slap my face.

"Zuke was dumb," she sneered.

"You didn't think so when you first met him."

"Oh yes, I did."

"What about all that across-a-crowded-room stuff?"

"It wasn't quite like that."

"Then what was it like? Tell me."

"All right," she said. "Zuke didn't slip his hand into mine at that party. It was the other way around. I brought him back here and sounded him out. He had this blind loyalty to Howie Danzig but I knew that I could break it down."

I nodded at the bedroom. "In there?"

"Of course not!" she snarled in disgust. "I never let him touch me. Do you think I'd throw away my trump card as easily as that? Zuke was desperate for me but I made him wait. *After* the contract was signed. That was the deal.''

''Meanwhile, you shunted Mardie Cutler into the house.''

''She was perfect. Zuke was already saying goodnight to his wife at the bedroom door by then. I knew that he'd go for Mardie in a big way if he saw her doing a workout in that leotard of hers. She fell for him completely, which was even better. When I had my own aerobics sessions with her here, she used to tell me all about it. I was her confidante.'' Her smile was callous. ''I didn't *need* to screw that jerk. Mardie was doing it for me.''

''She spied for you without even knowing it.''

''And helped to soften him up good and proper.''

''Do you always have to manipulate people, Suzanne?''

''If I can,'' she said, crossing to the drinks cabinet to pour herself a large gin. ''Mardie was a nice kid but she got in my way. My name was in that address book of hers, so I had it stolen. When she got in touch with you, it was only a question of time before she led you back in my direction. And I couldn't let that happen.''

''So you had her stabbed to death.''

''She was expendable.''

Suzanne took a long sip from her glass. She showed no hint of remorse. I was horrified to recall that I'd once made love to her. Everything about her was now totally repulsive.

''Why did Zuke have to be killed?''

''Because he let me down.''

''By not signing that contract?''

''By not honouring the terms that he'd agreed to. Don't forget, Alan, I'm a lawyer. Contract is everything to me. It's binding.''

''Not unless it has a signature on it.''

''He'd *promised* me!'' she exploded. ''He'd given me his word. It wasn't just Zuke that we were after but a whole team of golfers. He was the vital first step.''

''I know. Zuke was one of the greats. Even when he was playing badly, he still had charisma. Nobody on the tour had the influence he did. Sign up Zuke Everett and you'd tempt other golfers into the Kallgren fold. Sign up Phil Reiner and all you've got is Phil Reiner. Am I right?"

"More or less."

"What did Gamil Amir say over dinner?"

"No dice." She gulped down her drink."

"You can't cope with rejection, can you?"

"Zuke betrayed me!" she retorted. "He was going to sign right after the tournament and he blew the whistle on the whole deal." Scorn seeped in. "Because of one good round of golf."

"No, Suzanne, it was much more than that. It proved that he could still play. The long drought was over. Zuke didn't need you. He could get by on his own talent. That's what he told you, isn't it? After the third round."

"He was crazy."

"I remember you coming over to congratulate him and then turning away when he spoke to you. Now I know what he said. He told you where you could stick your offer. The deal was off." I pointed to the bedroom. "Including *that* clause in the contract. He rejected you as a business proposition and he rejected you as a woman."

She threw her glass violently at the wall. It smashed on impact and the fragments went everywhere. Moving to the table, she snatched up her handbag and tucked it under her arm.

"Do you know what was at stake for me?" she demanded. "Do you realise what was riding on that contract? Everything. I'd spent six months on him. Six months of careful preparation and hard work. We had to get Zuke Everett to join us and it was all down to me. If he'd signed, then others would have followed suit and Golden Haze would have taken flight."

"And Suzanne Fricker would have been up there with it."

"Yes."

"What did Kallgren offer you?"

"What I insisted on. A vice presidency. I'd have been made for life. If Zuke had kept his promise. Vice president of the Kallgren organisation. A position with *real* muscle at last. I'd have been up there at the top if only he'd put his name to that contract."

"But he didn't. What does that make you?"

"Someone who didn't quite bring it off. People like me don't stay too long on the Kallgren payroll."

"So the skids are under you."

"All because of Zuke Everett. I was trying to *save* his career and he repaid me by wrecking mine."

"Was that reason enough to have him killed?"

"Of course!" she said vindictively. "I showed them both. I taught Zuke that nobody tears up one of my contracts and I made a lovely big mess all over Mr. Kallgren's nice, clean tournament. I got back at both of them!"

"You might even have got away with it if I hadn't come along."

I moved towards her but she was ready for me. Opening her bag, she took out a revolver and pointed it at me. I halted in my tracks. Suzanne smiled at my discomfort. She used the revolver to indicate the briefcase lying on her desk, then she motioned me across. I obeyed the silent instruction.

"Open it."

"Why?"

"I want you to see what Zuke turned down."

I flicked the two catches and lifted the lid. Bundles of crisp new hundred dollar bills were stacked neatly inside. My surprise caused her to laugh. She gestured with the gun again.

"Take one out."

"What for?"

"I want you to count it."

Pulling out a bundle, I slipped off the band that was holding the bills together. With her standing over me, I thumbed my way through the money. It didn't take me long.

"$5,000," I reported.

"There are fifty bundles in there. A grand total of a quarter of a million dollars. It was Zuke's signing-on fee. Paid in cash as he requested. Non-taxable. All his. A quarter of a million. Exactly twice what he was getting from his other sponsors.''

I turned one of the bills over. The American eagle was printed on the back. I glanced down at the briefcase and ran a covetous hand over its contents. $250,000. Twice the money. It was ironic.

Zuke had been offered another kind of double eagle.

True to himself, he'd chosen the one out on the golf course.

''Well?''

''He did what he felt was right, Suzanne.''

''What about you?''

''Me?''

''What would you have done in the same situation?''

Instead of telling her, I showed her. With a sudden movement of my hand, I threw the bundle of loose bills up into her face and dodged to the left at the same time. The first bullet grazed my shoulder. Before she could fire a second, I knocked the revolver from her grasp with a downward blow. She dived after the weapon but I got there first and took charge of it. Suzanne backed away as I covered her.

The red telephone rang and she made a reflex move to answer it. Ordering her back with a gesture of the gun, I snatched up the receiver.

''This line is closed, Mr. Kallgren. For good.''

When the double funeral had been held, I was anxious to get away from Los Angeles. It held too many sad memories for me to linger there. The gloom was not comprehensive. Howie Danzig had improved slightly in hospital and was now expected to pull through. Valmai and Helen had worked out some kind of truce that seemed to benefit them both. Salgado and Nelms were pleased that the murders had finally been solved. Orgaz was delighted to be relieved of the task of looking after me. The motel management was thrilled that I was finally leaving.

Home thoughts excited me. There was Lynette to visit and Rosemary to confound and my father to despise. There was Carnoustie to bring stability and a sense of proportion back into my life. On the emotional front was a big, welcoming gap. Katie Billings might have gone in a blaze of glory but there would be other women in other places. With luck. I was optimistic.

Then there was Donnelly. The doom machine. I intended to confront him on Monday morning, pay off all my debts, stage a spectacular row with him and transfer my account elsewhere. That would teach him to appear in my nightmares.

Los Angeles International Airport was at full pandemonium level when I checked in. Valmai had come to see me off and she advised me about some additional presents I wanted to buy Lynette from the duty-free shop. As we headed towards the departure lounge, a brawny figure came hurrying over to us.

It was Patch Nelms. He carried a brown paper parcel.

"Don't go without this, Mr. Saxon."

"What is it?"

"Why not find out?"

I opened the parcel and took out my old baseball cap. My stomach lurched as I remembered seeing it covered in blood on Zuke's head. Nelms read my mind.

"Had it cleaned for you," he said. "Special."

"Thanks all the same."

I took the parcel to the nearest bin and dropped it inside.

Nelms grinned. "That's how *I* feel about the Yankees."

America can seem like a very alien place sometimes.

The detective walked away and Valmai frowned.

"What was all that about?"

"A private joke."

I leaned forward to kiss her on the cheek. Neither of us wanted a prolonged leave-taking. Most things were better left unsaid.

"Thanks for everything, Alan."

"Give my love to Louis."

"I will."

"Goodbye, Valmai."

"See you next time you come to California."

"It's a date."

But we both knew that we would never keep it. The man who had brought us together had died and our relationship had gone with him. Valmai had chosen to live near a windy beach with a mad dog. I no longer fitted into her world. If we saw each other again, there would be too many painful reminders to accommodate.

The TWA flight was on time and I was conducted into the first-class section. It gave me warm satisfaction to know that I'd be spending Kallgren's money as I flew away from him. What was even more gratifying was the fact that his bid to grab a large chunk of the golf world had failed.

We were soon airborne and I spared Los Angeles a final glance through the window. It was a poorer place for the loss of Zuke Everett. His death would be a source of permanent sorrow to me, but there was one mitigating factor. I let my mind dwell lovingly on it.

Early in the flight, the cabin was darkened so that a film could be shown. I saw none of it. My eyes were closed as I replayed a video of my own. It was a treasured record of a high-definition performance in which I'd been involved.

A master golfer on the 13th hole at Golden Haze.

That double eagle was my souvenir of Zuke Everett.

It would keep his memory alive forever.

About the Author

Keith Miles lives in Coventry, England. He is the author of several previous novels, plays, children's books and nonfiction books which have been published in England. DOUBLE EAGLE, the second book in this golf mystery series featuring Alan Saxon, follows BULLET HOLE.